Jericho's Road

Also by Elmer Kelton in Large Print:

Ranger's Trail
Texas Vendetta
The Way of the Coyote
Buffalo Wagons
Captain's Rangers
Eyes of the Hawk
The Good Old Boys
Hanging Judge
Llano River
Long Way to Texas
Massacre at Goliad
Shadow of a Star

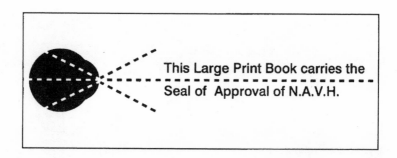

Jericho's Road

ELMER KELTON

Thorndike Press • Waterville, Maine

This is a work of fiction. All the characters and events portrayed in this novel are either fictitious or are used fictitiously.

Published in 2005 by arrangement with St. Martin's Press, LLC.

Thorndike Press® Large Print Western.

The tree indicium is a trademark of Thorndike Press.

The text of this Large Print edition is unabridged. Other aspects of the book may vary from the original edition.

Set in 16 pt. Plantin by Minnie B. Raven.

Printed in the United States on permanent paper.

Library of Congress Cataloging-in-Publication Data

Kelton, Elmer.
    Jericho's road / by Elmer Kelton.
       p. cm. — (Thorndike Press large print Western)
    ISBN 0-7862-7384-4 (lg. print : hc : alk. paper)
    1. Mexican-American Border Region — Fiction.
2. Cattle stealing — Fiction. 3. Texas Rangers — Fiction.
4. Ranch life — Fiction. 5. Mexico — Fiction.
6. Texas — Fiction. 7. Large type books. I. Title.
II. Thorndike Press large print Western series.
PS3561.E3975J47 2005
    813'.54—dc22   2004027605

For Jerry Hunt,
Art and Margie Hendrix,
avid collectors

National Association for Visually Handicapped
----------------------- serving the partially seeing

As the Founder/CEO of NAVH, the only national health agency solely devoted to those who, although not totally blind, have an eye disease which could lead to serious visual impairment, I am pleased to recognize Thorndike Press★ as one of the leading publishers in the large print field.

Founded in 1954 in San Francisco to prepare large print textbooks for partially seeing children, NAVH became the pioneer and standard setting agency in the preparation of large type.

Today, those publishers who meet our standards carry the prestigious "Seal of Approval" indicating high quality large print. We are delighted that Thorndike Press is one of the publishers whose titles meet these standards. We are also pleased to recognize the significant contribution Thorndike Press is making in this important and growing field.

Lorraine H. Marchi, L.H.D.
Founder/CEO
NAVH

★ Thorndike Press encompasses the following imprints: Thorndike, Wheeler, Walker and Large Print Press.

1

After several years as a Texas Ranger, Andy Pickard concluded that the average criminal he dealt with was about as intelligent as a jackrabbit. That said, even a dullard could pull a trigger and hurt somebody. A case in point was the reluctant prisoner trudging along ten paces ahead of Andy, dragging his feet and wailing about the insensitivity of law enforcement.

"It ain't fair," the handcuffed man whined. "You're a young man, barely growed, but you're ridin' my horse and makin' me walk."

Andy said, "You shot mine."

"I didn't mean to."

"I know. You were shootin' at *me*."

The prisoner stumbled over his own feet and almost fell. "How much further we got to go?"

"A ways yet. It'll give you time to consider changin' your occupation."

Deuce Scoggins had earned a reputation as a second-rate horse thief who could not tell a mare from a gelding and knew no better than to peddle them in the first town he came to after he stole them. His trail had led Andy across several counties along the Colorado River, but a string of angry victims had made the path easy to follow. Confronted, Deuce had fired one shot in panic, killing Andy's horse, then had thrown up his hands and begged for mercy. Andy had made him strip the saddle, bridle, and blanket from the dead animal and transfer them to his own.

"Where'd you get this horse?" Andy asked him.

"Won him in a poker game."

Andy doubted that. Deuce was not smart enough to win a poker game. He had stolen this horse like he had stolen just about everything else he had. Deuce's sweat-streaked shirt was much too large, loosely draped over thin shoulders, the grime-edged cuffs almost covering his dirty hands. He had probably lifted it from somebody's clothesline.

Andy asked, "Did you ever think about gettin' a job and makin' an honest livin'?"

"Work? I tried once. Ain't much I can do good enough that anybody'll pay me for it."

"You're not very good at this, either."

Andy wondered if he was being fair,

comparing Deuce's intelligence with that of a jackrabbit. He might not be giving the rabbit enough credit.

Deuce grumbled, "Even an Indian would treat a man better than this."

"You don't know Indians." Andy did. Through several of his boyhood years he had lived among the Comanches. "Be glad you *don't* know them. They'd make it a mighty short acquaintance."

The afternoon was almost done when they rounded a bend in the wagon road and saw the crossroads town ahead. Its largest buildings were a courthouse, a new jail, and a church.

Deuce brightened, seeing that his long walk was almost over. He said, "I heard their old jailhouse got burned down. It wasn't no nice place. I was in it once."

"Too bad you didn't go in the church instead."

"Can't you take these handcuffs off before we hit town? It's embarrassin' to let people see me this way."

"A little embarrassment might be good for you. There was a time when they would've necked you to a tree limb. As it is, they'll likely just send you to the penitentiary."

"I already been there. It ought to be

9

against the law to put a man in a hellhole like that."

Sheriff Tom Blessing stood in the doorway of the redbrick jail. Recognizing Andy, he grinned broadly and raised his big right hand in greeting. He looked more like a farmer than a lawman, for indeed he was a farmer first. Despite his years he still had the muscled body of a blacksmith. "Bringin' me a guest, Andy?"

Andy grinned back at him. "I hated for your new jailhouse to stand empty. The taxpayers have put a big investment in it."

Andy dreaded the handshake because Tom could bend a horseshoe double, and he could break the bones in a man's hand. He had been sheriff here so long that many people in town could not remember anyone else serving in that office. He showed no sign that he was ready to yield any ground to his age. He said, "Come on in here, Deuce. I've got a nice cell with your name on it, all swept out and waitin' for you."

Deuce sounded like a lost soul crying in the wilderness. "I'm hungry and I'm thirsty, and this Ranger has wore my feet down plumb to the bone."

Tom offered no comfort. "Write a letter to the governor." He led Deuce past barred iron doors and pointed him to a cell. When

Deuce was inside, Tom slammed the door hard. That reverberating impact always reminded Andy of a gallows trapdoor dropping. There was something coldly final about it.

Tom told Deuce, "I'll bring you a bucket of water directly. There's a slop jar under the cot. Make yourself at home." He winked at Andy.

Deuce was wanted in several counties, but Andy had brought him here because this was the nearest jail, and the sun was almost down. He did not care to risk camping with the prisoner on the trail. Here he could get a good night's sleep without worrying that Deuce might try to escape. Tom would keep the horse thief in custody until the several counties that wanted him sorted out their priorities.

Tom asked, "Did he give you any trouble?"

"Not after he shot my horse. He went to blubberin'. Thought I was fixin' to kill him. I let him keep on thinkin' so till I got the cuffs on him."

"Some Rangers would've shot him for killin' their horse. Whose is that you're ridin'?"

"No tellin'. Somebody's probably lookin' for him."

11

"I'll check my notices." Tom fingered through a stack of papers on his desk. "I got a message for you somewhere. Yeah, here it is." He handed a paper to Andy. "Your captain sent a wire to all the sheriffs around here, not knowin' just where you'd turn up. Wants you to report in to him."

Andy felt uneasy, wondering what the captain might want. Maybe the state's finances had turned tight again and the Ranger force was being trimmed. It had happened often before. His several years of service were no guarantee that he would escape the next cut.

He asked, "Reckon the telegraph office is still open?"

"I expect so. The operator's not anxious to go home of an evenin'. His wife's been burnin' the beans lately on account of him bein' a sorry poker player."

Andy mentally composed a brief message on his way down the street. In the telegraph office he wrote it out on paper, reporting the capture of Scoggins. He read it over and penciled out every word it could spare. The state disliked paying for long messages, so Ranger reports tended to be spare on detail. He remembered one Farley Brackett had sent: *Five fugitives met, three arrested, two buried.*

He told the telegraph operator, "If I get a reply, I'll be stayin' the night at the jail."

"I'll fetch it over soon as it comes."

Andy stayed to watch him tap out the message. He still marveled at the progress he had seen in just the few years he had been a member of the Rangers. It seemed unreal that he could write a few lines here and know they would be received miles away in an instant. The telegraph had done much to tighten up law enforcement across Texas. Word of a fugitive could race past him and alert officers to intercept him down the road.

Andy could not imagine how it might ever get much better than that.

Back at the jail he found Tom standing in front of the woodstove. The sheriff said, "I'm heatin' some leftover beans and corn bread for the prisoner, but I expect you'll want somethin' better. I'll go with you down to the eatin' joint soon as I get Deuce taken care of."

Tom had a farm a few miles out of town, but he often spent the night in the jail rather than make the ride twice, once out and then back in the morning.

Andy said, "If it wasn't already so late I'd ride out and pay a visit to Rusty Shannon. Maybe I'll do it tomorrow."

Tom smiled at the mention of the red-haired former Ranger. "I used to worry a right smart about Rusty. He pined away for a long time after Josie Monahan died. He's fared some better since he made up his mind to marry her sister Alice. She's been like a tonic to him."

"He deserves a run of good luck for a change. He had enough bad to do for a lifetime." Rusty had been like a brother to the orphaned Andy, teaching, counseling, providing a benchmark when Andy seemed about to lose his way. "If it wasn't for Rusty I don't know where I'd be now. In jail, like as not. Or dead."

Tom had a benevolent smile his prisoners seldom saw. "You never were that bad of a kid. All you needed was guidance."

Andy had been taken by Comanche raiders when he was a small boy. They raised him until he fell back into Texan hands at about the time his voice started to change. His reintroduction to the white man's world had exposed him to many pitfalls. Even now, in his midtwenties, he sometimes found himself facing situations where the choice was difficult to make. He had always leaned heavily on Rusty's advice. When Rusty was not around, he tried

14

to visualize what Rusty would do.

He said, "Too bad Deuce Scoggins didn't have somebody like Rusty to point the way for him when he was young."

Tom shrugged. "Might not've made any difference. There's some people that nobody can help. They've got no skill and no trade. They're too shiftless for honest work, and every time they come to a fork in the road they turn the wrong direction. I've seen a lot like Deuce, driftin' to God knows where. I've got to watch myself so I don't get to thinkin' the whole world is that way." Tom's eyes narrowed. "You've been a Ranger for a good while now. You ever find yourself gettin' cynical?"

Andy had to think a minute before he remembered what *cynical* meant. "I still find there's more good folks than bad ones. If I try, I can even feel a little sorry for Deuce."

"Don't tell him so. It might encourage him to get worse."

The telegraph operator found Andy sitting with Tom at a table in the restaurant, hungrily emptying a bowl of thick beef stew. He waved a sheet of paper. "Got a reply to your message. Thought you'd want to see it right away."

Andy read it slowly, his finger tracing the

15

lines. Rusty had been more successful in teaching him about farming and being a Ranger than about reading and writing.

"Any answer?" the operator asked.

"Just say, 'Will comply.' "

That ought to be short enough to satisfy the money counters, he thought.

The operator picked up a biscuit from the table and took a big bite of it as he went out the door. Tom asked, "New orders?"

Andy nodded. "Captain says our company is bein' cut again. Says headquarters in Austin wants to reassign me to the Mexican border."

Tom frowned. "If you've ever thought about resignin', this might be the time. A man can get killed down there."

"A man can get killed anywhere. Deuce might've shot me if he hadn't hit my horse instead."

"But it's like a holy war along the Rio Grande. Been that way since the battle of the Alamo and doesn't show any sign it's fixin' to change. You're automatically somebody's enemy on sight. It just depends on how light or dark your face is."

"Sounds like the Indian wars."

"The Indian wars are over with. This one's not. Do you speak any Mexican?"

Andy swallowed a mouthful of stew. "Just a few cusswords I've picked up."

"You'll have every chance to use them, and probably pick up a bunch more."

The captain had not given Andy a deadline for showing up in Austin. Because the horse he had taken from Deuce was undoubtedly stolen, he left it in Tom's custody and bought one at the livery barn. Rangers were obliged to furnish their own horses, but the state was supposed to pay for one killed in the line of duty. Andy trusted that he would be reimbursed. If not, he would still eat, though it might be a while before he could afford a new hat or a pair of boots.

Tom approved of the black horse. He rubbed his big hand down the back and the shoulder and finally patted the animal's neck. "Got long, strong legs. He'll serve you well in a chase."

"I hope I'm the one that does the chasin'."

"If not, you'll sure be glad for those good legs."

When Andy prepared to leave town the next morning, Tom said, "Sorry I couldn't provide you a featherbed."

The jail cot had been hard as a cement floor.

Andy smiled. "At least the price was right."

Tom said, "I'll ride with you as far as Shanty's farm. Then I'll be cuttin' off and goin' home."

"I'm glad for the company."

"If they send you by San Antonio, be sure to go and visit the Alamo. It'll help you understand the trouble you'll run into when you get to the Rio Grande."

Riding down the street, Andy saw two women pull a buggy up near a general store.

Tom said, "That's Bethel Brackett and her mother."

"I know." Andy hesitated, wondering if he should ride over and greet them. He realized they had seen him, so he had no choice. "Give me a minute, Tom."

Tom smiled. "Take all the time you want. If it was me and I was thirty years younger, I'd take the whole mornin'."

Dismounting, Andy extended his hands to help the older woman down. She said, "We had no idea you were in town, Andy."

"Passin' through on duty. You're lookin' fine, Mrs. Brackett."

He turned toward the younger woman, who had been driving the horses. Bethel seemed reluctant at first to accept his help.

"Andy Pickard, I ought not to speak to you."

"What did I do?"

"It's what you don't do. You don't ever come to see a girl. You could be dead and I wouldn't know about it for six months."

He thought her pretty, even if at this moment she was being petulant. He said, "If I ever die, I'll write you a letter and let you know."

"You could've let me know you were here."

"Didn't get in till late yesterday. Can't stay. I've got orders to report to Austin."

She frowned. "Even my brother Farley breaks down and sends us a few lines every six months or so. I'd write to *you* if I knew where you'd be."

"Half the time I don't know that myself." Andy could not tell whether she was angry or just a bit hurt.

She turned at the door. "If you run into my brother somewhere, tell him Mother and I are all right." She went inside, leaving him embarrassed and not knowing what to do about it.

Tom had watched quietly. He drew in beside Andy and said, "That little girl thinks a lot of you."

"Hard to tell it, the way she acts."

19

"A woman likes to have some attention paid to her, and you ain't done it. She'd follow you in a minute if you was to just ask her."

"Follow me to what? A tent camp in the brush with a Ranger company? She was raised better than that."

"You won't be a Ranger forever. Sooner or later you'll get a bellyful of cold camps and short rations. You'll start lookin' for a place to light."

"I don't know as I could ever be a farmer like Rusty. Followin' a mule down a corn row is too slow a life for me."

"Lots of Rangers go in for sheriffin' when they get tired of the service. They can uphold the law and still sleep in a decent bed most nights. If you was to decide to give it a try I'd hire you as a deputy."

"Much obliged, Tom, but so far I'm satisfied with what I'm doin'."

A former slave, Shanty York had inherited a small farm when his owner died. At first he had trouble keeping it because some neighbors objected to a black man's being a landowner. Several of them burned his cabin one night. Rusty and Tom and other friends rebuilt it and none too gently elevated Shanty's antagonists to a higher level of tolerance.

The old man looked frail. Nevertheless, he was working in his garden when Andy and Tom rode up. He seemed always to be busy so long as there was daylight to work by. Shanty took off an unraveling old straw hat and wiped a tattered sleeve across a black face shining with sweat. His broad smile displayed a solid row of white teeth. So far as Andy knew, he still had all the ones God had given him. "Mr. Tom! Andy! You-all git down and grab ahold of this hoe awhile."

He reached out his hand, and each man took it. For most people Shanty would precede their names with *Mr.,* as he did with Tom. But he had known Andy since the day Rusty had brought him home, a hurt and frightened boy who spoke only Comanche. Shanty had helped care for Andy's broken leg and patiently coached him word by word into remembering his forgotten English.

Tom exchanged a few pleasantries, then rode on toward his own farm. Shanty said, "You'll stay and eat with me, won't you, Andy?"

Andy said, "I wish I could, but I've got orders. Just want to drop by and see Rusty before I go."

Shanty kept smiling. "You don't need to worry none about Mr. Rusty. He's doin' fine, him and Miz Alice. I don't know as they've told anybody yet, but she's in a family way."

Andy chuckled. "The old rusty-haired son of a gun. I didn't know he still had it in him."

"It's in Miz Alice now. She glows like the sunrise."

It was useless to ask Shanty how *he* was doing. If he were on his deathbed he would declare that he was fine. His face gave little clue to his real age, but his short gray hair and the droop of his shoulders showed that he was getting old. Andy asked, "Anything I can send you from Mexico?"

"Any necessaries, I can get right here to home. Can't think of nothin' I'd want from way off yonder."

"The Rio Grande is pretty far, all right."

"Too far for these weary old bones. You be careful you don't come back speakin' Mexican. Took us long enough to get you over speakin' Comanche."

Andy reached into his saddlebag and lifted out a small sack. "Brought you some rock candy to sweeten your disposition." He knew the old man loved candy, but Shanty rarely splurged on such luxuries.

Shanty's eyes teared a little as he struggled for words. "I thank you mighty kindly."

Andy stalled, not wanting to leave. Every time he rode away he wondered if this might be the last time he saw the old man. He asked, "Would you like me to milk your cow for you before I go?"

"She's dried up for a little while. She's in a family way too." Shanty stared at him, his eyes serious. "You be careful, boy. They tell me there's lots of wicked goin's-on down along that river."

"There's wicked goin's-on everywhere." Andy reconsidered what he had said and wondered if his experience with law-breakers *was* making him a little cynical. Tom Blessing had warned him about that.

He turned once in the saddle to wave at Shanty, then reined the black horse in the direction of Rusty Shannon's farm. The familiar terrain brought back memories, most of them pleasant, a few he did not want to dwell upon. Not far from here he had been part of an unlucky Comanche raiding party, come down from the high plains to steal horses. In a skirmish with Rangers and settlers his horse had fallen on him. Rusty had recognized that he was white and took him to his farm to heal. At first Andy had given him reason to regret his generosity, trying to escape back to his Comanche friends. He had eventually realized that the Indians had reached the end of their time as free-roaming horsemen of the plains. He had gradually accepted his place in the white world, though sometimes he still found himself thinking like a Comanche, feeling like a Comanche. He leaned heavily upon instincts that were sometimes so strong they puzzled him.

Like now, for instance. He sensed a horseman's approach before he saw him. As he crossed over a rise in the wagon road he saw a man on horseback, moving diagonally toward him. He recognized one of Tom Blessing's brothers. They stopped and visited a few minutes, but Andy did not mention what his instinct had told him. Most people did not know how to accept it.

Riding by Rusty's field, he saw that the corn was tall and green, promising a good yield. He remembered a time he had found the crops beaten into the ground by a hail so devastating that Rusty had reenlisted in the Rangers awhile to make up for the financial loss.

Alice stood in the cabin's open dog run, slicing a ham suspended from a rafter. She did not see him right away. She was a slender woman with light brown hair almost to her waist. He had always considered her handsome, though her sister Josie might have been prettier. Josie's death had dealt Rusty a blow that for a time threatened to break his spirit. Eventually he had worked his way up from the darkness and had come to accept Alice.

Andy had been pleased, though he had one reservation: he feared Rusty might regard her as second best, a substitute; that Josie still held first place in his heart. Alice deserved better than that.

She gave Andy a sisterly hug, then pushed him off at arm's length to look him over. "Don't the Rangers ever feed you? You look like you haven't eaten in a month."

He grinned. "I eat Indian style. When I can get it, I eat all I can hold. When I can't get it, I live off of what I ate before."

"I'll slice some more ham and see how much you can eat for supper. I've managed to put some weight on Rusty. If you'll stay around a week or so I'll fatten you up too."

"Can't. I've been ordered to Austin."

She appeared disappointed. "A few days of company would be good for Rusty. He hasn't been away from the farm much since plantin' time."

"I guess he figures he did enough travelin' when he was a Ranger. A man can get awfully tired of it."

"Don't you get tired of it, Andy?"

"Now and then. But soon as I rest up a little I'm ready to go again."

"There'll come a day when you'll decide it's been enough, like Rusty did. You'll want to settle down." Her eyebrows lifted. "Are you goin' to see Bethel Brackett before you leave?"

Andy looked down. "Already saw her, in town." He abruptly changed the subject. "Where's Rusty at?"

Her eyes told him she still wanted to talk about Bethel, but she said, "He went lookin' for a heifer. He thinks she's had her calf, and she's hidin' it out."

"Summer calves can be hard to raise."

"A farmer is ready to take a rain or a calf any time."

She went into the kitchen side of the cabin. "I'll start supper when I see Rusty come to the barn. How about some coffee while you wait?"

"I can get it myself."

Rusty had done his bachelor cooking at the fireplace, but Andy noted that a new iron stove had been installed. A shop-made

26

table and sturdy wooden chairs replaced the crude homemade kitchen furniture that he remembered.

Coming up in the world, he thought.

He watched Alice, trying to discern sign of her pregnancy. All he saw was a brightness he had not found in her eyes before. He said, "Shanty tells me there'll be three of you by-and-by."

She looked startled. "How could he know? We haven't told anybody."

"Guess he saw it for himself. He said you glow like the sunrise." He studied her face. "I believe he was right."

"I have reason enough. I'm happy here. I couldn't ask for things to be any better."

Andy looked at the mantel. Always before, he had seen a picture of Josie there. It was gone now.

Alice turned to see where his gaze was directed. She said, "Lookin' for Josie's picture? Rusty took it down. He said he didn't need a picture to remember, or to keep pushin' the past into his face. Said yesterday's gone. Today is all we've got."

"You think he really sees it that way?"

He saw a flicker of doubt in her eyes. "Sometimes when he holds me I can't help feelin' that he's thinkin' of Josie." She blinked and turned away. "I've tried real

27

hard to be a good wife to him. Lord knows he deserves it. I wouldn't ask him to forget Josie, ever. But maybe with time I can be as much a part of him as she ever was. Even more."

"Maybe you already are."

"No, not yet, but I will be. I'm a Monahan, and you've never seen a Monahan give up."

Andy heard a milk cow bawling. He walked to the door and saw that Rusty had ridden up to the log barn. He said, "I'll see if he needs any help."

"Tell him supper will be ready by the time he gets through with the milkin'."

Rusty pumped Andy's hand as if they had not seen each other in years. It had been only a few months since Andy had ridden by here on his way to an assignment. They exchanged small talk about crops and rain and local politics. Andy squinted. "I see a little more gray in your hair."

"You've got the sun in your eyes."

"Alice looks fine."

"She does, doesn't she?"

Andy pointed toward the milk cow. "You'll be needin' all the milk Old Boss can give. I understand you-all are expectin'."

Rusty was surprised. "Alice told you?"

"Shanty did. That old man sees things nobody else can."

"He ought to. He's been around since the Colorado River was just a creek. What brings you over this way?"

Andy told him he was due for reassignment to a company on the Rio Grande. That brought concern to Rusty's eyes. He repeated what Tom Blessing had said: "A man can get himself killed down there."

"A little risk never stopped *you.*"

"It would now." Rusty glanced toward his cabin. "I've got responsibilities."

"I don't."

"You've got a responsibility to yourself. If you stay too long you're liable to get all shot up and have to quit anyway. Then you may be too crippled to do much of anything else."

"I'm doin' a job that needs to be done. When I stop feelin' that way I'll turn it back to them like you did."

2

As cities went, Andy always found Austin agreeable provided he did not stay long. His first visit here had been with Rusty and Tom Blessing. He had spent his early years in Indian villages and later in the sparse farming community where Rusty lived. The size of this city had amazed him. It was the state capital, Texas's seat of power. That fact had been driven home to him by a tempest that boiled up in 1873 upon the transfer of the governorship from the state's reconstruction administration back to the Texans who had supported the Confederacy. Many former Rangers, cast adrift after the war, had participated in the forcible removal of a reluctant Unionist governor.

The place looked peaceable now after several years of stable and generally benevolent government. Andy rode up Congress Avenue toward the capitol building. The street was wide enough that several spans of mules or oxen could turn a wagon around without crunching its wheels against the wooden sidewalks. After seeing the town several times, Andy was still in awe of the wagon and carriage and horseback traffic and the busy-looking pedestrians along the street. It took a lot of people to govern the state, he thought. Or perhaps, as Tom had once suggested, it took one to do the work and two to watch him.

He paused in apprehension at the door of the Rangers' state office, wondering what was in store for him. He straightened his back and stepped inside, trying to look confident. A clerk sitting at a rolltop desk turned and viewed him over the rims of reading glasses set low on his nose. His annoyance over the interruption was but thinly veiled. "Yes?"

"I'm Private Andy Pickard. I was ordered to report here for reassignment."

The clerk did not recognize the name. His face was pale, the mark of a man who spent his days in an office rather than out in the field. Andy wondered if he knew which end of a gun the bullet came out of. After riffling through some papers he withdrew one and studied it. "Oh yes, Pickard. Do you know Major Jones?"

"Met him. He's visited camps where I've been." Major John Jones was well-known for spending a minimum of time in the office. He was usually on the trail in his buggy, inspecting the far-flung Ranger outposts that were his responsibility.

The clerk said, "Luckily you have chosen a day when the major is in. Unfortunately at this moment he has company. You may sit if you choose to wait."

Andy seated himself in an uncomfortable straight-backed wooden chair that he supposed was meant to discourage long visits. He became aware of loud and angry voices beyond the door of the major's office. He glanced at the clerk, asking a silent question. The clerk rolled his eyes. "The major is having a discussion with a representative of the treasurer's office. The gentleman is explaining why the Rangers must do more but do it with less money and fewer men."

Andy could not follow all that was being said, but he caught words like *stingy* and *waste* and *efficiency*. The latter seemed to receive special emphasis.

The door swung open. A man as pale-faced as the clerk strode out but turned to fling final words back at the major. "If it were up to me we would disband the Rangers. That would stop this needless drain on the state's resources."

Major Jones followed him, shaking his

finger. "And I hope the next person to face a holdup man is yourself. I'd like to see how long it would take you to call for the Rangers."

A gust of hot wind seemed to follow the treasury representative's retreat.

Major Jones's fists were clenched. He said, "There goes a man who can make me forget the biblical injunctions against profanity."

As his anger subsided he became aware of Andy standing at attention. He said, "I remember your face, but your name is a puzzle to me."

"Private Andy Pickard, sir. I was ordered to report to you for reassignment."

"Oh yes." The clerk handed Jones a couple of sheets of paper. Jones glanced at them, then beckoned Andy into his office. He was known for quick perception and attention to detail. He could drop in on a camp unannounced and in a few minutes have a firm grasp on the situation there. If he found shortcomings he saw to it that they were being corrected before he left for the next place to be inspected. He believed in Ranger regulations, but his own conduct was based on higher rules. If he visited a camp on a Sunday, he personally conducted religious services.

The major was a small man, but he had a firm handshake and a strong, steady gaze that seemed to see into the hidden part of a man's mind. "Have a seat, Pickard."

Some officers might offer a man a drink at this point, but not Major Jones. He said, "As you may know, the legislature has seen fit to cut our budget again. Some from the settled parts of the state say we don't need Rangers now that the army has the Comanches and other hostiles safely tucked away on their reservations. I have argued to little avail that outlaws present as much of a challenge now as the Indians ever did. Would you not agree?"

Andy was inclined to defend the Indians, but he knew that was not what the major wanted to hear. "Yes, sir."

"I am keeping as many Rangers as I can, given the funds the state has allotted to me. Your record tells me you are one whose services I should retain. I am transferring you to a region that needs all the law enforcement it can get. Are you familiar with the Nueces Strip?"

"I've heard of it. Never been there."

The major turned to a map of Texas on the wall behind his desk and put his finger on the lower part. "It is that region between the Nueces River and the Rio

Grande. Mexico still claims it in spite of the treaty Sam Houston won from Santa Anna. The scarcity of law has made it a gathering ground for robbers and cutthroats from both countries."

"I heard Captain McNelly whipped them a few years ago."

"Leander McNelly and his men put down much of the worst trouble, but fighting still goes on. Mostly it's between the races — white against Mexican, Mexican against white." He lowered his chin and stared hard at Andy. "How do you get along with Mexicans?"

Andy shrugged. "All right, I guess. Never knew very many. They haven't settled much where I come from." He had known a few Mexican boys among the Comanches. Like himself, they had been captured on raids and gradually assimilated into the tribe as potential hunters and warriors.

Jones said, "Mexicans dominate the Nueces Strip, at least in numbers. Some still consider themselves to be living in Mexico and not subject to American law. At the same time many Americans in that section do not recognize that Mexicans have legitimate rights, especially ownership of property. They drive them from their

35

lands, or try to. They would like to see every Mexican banished to Mexico, or killed. It is not for us to choose sides. It is our responsibility to put down violence from whatever quarter it may arise."

"Sounds like that would take a lot of Rangers."

"Far more than we have, which sometimes drives us to actions we would not normally consider. Captain McNelly used extreme measures, but the situation called for them. He was up against desperate men."

"What do you mean, extreme measures?"

"At the worst, summary executions. We would prefer to observe all the niceties of the law, but outlaws respect only force. McNelly knew how to get their attention. He stacked the bodies of a dozen dead bandits in the town square in Brownsville. Afterward he conducted a raid across the river into Mexico and shot every suspect he came across. No doubt he killed some who did not deserve it. They were simply in the wrong place at the wrong time. This caused us no end of diplomatic trouble. It is easy to criticize him now from the comfort of an Austin office, but you have to give him credit. He put a damper on border jumping for a while."

Andy was troubled by the thought of shooting suspects. "It's been preached to me over and over that everybody has a right to be tried by a jury."

"No bandit summons a jury before he shoots someone. Mind you, I do not advocate summary justice. However, under extreme circumstances we may have little choice. Now, after what I have told you, do you think you can handle this assignment?"

Andy nodded. "I'll do my duty as I see it, sir."

"Your commanding officer may sometimes see it differently than you do. If so, will you obey him?"

"If I can't, I'll give him my resignation."

Jones mulled that over. "Well enough, but surely you would not desert him in a crisis."

"I won't quit in a fight, but I might resign afterward."

Jones dipped a pen in an inkwell and began to write an order. "How soon can you start?"

"Right now. I'm travelin' light."

"It is a long way to ride alone. I have assigned another Ranger of your acquaintance to the same place. Find him and you can travel together."

Andy thought of several he hoped it might be — Len Tanner or either of the Morris brothers.

Jones said, "His name is Farley Brackett."

Hearing that name was like biting into a sour apple. Andy and Farley had ridden together on several missions, but their relationship had always been prickly.

Jones said, "From all I know of him, Brackett is a good man to have at your side in a fight."

Andy knew that to be true but was tempted to tell Jones that Farley started some of those fights himself. The war had left a visible scar on his face and invisible scars on his soul. In the first years after the Confederate defeat he had been an unreconstructed rebel, a constant thorn in the side of Union authorities. He had brought trouble to Rusty Shannon's door and therefore to Andy as well.

The major handed Andy the order he had been writing. "Stop at Ranger headquarters in San Antonio as you pass through. They can tell you exactly how to find your camp on the Rio Grande. It is moved from time to time."

"Yes, sir." Andy sensed that the major

was finished with him. He thought he should salute or something, but he simply backed to the door.

The clerk was waiting for him. He said, "I hope you've got a little money."

"A little. Not much."

"It'll have to stretch. We have no traveling money to give you."

"I don't eat much."

"That's good. You may have to live off of the land."

That was neither new nor news to Andy. "Any idea where I'll find Farley Brackett?"

"He put his horse in a stable down the street. Beyond that, I suggest you investigate all the dramshops."

Brackett did not have a reputation as a drinking man, but perhaps that was because he seldom had the opportunity, Andy thought. Whiling away the hours in Austin might tempt him to make up for time lost in dry and spartan Ranger camps.

Andy went to a livery barn where he and Rusty and Tom Blessing had stabled their horses on a visit several years ago. He recognized the proprietor as the same dried-up little man who had been there before, charging a shameless price for oats, hay, and corral space. Andy said, "I'm lookin' for a Ranger named Farley Brackett."

The hostler pointed to a stall. "His horse is here. I doubt Brackett has gone far afoot. Most of the Rangers I know had rather be whipped with a wet rope than to walk a hundred yards."

"If he comes in, tell him Andy Pickard is lookin' for him."

The hostler eyed him with curiosity. "You've got some older, but I believe I remember you. Ain't you the one that spiked them Union soldier boys' cannon so they couldn't use it to keep that Yankeefied governor in office?"

Andy suspected a lot of people in Austin remembered that incident. It had been a wonder someone was not killed. "I didn't spike the cannon, but I was with the ones that did."

"It was a hell of a show for a little while. Too bad it fizzled out before anybody got a chance to kill one of them damn Yankees."

Like many Texans, the hostler was still engaged in the war between the states, at least with words. Living among the Comanches at the time, Andy had been only dimly aware of the war. He knew a lot about its aftermath, however. To some degree it was still going on, just as the war between Texas and Mexico continued along the border years after it had been relegated to the past elsewhere.

He walked back over to Congress Avenue and entered the first bar he came to. It was moderately busy. He noted that most of the patrons wore suits. Men who wore suits in Austin were usually either lawyers or state employees. No wonder people complained about the waste of their tax money, he thought. This was a weekday. These men were supposed to be working.

Farley was not there. Andy waved off a bartender's question and returned to the street. A second barroom gave him no better result.

As he approached the third he heard a familiar voice raised in challenge: "I don't give a damn whether you like Rangers or not."

The reply came in an equally angry voice, though the words were muffled. Andy heard boots striking hard upon a wooden floor. A man hurtled out through the open door, speeded along by strong hands that gripped his collar and the seat of his britches. He sprawled on his stomach in the street. Farley Brackett stood in the doorway, making a show of dusting his hands. He said, "Come back in and I'll finish windin' your clock for you."

The man sat up but for the moment looked too confused to continue the contest.

Farley's eyes reflected surprise as he recognized Andy. "Badger Boy! What the hell you doin' here?" He did not appear pleased.

Badger Boy was an English version of the name by which Andy had been known among the Comanches. No one used it anymore except Farley, and he usually said it in a mocking way.

"Lookin' for you. I ought to've known to wait and listen for a fight."

"Wasn't no fight to it. I was just standin' there havin' me a peaceful drink when that gink asked me if I wasn't a Ranger. Don't know how he figured out I was. They never have got around to givin' us any badges."

"Some people claim they can tell a Ranger on sight, just by the way he walks and talks."

"I wasn't talkin' at all till that bird started to hooraw me. He said he never seen a Ranger that didn't smell like a skunk."

"If you try to whip everybody that doesn't like us, you'll be too busy to do anything else."

Farley transferred his irritation from the

stranger to Andy. "You're a little young to be preachin' gospel to me, Badger Boy. I've been shot and shot at more times than you've had birthdays."

"A little preachin' might do you good, but I know you wouldn't listen to it."

"That, I wouldn't," Farley said, and went back into the bar. Andy remained on the sidewalk, debating with himself about following. He considered riding on alone and letting Farley follow in his own good time or not at all. He knew from past experience that Farley could be poor company, chronically dissatisfied and critical. But the major might not be pleased. He liked his Rangers to work together as a team, not pull against one another like stubborn mules.

He walked into the room and found Farley leaning against the bar, a drink in his hand. The war scar on the side of his face accentuated his frown. "You still here? I figured you left."

"The major says we're supposed to head south and report for duty on the border."

"I don't remember him sayin' I had to ride with *you*. Every time we work together somethin' bad happens to me. You're a damned jinx."

"I'm not crazy about the notion either,

43

but if you don't like it you can resign."

"That'd make you happy, wouldn't it? Well, I'm not quittin'. Go find you a girl or somethin' and leave me in peace for what's left of the day. We can start the trip fresh in the mornin'."

Andy doubted how fresh Farley would be if he spent the evening in this bar or some other, but that was Farley's problem. "I've got my horse in the same stable as yours. I figure to leave soon after daylight."

Walking outside, he met the stranger Farley had thrown out. The man seemed to have gathered his wits, and his expression indicated that he did not consider the argument settled. Andy pointed his thumb at the door. "He's still in there," he said. He stood around a few minutes, listening to the sounds of a vigorous scuffle and the cheers of bystanders from inside.

Farley tumbled out the door and fell on his back on the sidewalk. Andy looked down at him and tried not to grin. "Enjoy yourself."

Farley rolled over and pushed to his feet, muttering under his breath. Face crimson and fists clenched, he stalked back into the barroom.

Andy's growling stomach reminded him that he had not eaten anything since breakfast. He had noticed a restaurant as he walked down the street. He met a policeman hurrying along the wooden sidewalk. The officer said, "Somebody told me there's a fight down thisaway."

Andy pointed. "You might look in that bar yonder. There's a right smart of noise comin' out of it."

By the time Farley got himself untangled from this mess he might be ready to travel, Andy thought.

Awake at daylight, Andy sat on the edge of the wagon-yard cot and looked at Farley, still sleeping, his blankets spread on a pile of hay. "Time to get movin'."

Farley did not respond. Andy had heard him come in during the night but had no idea what time it was. Farley had been talking to himself.

Andy said, "I'm fixin' to go get some breakfast. Then I'm hittin' the trail with or without you."

Farley still did not respond. Andy could see his chest rise and fall with his breathing, so he knew at least that Farley was not dead.

The hostler had a fire going in a small iron stove in the front office, a steaming pot on its top. He told Andy, "Got coffee here."

45

"Thanks, but I'm goin' for breakfast."

"You might want to take some coffee to your partner. By the looks of him as he staggered by here in the wee hours, he's liable to need it."

"His legs ain't broke. Let him come and get his own coffee."

The hostler seemed startled at Andy's lack of concern for Farley. "I thought you was Rangers together."

"Rangers, but not together any more than we have to be."

After breakfast Andy brushed the black horse, then saddled him. Farley was sitting up but still on his blankets. He appeared to have trouble focusing on Andy. "Where you goin' so early?"

"South, like we were ordered. You can catch up to me or not, that's up to you."

Farley rubbed a hand over his bruised and swollen face. His knuckles were red, the skin broken. "I must've had fun last night. I just can't remember much about it."

"Last time I saw you it looked like you were comin' out second best against a man who didn't like Rangers."

"It taken me a while, but I finally convinced him. It's what happened afterwards that I can't remember much about. The last I knew, him and me had a couple of drinks together, us and some policeman."

"A couple?"

"Maybe three. I never let myself get drunk."

Andy tied his blankets behind the saddle and started to lead the horse outside. Farley called, "Ain't you goin' to wait for me?"

"No." Andy mounted in the street and turned south to intersect the San Antonio road. He crossed the Colorado River on a wooden bridge and turned to look back northward toward the capitol building. Though he liked Austin, he never felt at ease in large cities. This one was home to maybe five or six thousand people.

He was a couple of hours down the trail when he heard a horse coming up behind him. "Badger Boy! Wait up."

Farley pulled in beside him. "Damn it, you'd make a man kill his horse tryin' to catch up with you."

"Told you I was leavin' soon after daylight."

"You could've waited. I was sick this mornin'."

"You look like a herd of cattle ran over you. For all I care you could've stayed in Austin."

"I was just havin' a little fun. Looks to me like I've earned it. Don't get much chance when we're out in the field."

"It's a good thing the major didn't see you."

"He knows that a man has to let off some steam now and again. Else he'll blow up like a boiler with the valve stuck."

Andy remembered how Farley had let off steam in the early years after the war, provoking the carpetbag state police into one fight after another. He had been like a wolf luring dogs into chasing him, then turning on them in a fury of slashing teeth. They had learned to pursue him only at a safe distance. Now he directed his belligerence at lawbreakers for the most part. That made him useful to the Rangers, though he tended to act first and plan later.

After a long, smoldering silence Farley remarked, "That's a good-lookin' black horse. Where did you steal him at?"

Farley had never gotten past a bone of contention involving a sorrel horse his father had given to Rusty Shannon and that Rusty had passed on to Andy. Farley always contended that the horse was his own and that his father had no right to give him away.

Andy said, "I always figured if you're

goin' to steal a horse, you'd just as well steal a good one."

The wagon road south from Austin skirted the eastern edge of rough limestone hills where the Edwards escarpment rose out of the western portion of the coastal plain. To the east lay farming settlements along the Colorado and Brazos rivers. To the west, stock farmers and ranchers were freely expanding their operations now that they no longer slept with their guns, worrying about Indian raids. German enclaves such as Friedrichsburg and Neu Braunfels had sunk deep roots. The hill country had appealed to Andy from the first time he saw its long green valleys, its bubbling springs, its clear-running creeks and rivers. Someday, if he ever left the Rangers, he thought he could make a life for himself there.

Traveling at a pace that would not be hard on the horses, Andy and Farley took two days traveling from Austin to San Antonio. Farley said, "Last chance for a little relaxation. Ain't goin' to be much fun from here south."

"If you'd had much more fun in Austin you'd still be there."

"It'll be all business when we get to the

border. Go on ahead if you want to, but whatever trouble they got down there can wait another night or two."

Andy did not feel like arguing. "We can tell them we needed to rest the horses." He would welcome the chance to look around the historic city. "We'll need to find Ranger headquarters."

"Tomorrow is soon enough. If they know we're here they'll want us to start south right away whether our horses are tired or not."

Andy had never been to San Antonio, though he had heard many stories about its turbulent past. The town had been a cross-roads of early Texas history. Several pitched battles had been fought there, first for Mexico's freedom from Spain and later for Texas's freedom from Mexico. Though other cities in the state were rapidly gaining in importance, San Antonio remained the jewel in its crown — if a sprawl of picket *jacales* and single-story buildings of stone and adobe could be considered a jewel.

As soon as they found a convenient wagon yard and put their horses away, Farley disappeared. He had been to San Antonio in his hell-raising days after the war and knew where he wanted to go.

Andy asked the stable's manager how to find the Ranger headquarters, then walked about, familiarizing himself with the center of town. Street traffic was heavy. A man had to look both ways before crossing over lest he be stepped on or rolled over by horses, wagons, and ox-drawn carts with high, solid wooden wheels that groaned and squealed on dry hubs.

He had known the population would be heavily Mexican, but seeing it for himself made him feel like an outsider. As a boy with the Comanches he had listened to Kiowas talking. He had felt helpless because he could not understand a word. He found himself just as lost trying to decipher some meaning from the Spanish he heard spoken all about him.

He had learned Comanche and relearned English. With time he should be able to pick up at least enough Spanish to get him by, he thought.

A strong German element was also evident, spilled over from early immigrant settlements founded in the 1840s. He despaired of ever learning to speak German. Spanish would be challenge enough.

He came unexpectedly upon what he recognized as the Alamo, at least the battle-scarred remains of the church that had

51

been the center of the original mission complex. Much of the rest was gone, lost to new construction and bustling commercial uses. He was disappointed to find that even the old sanctuary had been turned into a warehouse. He thought it an undignified fate for a building where brave men had fought, bled, and died for Texas. Perhaps it would someday be turned into a shrine befitting the blood sacrifice that patriots of both Texas and Mexico had made there.

In the Ranger office Andy looked at a map that appeared to be the same as the one on Major Jones's Austin wall except that more trails had been added, some ranches and small towns penciled in. A lieutenant traced one of the trails with his finger. "With some exceptions, you'll find most white ranchers friendly to the Rangers. With some exceptions, you'll find most Mexicans distrustful and unfriendly. Both sides have cause." He turned back to face Andy. "Have you got anything against Mexicans?"

"Major Jones asked me the same question. No, I don't."

"Many people do, Rangers included. It's not one-sided, though. Many Mexicans have a hard grudge against whites too. Especially Rangers. They say we use our authority and our guns to help the gringo ranchers run them out of the country."

Andy reflected a minute. "Do we?"

"We're not supposed to, but some take it to be their duty. Old wars don't die easy. They linger on like an incurable disease."

"I try to treat everybody just alike."

"That's a fine ideal. I hope you can live up to it when you've been on the river awhile. A man can lose his religion there if he doesn't get killed first."

Andy was not sure just what his religion was. Old Preacher Webb and others had counseled him about Christianity, but remnants of Comanche beliefs lingered as well. Sometimes the two seemed much the same. Other times they conflicted.

Andy asked, "When I get down there, what'll my duties be?"

"They'll be whatever Lieutenant Buckalew tells you to do. If he says ride, you'll ride. If he says shoot, you'll shoot. Don't waste his time or yours askin' questions."

"Yes, sir."

"When the lieutenant isn't around, you'll take orders from Sergeant Donahue. You may find that the lieutenant and the sergeant don't always see eye to eye."

"In that case, which one do I listen to?"

"The one who's there at the time." The officer turned toward a small safe. "How long since you've been paid?"

"I was out on assignment the last payday. And I had to buy a horse. About all I've got in my pocket is a whittlin' knife."

"I'll advance you a little travelin' money against your wages. We can't have a Ranger beggin' his way down the road. Keep account of your expenses. Maybe the state'll see fit to reimburse you. Or maybe not."

Andy normally wasted little time worrying about money, but once in a while the need could not be ignored. He had feared he would have to accept a wound to his pride by asking Farley to lend him a few dollars. But Farley might have no money left either after a couple of days and nights in San Antonio. It would give Andy deep satisfaction if Farley had to touch *him* for a loan.

His stomach rumbled loudly enough that he was sure the officer must have heard. He asked, "Where can I get a decent meal cheap?"

The lieutenant seemed to approve of the word *cheap*. "There's a fair-to-middlin' chili joint down the street a couple of blocks and around the corner. It's not the Menger Hotel, but it's fillin'. And the cook washes his hands once a day whether they need it or not."

"Sounds like the place for me."

He started to leave, but the officer snapped his fingers and said, "Almost forgot. There's another Ranger who'll be headed the same way as you and Brackett. He came up to deliver a prisoner. Maybe you know him. Name's Len Tanner."

Andy grinned. "I've known him since I was this high." He held his hand flat at chest level. "I lost track after he got transferred away from my camp. Where do you reckon I'll find him?"

"Go where you hear the loudest talkin'."

Len had a reputation for a loose jaw. He could talk the bark off a live-oak tree. Andy had first gotten to know him when an accidental horse fall and broken leg took him out of Comanche hands and thrust him back into the life of a white boy. A jovial spirit who came and went as the mood struck him, Len had spun enticing tales of high adventure and eventually had talked Andy into joining the Rangers.

The café's proprietor had laughing eyes that offset the fierceness of his black beard. His body was shaped like a pickle barrel.

He asked, "Cowboy?"

"Nope," Andy said. "Ranger."

"Ain't nothin' too good for a Ranger. I'll give you a choice: beefsteak or chili. Same price."

"That bein' the case, I'll take the beefsteak."

The man laughed. "Some of the biggest ranchers in South Texas come in here to eat. It's the only time a lot of them ever eat any of their own beef."

Andy took that to imply that most preferred to eat their neighbors' cattle. It also implied that the operator of the chili joint was not choosy about the source of his meat supply.

Andy said, "It doesn't sound like rightful ownership means much around here."

"Not unless a man is ready and willin' to fight for what belongs to him. There's people here who can steal your socks without takin' your boots off."

The cook poured a cup of coffee for Andy without being asked. A cast-iron skillet clanged as he placed it atop the stove. He plopped a huge spoonful of hog lard in it to heat and melt. He said, "The secret to a good steak is to fry it deep in plenty of hot grease."

Enough of it, Andy thought, and he

could develop a belly like the cook's.

The cook said, "I ain't seen you before. Where are you stationed?"

Andy told him he was being reassigned to the border. The man's face went serious. "The trail down to the Rio Grande can be risky, especially the lower part. The more Rangers the better. You never know who's liable to pop out of the brush lookin' for somebody to shoot."

"I'll have another Ranger with me. Maybe two if I can find Len Tanner."

The name brought a flicker of recognition from the cook. "I believe that old boy was in here yesterday. He talked till my ears hurt."

"That's him."

The cook turned Andy's steak over in the skillet. "If I was you I wouldn't noise it around too much about bein' a Ranger. I rode awhile with McNelly's outfit. Down in that border country the Mexicans called us *rinches,* and they didn't say it sweet. I decided to move up here for my health."

Mention of Captain McNelly stirred Andy's curiosity. "What kind of a man was he?"

"As good a feller as I ever knew. He had a hard job to do, and he done it despite bein' sick most of the time. Some days he was almost too weak to stay in the saddle, but he wouldn't let go. He meant to clean up the border if he had to kill half the population. He *did* kill a lot of them. Some claim he went too far." The cook shrugged. "All I can say is that bandit raids tapered off right smartly by the time he got through."

Andy said, "From what I hear, they're back. Maybe not as strong as before McNelly, but bad enough."

The cook lifted the steak on a fork and dropped it onto a platter. "Want a little advice? No extra charge."

"Sure."

"Don't trust every smilin' face you see. You never know for sure who's your friend and who wants to see you dead. When in doubt, shoot first."

Andy asked, "What if I kill somebody innocent?"

"There's damned few innocent people down there. They might start that way, but they get over it."

Andy's back was to the door, but he sensed that someone had entered the room behind him. The voice was Farley's, and he sounded agitated. "Eat quick and let's get movin'."

"I thought you had some celebratin' to do."

"Done done it. I'm ready to go."

"What's the big hurry? It's already late in the day. We can't get far before dark."

"We can get far enough. I'll go fetch our horses while you finish your supper."

Farley left in a trot. The cook said, "Don't eat too fast. Ain't good for the digestion."

"I just hope he didn't kill somebody."

Before Andy had finished eating his steak and red beans, Farley was back and leading Andy's black horse. He shouted from outside, "Come on. Let's move."

Andy kept his seat until he had emptied the platter and finished his coffee. He paid the proprietor out of the money the lieutenant had advanced. The cook said, "Mind what I told you. They'll smile when you're lookin' and stab you when you turn your back."

Farley was fidgeting as if he had ants in his underwear. "You damned sure took your time."

"I don't see why we have to rush away from here like a couple of thieves."

Farley did not answer. He set his horse into a long trot. He did not bother to look back and see if Andy was following.

Andy caught up to him as they passed through the southern outskirts of town. "Who did you shoot?"

The question surprised Farley. "I never shot nobody."

"The way you left, I thought maybe you did."

Farley looked back. "It wasn't nothin' like that. I ran into an old friend of yours, and I was afraid he'd want to ride with us. I can't listen to Len Tanner all the way to the border. I might shoot him to shut him up."

Annoyed, Andy said, "All this rush was to get away from Len? Where did you find him?"

"I was visitin' a couple of ladies I know. He was there doin' the same thing. You're too young to understand."

"I'm old enough. Seems to me like you ought to find yourself a good woman and leave those other *ladies* alone."

"What woman would look twice at this scarred face unless she was paid to do it?"

"There's bound to be some. You've been searchin' in the wrong places."

"And you're stickin' your nose in where you've got no business."

Andy choked down his irritation. Though Len's chatter could be a trial, he would prefer it to riding with a morose Farley Brackett. "I've got half a mind to go back and find him."

"If you do, you'll go by yourself."

"That might be an improvement."

Farley grumped, "You're damned hard to get along with. Must be you ain't got all the Indian out of you."

3

Andy looked back a couple of times as they put the historic old town behind them. He hoped he might see Len catching up. He said, "Len's a good Ranger, you can't take that away from him."

Farley said, "That don't mean I've got to appreciate his company. A man can put up with just so much jaw."

Andy knew of no one who disliked Len except some of the criminals he had sent away to board with the state. Farley was a good Ranger too, but Andy knew many people who did not care for much of his company, himself included.

He asked, "When are we goin' to stop and camp?" He hoped Len would catch up.

Farley said curtly, "You already had your supper, and I brought mine with me." He held up a pint bottle.

Andy had rarely seen him drunk, for Farley could hold a prodigious amount of whiskey without showing its effects. He had a stern will that did not permit interference with whatever he set his mind to do. Len, on the other hand, did not drink on duty or when he thought he might be called to duty. Even a modest amount of whiskey could start him to singing in a voice loud but seriously off-key.

At dusk Farley said, "We better call it a day. We been pushin' the horses pretty hard."

Farley had been pushing. Andy had just been trying to keep up.

Farley added, "We don't need no fire. It's warm enough, and we ain't cookin'. A fire just draws visitors."

Andy knew Farley was concerned about just one visitor, Len. They pulled off the trail a little way, unsaddled and hobbled their horses. Dragging one foot, Farley smoothed the rocks from a small patch of ground and spread his blankets. He hoisted the bottle without offering to share it. Andy would have refused it anyway. He had not developed a liking for whiskey and could not understand why others so readily did. It always burned his throat on the way down and kindled a fire in his stomach when it got there.

Farley said, "I don't suppose you seen my mother and sister before you left?"

"I did."

"How were they?"

"Fine. They're the *likeable* members of the Brackett family."

Farley accepted the implication without visible reaction. "You serious about Bethel?"

"I might be if I wasn't a Ranger."

"That's easy fixed. You could quit."

"If you don't like me ridin' with you as a Ranger, you sure wouldn't like havin' me for a brother-in-law."

"I'd seldom ever see you."

Andy said, "I guess that's right. You hardly ever visit your womenfolks."

"It's better that way. All I ever brought them was trouble."

Andy kindled a small fire. Farley demanded, "What's that for?"

"I want to boil a little coffee after that ride."

"Never could see why some people got to have coffee all the time. It's too much trouble. With whiskey, all you have to do is pull the cork."

Andy heard the strike of a horse's hooves and saw a lanky rider approaching in the dusk. A familiar voice shouted, "Hello, the camp. You there, Andy?"

Farley groaned. "Oh hell."

Andy stood up and waved his arm.

"Come on in, Len."

Len Tanner swung a spindly leg over his horse's rump and stepped to the ground. "I'd about give up on catchin' you fellers. I thought you'd wait for me in town."

Andy saw no need to explain and hurt Len's feelings. "Farley was in a hurry to leave. It's a right long trip to the river."

"I know. I had to deliver a prisoner all the way up to San Antonio. He was wanted for usin' his knife a little too free. That's a common failin' in this part of the country. Got some of that coffee left? I ain't had no supper."

Farley muttered, "I suppose after a few days in town you was too broke to feed yourself."

Andy figured Farley might be right about that. Wages slipped through Len's fingers like sand. He always said he could travel lighter without the weight of silver in his pockets. He was too skinny to carry much extra weight anyhow.

Len said, "I'll ride with you fellers if you'll have me. It always shortens the miles when I've got somebody to talk to."

Farley grunted and moved to where he had spread his blankets. "I'm hittin' the soogans. If you find me gone in the mornin' it'll be because I made an early start."

65

Len said, "Eager, ain't he? He wouldn't rush if he knew the border. It was easier fightin' Indians. At least when you saw one you knew he was your enemy. Down yonder you're never sure."

Andy asked, "How come you to transfer from the San Saba? That was a nice place to be stationed."

"The captain volunteered me. I guess they needed a man with experience."

More than likely the captain had heard Len's stories one time too many, Andy thought.

They set out the next morning soon after daybreak. Len began to tell about his experiences since he had been sent down to the border. Andy listened eagerly, but Farley quickly lost patience. He stopped and dismounted, lifting his mount's left forefoot and examining the shoe.

"I think there's a stone lodged in here," he said. "You-all go on. I'll catch up to you by-and-by."

Andy suspected Farley was trying to get out of earshot. He would probably drag along behind. Andy had rather listen to Len's stories than to Farley's grumbling anyway.

He had noticed a bright, shiny star on Len's shirt. Sometimes Rangers made their own badges. "Where did you get that?"

"A Mexican cut it for me out of a silver peso. Looks pretty good, don't it?"

"Looks like a target."

"Ain't nobody hit it yet. Been a couple tried."

"White or Mexican?"

"One of each. Most Mexicans don't like Rangers, and a lot of whites don't like Rangers gettin' in their way when they're tryin' to take what belongs to the Mexicans. We get shot at from both sides."

By noon Farley had not caught up. Andy could see him poking along a couple of hundred yards behind. Len asked, "Reckon we ought to stop and wait for him?"

"He likes his own company. Let him make the most of it."

"I figure he must've been born in the dark. Me, I was born in the daylight."

Andy enjoyed studying the changing landscape. It was gently rolling, mostly open except for watercourses lined with trees and many varieties of brush. Wide areas were flat enough for farming, though little had as yet been broken by the plow. Cattle of many hues grazed the tall, summer-curing grass. Some hoisted their tails and ran for the thickets. Others watched placidly as the riders passed, for this was a much-used public roadway. They were accustomed to wagon, cart, and horseback traffic.

He said, "Sure looks peaceful."

Len shook his head. "Wait till we get down into the brush country. Plant, animal, or human, everything there is lookin' for a chance to draw blood. They've all got stickers, horns, knives, or shootin' irons."

Farley grudgingly rejoined them as they stopped at an abandoned adobe hut from which windowsills and the roof had been removed. The mud walls were gradually disintegrating, most of their plaster covering gone.

Len said, "Sure feels good to sleep indoors now and again."

Farley spread his blankets outside, by himself.

As the next day waned toward dusk they began looking for a place to stop. They came upon a little creek that appeared to be a favored camping site. A half dozen Mexican ox carts were there. A couple of dark-skinned men walked out to meet the riders. They spoke in Spanish. Andy could not understand a word.

Len said, "I've picked up a little Mexican lingo. They're invitin' us to share the camp with them."

Andy asked, "They can see your badge. I thought all Mexicans hated Rangers."

"Just the same, they'd feel safer camped with us. There's gringos around who would be glad to do them harm."

Farley said, "They might wait till we're asleep, then carve their initials on our gizzards."

Len argued, "They're just freighters, haulin' goods from the Gulf of Mexico to San Antonio. They know if they hurt anybody they couldn't get away. An ox team travels awful slow."

"I don't trust anybody I can't understand. We need to find a place where we're by ourselves, or at least with people who talk our language."

Andy said, "The worst people I ever knew spoke our language real plain. They just didn't think the same way we do."

Farley snorted. "Stay here for all I care. I'm goin' on."

Andy glanced at Len and shrugged. They traveled a while longer. Farley turned from the road and followed a cow trail about a quarter mile. "Them people might come huntin' for us after dark. They'll play hell findin' us out here."

Andy was not keen on making a dry camp. He asked, "What have we got that they'd want?"

"Our horses. Our guns. We're gringos, and we're Rangers. That by itself might be enough."

Len said, "Can't fault anybody for bein' what they was born. The big dealer dealt us each a hand the day of our birth. It's up to us to play it out the best we can."

Farley said, "I was born cautious."

Not all that cautious. Andy remembered when Farley's reckless disregard for reconstruction law had made him a target of the carpetbag state police and brought bad trouble down upon his family. But Farley was selective in what he chose to be cautious about.

Len said, "If you-all are nervous about my badge, I'll take it off." He stuck it in his pocket. "If anybody jumps us now, it won't be because we're Rangers."

Toward noon the next day Andy began seeing dust rising in the south. It troubled him for a time because it was too localized to be a dust storm.

Len said, "It'll be a trail herd on its way north. Lots of them swing by San Antonio to supply their wagons."

The point man, riding at the front of the

strung-out herd, was white. He gave the three Rangers a silent and distrustful study, then moved on past them. Len observed, "It's a steer herd bound for the Kansas railroad, I'd guess. Cow herds are generally headed farther north, like to Wyomin' and Montana."

Wyoming and Montana were exotic-sounding names to Andy. He said, "I wonder how it'd be to go up there ourselves."

Len shook his head. "The sight of a snowflake makes me shiver. Feller told me one time he was up in Wyomin' and seen a hat movin' along on top of the snow. When he went to look, he found a cowboy under the hat, and the cowboy was on horseback."

Andy grinned. Len declared, "It's the gospel truth. At least that's what the feller told me."

Farley's face was without expression. Andy could count on one hand the number of times he had ever seen Farley smile at a joke, or anything else. Farley nodded toward the cattle. "Notice how many different brands they've got on them?"

Len said, "A lot of those are Mexican brands." He pointed out that they were larger and more intricate than most of Texas origin.

Andy asked, "You think they're stolen?"

"Let's say they was got awful cheap. They swum the Rio Grande in the dark of the moon. Come daylight, they was citizens of Texas."

Andy said, "Maybe we ought to arrest this whole outfit."

Farley said, "Didn't the Comanches ever teach you how to count, Badger Boy? There's a dozen or fifteen of them and just three of us. I doubt you'd find a churchgoin' man amongst them."

Len said, "There's a chance these people bought the cattle in good faith from somebody else who brought them across the river. Anyway, the Mexicans they belonged to may have made up the loss already, swimmin' Texas cattle back in the other direction."

Farley said, "Sounds like everybody breaks even."

"Not everybody. There's losers, and they're generally the little fellers. Besides, it's bigger than just cattle. People get killed."

A swing rider approached. He had a sober bearing that indicated he might be the boss. He said, "I hope you-all ain't Rangers."

Andy said, "Why? What difference would it make?"

The drover spat. "The Rangers gave me trouble over the Mexicos in this herd. I had to pull strings in high places."

Farley said, "We're Rangers, but we ain't been given any orders yet. It's no hide off of our butt if you take these cattle to Timbuktu."

The trail man said, "Kansas is far enough. Time we get there they'll all be talkin' American."

The Rangers pulled away from the herd to get out of the dust. It struck Andy as curious that more than half the horsemen appeared to be Mexican. He said, "If these cattle were stolen from south of the river, the Mexicans with this outfit are robbin' their own countrymen."

Len said, "Some don't feel like they owe Mexico nothin', or Texas either. Santy Anna stabbed them in the back. After preachin' that his soldiers ought to be proud to die for Mexico, he gave away Texas to save his own hide. They don't see that anything is wrong if they can get away with it. That includes shootin' a Texas Ranger or a Mexican *rurale*. It's open season on anybody who gets in their way."

"Some of these drovers are gringos."

"Thieves don't pay much attention to each other's color as long as they're all fillin' their pockets. Afterwards they may try to cut each other's throats. Why, just last spring . . ." He started retelling a story he had already told twice on this trip.

Farley dropped back a hundred yards.

Len dismounted in front of an abandoned adobe house. He rubbed his mount's right foreleg. "Feels to me like my horse is comin' up lame."

Andy looked to the west, where the sun cast a rosy glow through low-hanging clouds. "He may just be gettin' tired. It's time we stopped for the day and gave the horses a rest."

Farley argued, "We've got an hour of daylight left."

Andy said, "You want Len to have to walk and lead his horse?"

"It wouldn't hurt him none. Might make him tired enough to quit talkin'."

Len said, "You go right on ahead if you want to. I ain't goin' to ruin a good horse."

Andy said, "I'm stayin' with Len."

Farley seemed about to argue the point but gave in. "You two need lookin' after. Anyway, they ain't goin' to pay us extra for reportin' in early."

Andy saw a well beside the house and led his black horse over to examine it. Looking down into the water, he saw no sign that it harbored any drowned rats or other small animals. Though the house appeared not to have been occupied in a long time, the windlass had a reasonably new rope. It was probably a gift from someone who passed this way often. Andy turned the handle and brought up a bucket of water. He poured it into a small wooden trough and brought up a second bucket so there would be enough for his horse. He cupped his hands and tentatively tasted the water to be sure it was good before he drank his fill.

Len started to walk through the door but stopped abruptly and stepped back. Andy heard a buzzing sound that he recognized instantly as a rattlesnake's warning. Len said, "I believe I'll sleep outdoors tonight." He handed his reins to Andy. "But I'll make sure this gentleman doesn't come out huntin' for me." As soon as Andy had led his and Len's horses away, Len shot the snake.

Holstering the pistol, he said, "Welcome to South Texas, where everything scratches, stings, or bites."

They searched around for sign of more

snakes, then hobbled the horses. Andy built a small fire in a rock-lined hole that travelers had used before him. He let the fire burn down to red coals, then set a coffeepot on top of them.

He said, "Indians would make supper out of that snake. It tastes a little like chicken."

Len grimaced. "Help yourself. I've been hungry lots of times. I've eaten mesquite beans and jackrabbit. I've eaten horse and mule meat, but I ain't never been hungry enough to eat a rattler." He went on to describe at length a couple of times when he was desperate enough that he almost ate the tops from his boots.

Muttering to himself about liars and those who listened to them, Farley went out to gather some dry wood. He came back and dropped several dead mesquite limbs near the fire. "Riders comin'," he said. He went to his saddle lying on the ground and pulled his rifle from its scabbard.

Andy followed his lead by drawing his pistol. He counted seven horsemen, one a smooth-faced boy of fourteen or fifteen. The others were older and had not felt a razor in at least a couple of weeks, nor water either except to drink.

Farley said with some relief, "At least they're Americans."

Len's right hand rested on the butt of his pistol. "That don't guarantee nothin'. They may not like the law, so we better not tell them we're Rangers. They've got us outnumbered."

The riders stopped a respectful distance from the Rangers' camp. One rode forward with his right hand raised in a sign of peace. He slouched in the saddle. "Howdy. Looks like you-all have made yourselves to home."

Farley did not offer a welcome. "You got any quarrel with that?"

The rider shook his head. His whiskers were coal black, a sharp contrast to the washed-out gray of his eyes. "None at'all. We're just travelers like yourselves, lookin' to water our horses before we ride on a ways more."

Farley said, "The water's free for everybody."

The man said, "We come upon a bunch of Meskins back yonder. They eyed us like coyotes that found a mess of quail. I've got a hunch they been trailin', waitin' to hit us in the night when we're asleep. It'd ease our minds if we could camp with you-all."

Andy saw doubt in Len's and Farley's eyes.

The visitor said, "The more there is of us, the safer we'll all be."

Farley was slow to lower his rifle. "Maybe. What say you-all camp over on the other side of the house?"

The man waved his arm, and the other six rode in closer. He said, "My name is Burt Hatton. Me and the boys here, we just delivered a herd to San Antonio. There's people that'd gladly shoot us for the money them cattle brought. Failin' that, they'd at least try to take our horses."

Andy did not like the looks of the men. They reminded him of a wolf pack circling a small buffalo herd and looking to bring down a calf.

Len was uncharacteristically silent. As the men moved away, he said, "Andy, you look like you smelled a skunk."

"It's just a feelin' I've got."

"Me too. Seems to me like I've seen that hombre before. With all the whiskers it's hard to be sure."

The drovers made camp on the opposite side of the adobe ruin. Once their horses were unsaddled and hobbled, Hatton walked back over to the Rangers' campfire. He asked, "You-all headed for the border?"

Len was usually the first to speak, but he kept his silence. His badge remained in his pocket.

Farley said, "We thought we'd go down there and take a look around."

"I hope you've been told what kind of country you're gettin' into."

"We've got a pretty fair notion."

"You'll find more Meskins than white people. Damned shame, seein' as this country is supposed to be American. We've chased a lot of them across the river, but they keep birthin' more and more of them here. Seems like they're bound and determined to outbreed us. A white man has got to keep his guns strapped on all the time."

Andy was a little disturbed by Hatton's tone. "If a man owns his land, how can you run him off of it?"

"They'll sell out when you put the proposition to them right. A Meskin gets real agreeable if you stick a pistol up against his ear and cock the hammer back. Especially if you can bribe a couple of Rangers to stand behind you."

Andy saw anger rising in Len's eyes. He had seldom seen Len yield to ill humor. Len turned away from the campfire. "I'm goin' to see about the horses."

Andy followed him. He kept his voice

low. "A Ranger wouldn't ever do that. Would he?"

Len frowned. "There's some that might. They think the border country would be a lot better off if all the Mexicans was moved to the other side."

"That's what they did to the Indians. They pushed them all north of the Red River." Resentment stirred when he thought about his Comanche friends forced into exile on a cramped reservation away from their former range. Yet he realized it had been the only way to curtail their raiding.

Len said, "The law says you can't put people off of their property, but some gringos ignore the law. They tell the Mexicans they can either leave or die. More often than not they sell out for whatever they can get. It usually ain't much."

"I wouldn't be a party to such as that."

"Me and you, we're just privates. We've got no say. If a sergeant says 'Fire,' all we can do is ask what at." Len looked worriedly back toward camp. "I'd swear that Hatton looks familiar."

"Maybe he's in your fugitive book."

Rangers carried a book with handwritten descriptions of fugitives. They consulted it often and kept it as up to date as possible.

They took special pleasure in marking off a fugitive as captured or killed.

Len said, "Might be. I'll read it after a while when that bunch can't see me."

Andy returned to the campfire. He heard Hatton talking to Farley about border outlaws. "There's one in particular you better be on the *cuidado* for. Guadalupe Chavez has got a big ranch over yonder, stocked with good Texas cattle his bunch has stole. Used to have considerable land on this side of the river too, but Jericho Jackson ran him off of it."

Andy asked, "Who's Jericho Jackson?"

Hatton seemed surprised that Andy did not know. "Just about the biggest man on the Texas side of the border these days. Took over a large part of what Chavez claimed north of the river. He ain't a man to be crossed, not even by the likes of Guadalupe Chavez. They're blood enemies."

Andy said, "This Chavez, what kind of man is he?"

"A real bad hombre. His pistoleros come across the river lookin' for somethin' to steal and gringos to kill. He tells his people that someday he'll fly the Mexican flag again over everything from the Rio Grande to San Antonio."

Len said, "I hear that Jericho Jackson ain't no angel either. It's like he built a wall around his ranch and don't let anybody in that ain't an outlaw like he is."

Andy said, "I remember Preacher Webb talkin' about a place called Jericho. It had walls, but they fell down."

Len nodded. "That was on account of a soldier called Joshua, but I ain't met anybody around here by that name."

Hatton's eyes flashed in irritation. "I wouldn't go talkin' against Jericho. It can get a man hurt." He pushed to his feet. "Maybe the boys have got supper fixed." He stalked away.

Farley turned on Len. "What did you provoke him for? He was tellin' us things we need to know."

"I remember where I've seen him before. He was with a bunch we caught drivin' stolen horses. We got most of the horses back, but the ones they rode was faster than ours. We suspected they was workin' for Jericho Jackson, but it's hard to get anything on him. People like Hatton do his dirty work for him."

Farley chewed on what Len said. "You reckon there's paper out on Hatton?"

Len grunted. "There ought to be. I'd wager that the cattle they delivered to San

Antonio still had Rio Grande mud on them. We better stand guard duty tonight, or we're liable to find ourselves dead in the mornin'. Or at least afoot. Notice the way he kept lookin' at our horses?"

Farley said, "I figured since the men was all white that we had no need to worry."

"White, Mexican, down in this country there's meanness enough to go around."

Andy asked, "So what do we do?"

Len made a wry smile. "What would your Comanche brothers do if they smelled Apaches?"

"They'd sleep with their eyes open and a war club in their hands."

Len said, "We'll do better than that. After good dark we'll move our horses, then we'll keep watch."

Andy half expected Farley to put up an argument because the idea was Len's, but he didn't. They made a show of stringing a rope between two trees and tying their horses and the pack mule to it. Before moonrise they quietly led the animals farther out into the brush and retied the picket line. They returned to camp but remained in the shadows beyond the campfire's dying light.

After a time Andy felt himself dozing off.

Farley punched him with his elbow. He whispered, "Rub a little tobacco in your eyes. That'll keep you awake."

And maybe blind me, Andy thought. He declined the offer of Farley's tobacco.

He felt himself nodding again just before Len gently shook him. "They're comin'."

The fire had burned down to flickering coals that yielded little light. Andy could make out shadowy figures moving stealthily into the Rangers' camp.

He recognized Hatton's voice, raised in disappointment. "They're gone."

Someone else said, "They can't be gone far. Their camp stuff is here."

Farley raised up. "Yes, we're still here, and you sons of bitches ain't gettin' our horses."

Pistols blazed on both sides, and then a rifle. Men shouted and cursed. A youthful voice cried out in mortal pain. Hatton's men backed away, quickly lost in the darkness. Andy heard Hatton shout, "Pick him up and let's get out of here."

The smell of gun smoke was pungent. Andy heard horses moving away from the Hatton camp. His heart pumping with excitement, he said, "We must've hit somebody."

Farley said, "I thought they would just

come after our horses. But they was after us too."

Andy said, "No witnesses, no charges."

Len said, "No use tryin' to follow them in the dark. I can't see that they done us any harm."

He was mistaken. At the picket line they found Farley's horse down. Andy knelt to examine it and found it was dead. "Stray bullet must've got him."

His first reaction was relief that his black horse had not been hit. But he realized that this would complicate the completion of their trip.

Farley declared, "Damned if I intend to walk all the way to the river."

Len said, "We can borrow a horse at the McCawley ranch, a little ways south. Till then we'll take turns walkin'."

Farley asked, "Who's McCawley?"

"Big Jim McCawley. He married into the Chavez family."

The name got Andy's attention. "Chavez?"

"He married Guadalupe Chavez's sister, but don't hold that against him. There was a time when even Lupe Chavez was considered good folks. That was before Jericho and others tried to take everything away from him and his family."

Farley said, "I don't know as this is a good idea, havin' truck with Chavez's kinfolks."

Len shrugged off Farley's objection. "Big Jim's always been friendly to the Rangers. We've brought back stock of his that was run off by thieves."

"I'd be friendly too if they recovered my property."

"You'll be surprised how many *ain't* friendly." A smile spread across Len's face. "Once you see Big Jim's daughter Teresa, you'll be glad we went there."

Andy said, "You sayin' she's pretty?"

"Wait till you see her eyes. Dark as coffee beans. They melt me plumb down into my boots."

Farley said, "But she's Mexican, ain't she?"

"One look at her and you won't even think about that."

"Mexican is Mexican."

4

Hatton and his men had galloped more than a mile when Burt Hatton shouted for a stop and reined his horse around. "Let's see about that damned kid."

Jesse Wilkes held the wounded boy to prevent his falling from the saddle. "I'm afraid he ain't goin' to make it."

Hatton listened for sound of pursuit but heard none. He dismounted and raised his arms. "Lift him down to me." He lowered the groaning youngster to the ground. "I wish to hell you'd stayed home like you was told. Let's have a look at you."

He felt the warm stickiness of blood on his hands. He fished a match from his pocket and struck it for light. In the few seconds that it burned, he saw what he had feared. He heard a faint bubbling sound. "Of all the bad luck, they got him in the chest."

Wilkes said, "I'm afraid he's goin' to die."

Hatton made no comment.

The boy whimpered, "Where's Aunt

Thelma? Take me to Aunt Thelma."

"You'll be all right," Hatton said, knowing he lied. "We'll carry you to a doctor."

"It hurts. Oh God, it hurts."

Wilkes was always finding fault. He said, "It was a mistake to let the boy come along. Jericho told us not to."

Hatton retorted, "We didn't let him come. He done that on his own."

The boy was a nephew of Jericho's wife. Given the responsibility of raising him, she had spoiled him so that he took advice from nobody except her. He had begged to help Hatton and his crew drive the cattle to San Antonio. It should not have been a dangerous trip. It became so only when Hatton took a notion to bushwhack three strangers for their horses and gear. It had looked easy.

Whose damn-fool idea was it in the first place? Hatton asked himself, though he knew it had been his own. He had not intended for Jericho to know about it. Hatton and the others would not have had to split their booty with him.

The boy cried, complaining about the pain until his voice began to fade.

Fearfully Wilkes said, "He's dyin', Burt. Do somethin'."

"Damn it, shut up."

In a few minutes the kid shuddered and was gone. Hatton shuddered too, and cursed under his breath. "Just my luck."

Wilkes said, "Better it had been one of us. It'll be hell to face Jericho. He's been known to kill a man for bringin' him bad news." He looked at Hatton, making it plain he expected Hatton to be the one to carry the message. "You know how he dotes on that woman of his, and she dotes on this boy."

Hatton frowned, considering his options. An idea took a little edge from his dark mood. "He don't have to know how the shootin' came about. We can tell him we got ambushed, and it wasn't our fault."

"Jericho'll see right through you. His eyes cut like a knife. Why would anybody pull an ambush on us?"

Hatton's spirits lifted a bit more. "Jericho hates Lupe Chavez like he was strychnine. He'll believe it if we tell him we ran into some Chavez bandits. We'll tell him they didn't give us a chance."

"*You* tell him. I wouldn't lie to him for a hundred dollars. What about the kid? We goin' to take him all the way home?"

"It's too far, and the weather is too warm. Come daylight we'll find a place to bury him. Jericho is goin' to ask a lot of questions. Everybody remember: Chavez's outfit ambushed us."

Wilkes grumbled, "I still say he won't believe it."

Hatton's voice was deep and dangerous. "You tell him different and I'll kill you."

Big Jim McCawley's place was not fancy, but it was large. A long Mexican-style rock house dominated a gentle knoll. It was surrounded by smaller, flat-topped buildings, mostly adobe, some of pickets, scattered haphazardly down the slope. Off to one side lay corrals with fences of stacked stones or upright tree branches bound tightly together with rawhide thongs dried to the hardness of steel. Everything appeared to have been built from raw materials close at hand.

Andy and Len walked their horses so Farley could keep pace afoot. He chose to lag behind a little so he did not have to listen to Len's long-running commentary on everything from the weather to the crowned heads of Europe, and now and then a detailed description of Teresa McCawley. Andy carried Farley's saddle and roll. Len carried his bridle and blanket.

Len said, "He ought to be gettin' in a

little better humor now that he can see the ranch."

Though Farley had ridden for long stretches while Andy and Len took turns walking, Farley had been grouchy as an old badger awakened from sleep. He seemed somehow to blame Andy and Len for the loss of his horse, though Andy knew that was illogical.

Once while Len was taking his turn at walking they came upon a long-horned cow with her calf. Not accustomed to seeing a man afoot, she took Len for a threat to her offspring, lowered her head, and charged. Len's long legs carried her in a wide circle until she gave up and trotted away with her calf, wringing her tail in agitation.

Farley almost smiled.

Andy asked Len, "You sure McCawley will lend Farley a horse?"

"Better than that, I'll bet he'll give him one. He'd take the shirt off of his back for somebody in need. He was a Ranger himself once, long before the war."

Andy saw dust rising from behind a corral fence. As the breeze swung around from that direction he could hear men yelling encouragement. He saw a figure bobbing up and down, riding a pitching horse. He said, "Maybe Farley can have that one."

Len said, "It'd give him somethin' to cuss at besides us." His grin showed that the thought pleased him. He pointed his thumb toward a corner of the corral. "I see Big Jim over yonder."

A large man stood outside, watching the show from between the upright tree branches that constituted the fence. In size and stature he reminded Andy of Sheriff Tom Blessing. The rancher turned his head as the two riders approached. His big hand dropped quickly to a pistol on his hip, then eased away as he decided the visitors presented no threat.

Len raised his hand. "You know me, Mr. McCawley. Name's Len Tanner. I'm a Ranger."

McCawley's eyes lighted up. A pleasant grin spread across a face ruddy and deeply lined, seasoned by many years of sunshine and hard weather. Gray hair in need of a trimming curled over his ears. "Sure, I remember you." He shook Len's hand, then shifted his attention to Andy.

Len said, "This is Andy Pickard. The tired-lookin' bird draggin' his feet back yonder, that's Farley Brackett. Him and Andy are Rangers too."

McCawley looked at Farley's saddle, which Andy held in front of him. "A saddle by itself ain't worth much. How come your man ain't got a horse to go with it?"

Andy was content to let Len do the talking. Len explained that they had been set upon by outlaws. "There was one that called hisself Hatton. I'm pretty sure he was with a bunch of horse thieves that our scoutin' party jumped a while back on the river."

McCawley's eyes went grim. "Hatton. Yes, I know him. He runs with Jericho Jackson's coyote pack. I had him in my sights once, but my horse scotched and I missed."

"I heard somebody holler like he was hit, but I don't know if it was Hatton."

Andy rode up to the fence and looked over. The bronc had stopped pitching. It was circling the inside of the corral in a lope, its bay hide shining with sweat. A grinning Mexican cowboy held a hackamore rein high and tight. Three other cowboys stood inside the fence, watching, hollering for him to spur the bronc in the flanks. One was Mexican, two were white. Having heard so much about racial strife in the borderland, Andy was a little surprised at the camaraderie.

McCawley said, "That's Pedro Esquivel in the saddle. He's *puro jiñete,* a natural bronc rider." He turned and saw Farley at last approaching the corral. "I suppose your man is hopin' for a horse?"

Andy said, "Yes, sir, but not that one."

McCawley smiled. "I've got several he can pick from. Nothin's too good for a Ranger."

Len said, "We'll see that Farley either pays you or brings your horse back."

"No need. It's a small thing against the debt I owe the Rangers. If the horse stayed here some thief would probably take it anyhow. We get hit by all kinds, Mexican and white."

Andy knew instinctively that he was going to like this man. The more he looked at him, the more he was reminded of Tom Blessing, solid as an oak, comfortable as a well-worn pair of handmade boots.

Farley trudged up to the corral, shoulders drooped in weariness. Sweat rolled down his face. Len introduced him to the rancher and said, "Mr. McCawley's goin' to fix it so you don't leave here afoot."

Farley always seemed to have trouble expressing gratitude. "I'll pay you when I can."

"I already told your friends that it's a gift."

Farley shook his head. "I'll pay you. I don't like leavin' debts behind me."

McCawley shrugged. "Whatever suits you." He looked at the western sky. "It'll be sundown directly. How about you-all comin' up to the big house with me? We'll have supper pretty soon."

What he called the big house was modest in size and far from new. The stones that constituted its walls were of varied sizes and hues. The building had been constructed for utility rather than for beauty. It reminded Andy of houses he had seen in San Antonio.

McCawley said, "I've promised my wife, Juana, a new house for years, but we're land-rich and cash-poor. If we could stop the raidin' and thievin', maybe I could lay aside enough money to build what she deserves."

The place might be old, but evidently McCawley's wife was making the best of it. A well-tended flower bed reached across the entire front, broken only by the doorway. It held roses, brilliant crepe myrtles, and several other colorful and eye-pleasing plants Andy could not identify.

The three Rangers removed their hats as

they stepped over the threshold, past a heavy wooden door carved with cattle brands and horse figures. A heavyset, middle-aged Mexican woman spoke to them in Spanish, took their hats and placed them on a rack in the nearest corner. Andy assumed at first that she was McCawley's wife, then realized she was a servant.

McCawley said, "Juana's in the kitchen. You-all come on back." He led them into a room dominated by a large fireplace where the cooking was done. Andy remembered that Rusty Shannon had bought an iron stove for Alice. Maybe McCawley was waiting for that new house before he installed so modern a convenience. Through a window he saw an outdoor Mexican-style baking oven in an open patio.

The room smelled of fresh bread, reminding Andy that he had eaten nothing since breakfast but a strip of jerky.

A slender, black-haired woman was bent over a table, slicing strips from a hindquarter of beef. McCawley said, "Juana, we have company."

She turned. Andy saw that she was no longer young, but she still had smooth olive skin and large, expressive brown eyes so dark that they looked black. She smelled faintly of lilac perfume. Or maybe it was the flowers in pots scattered not only in the parlor but in the kitchen.

"My wife," McCawley said.

Andy felt awkward, not sure he should speak English to her. But he knew no Spanish. He bowed from the waist. "How do, ma'am? I'm pleased to make your acquaintance."

Len said, "Howdy, Miz McCawley."

Farley grunted something unintelligible.

She said, "Welcome to our home, gentlemen. If you would like to wash up, you will find water and soap and fresh towels in the patio. Supper will be ready in a little while."

McCawley said, "These men are Rangers."

She smiled, skin crinkling at the corners of her eyes. "Then you are doubly welcome. Our house is your house."

The Spanish-style patio sat in the center of the house. Flowers of many hues had survived summer's heat beneath the edge of the overhanging roof.

Len commented in a loud whisper, "She talks English purt near as good as me and you, don't she? I'll bet she was somethin' to look at when she was twenty years younger."

Andy said, "She still is." For a moment a

vague image came into his mind's eye, a faint recollection of his mother. She had been killed by Indians when he was a small boy. He had no clear memory of her face, but sometimes he imagined he could hear her voice. He thought he heard an echo of it in Mrs. McCawley's. "She seems like a real pleasant woman."

Farley said, "But she's a Mexican."

Andy hoped McCawley had not overheard, but he had. The rancher said, "Yes, she's Mexican. There was a time when her family owned all this land." He made a sweeping motion with his hand. "Don Cipriano Chavez, her father, fought beside Sam Houston against Santa Anna. But that didn't help him when Americans decided they wanted his land. They killed him and Juana's first husband, and they tried to take away the property he had on this side of the river."

Len asked, "Then how come you to have this ranch?"

"After I married Juana, most of the land grabbers left this place alone. They knew I was a Texian, and I proved I would fight them. Some people called it a marriage of convenience, to save what her father left to her. But it was a lot more than that." McCawley looked back toward the door, his expression softening. "I was just a wanderer. I had no real aim in life except to survive. She gave me purpose. The land is in my name now, but it'll always be hers. And the children's."

Andy asked, "How many children?"

"I have a daughter and a stepson. Our daughter, Teresa, will be here in time for supper. She teaches the ranch children in a schoolhouse we built here."

"And the stepson?"

McCawley frowned. "Tony is away, with his uncle." His expression indicated that he did not want to dwell on this topic. Andy did not press him on it. He said, "You said bandits hit you pretty often."

"White renegades feel like this ranch is Mexican because of my wife. Mexican bandits feel like it's an American outfit because of me. We're fair game for all of them. Especially Jericho's bunch."

"Can't the Rangers stop him?"

Andy saw Len shake his head.

McCawley said, "Some of them don't want to. Jericho never lets himself get caught at anything he could go to jail for. He's like a general who runs an army from the rear and never goes out on the battlefield. And because he concentrates most of his attention on ranches in Mexico, a lot of the Rangers look the other way. They've never forgotten the Alamo and Goliad."

Andy said, "I thought McNelly stopped most of the bandits, white *and* Mexican."

"For a while. But he's gone."

Mrs. McCawley stepped out into the patio. "Teresa's here, and supper is ready."

McCawley motioned toward the door. "After you-all."

Andy waited for Len but not for Farley. His attention went immediately to a pretty girl with long black hair. McCawley introduced her as his daughter, but Andy had realized that the moment he saw her. She had the same dark brown eyes as her mother. They looked at Len and Andy, then dwelled for a moment on Farley before shyly cutting away. She waited for the men to sit. Farley did, but Andy and Len stood until she decided to seat herself. Andy was surprised at Len's sudden good manners.

Mrs. McCawley was last to the table. Light from the window revealed strands of gray hair that Andy had not noticed at first. She bowed her head and recited a prayer in Spanish. She crossed herself at the end of it, as did her daughter.

McCawley said, "Eat hearty. One thing we've got plenty of is beef. There ain't enough bandits to take it all."

Conversation lagged at first. Andy was too hungry to talk until he had emptied his plate. He was slower eating the second helping. He noticed that Teresa kept taking quick glances at Farley. He supposed she might be fascinated by his scar. It made him look a bit dangerous. Andy had been told that many women were drawn to men who looked dangerous.

To McCawley he said, "You've mentioned havin' trouble with Jericho. What about Guadalupe Chavez?"

A look passed between McCawley and his wife, and McCawley considered before he answered. "Some of Lupe's countrymen run off stock from time to time, but he leaves us alone."

Andy noticed that McCawley used the familiar form of the name, Lupe instead of Guadalupe.

Mrs. McCawley said, "My father was Cipriano Chavez. Lupe Chavez is my brother."

Andy stared at the girl. Her gaze was studiously fixed on her plate, though she had stopped eating. He thought she looked too innocent to be kin to a bandit whose name was known up and down the border. He remembered something the hole-in-the-wall cook in San Antonio had said, that very few innocent people lived on either side along the Rio Grande.

He remembered something else. McCawley had said his stepson was with an uncle. That uncle must be Guadalupe Chavez, Andy thought.

He had a feeling that whether or not his service on the river was pleasant, it should at least be almighty interesting.

After supper McCawley led the Rangers out onto the broad front porch, where he lighted a pipe while Len and Farley smoked cigarettes. He said, "You-all heard enough in there to raise a lot of questions. I feel like I owe you some answers."

Andy said, "You don't owe us nothin'."

"I want you to understand how things are. I was poor as a whip-poor-will when I first came to this part of the country. That was back in the fifties. Jobs were scarce. I served a little while with the Rangers, but half the time the state couldn't afford to pay me. Old Don Cipriano had land on both sides of the river, and he put me to work as a vaquero. By that time Americans were movin' into this part of the country in considerable numbers. They wanted land. They found that most of it was owned by Mexicans, so they started pushin' them

102

out. The old man thought they'd leave him alone because he'd fought for Texas independence.

"Some of those Johnny-come-latelys hadn't fought for Texas, but they thought they had a right to whatever part of it they wanted. They took control of the courthouse and ruled that the old man's land grant wasn't legal anymore. When he fought back, they ambushed him and Juana's husband. Lupe hunted down the leaders and left them layin' dead as a skinned mule. Then he took a fast horse and went to Mexico."

Len said, "And after that you married Mrs. McCawley?"

"When a respectable time had passed. I was in love from the first time I saw her. Besides, I was grateful to the old man and wanted to save his land for her if I could. I had to face up to some hard men. I even had Jericho in my sights once. I ought to've killed him, but I let him go because there was a time when we used to be friends." McCawley looked regretful. "He's hated me ever since. I guess he figures he's beholden to me, and it grates on his soul to owe anybody."

Andy said, "At least you've given Lupe Chavez a reason to like you, marryin' his sister and savin' her land."

"No, Lupe doesn't like me. To him I'm just another gringo, and he hates them all. He'd be glad to come to my funeral if he didn't have to kill me himself. He leaves me alone on account of his sister."

Farley asked, "But you're American. Ain't it tough, standin' up against your own kind?"

"People like Jericho aren't my kind."

Andy thought he understood. "For a long time I thought of myself as Comanche. But there were some Comanches I had no use for." He explained to McCawley about the years he spent with the Indians.

McCawley said, "Then maybe you can understand the position I'm in. Sometimes I feel like I belong to both sides, and other times I don't belong to either one."

After dark the Rangers unrolled their blankets in the yard. Len lay on his back, looking up at the stars. He asked Andy, "What color would you say Teresa's eyes are?"

Andy said, "Brown. Dark brown."

"But they're not brown like anybody else's. They're different. They're . . ." He considered for a moment. "Damned if I can say just what color they are. But they're the prettiest eyes ever I seen."

Andy said, "Sounds to me like you're in love. But as I remember it, you've been in love lots of times before."

"Not like this."

Farley said, "She's Mexican."

Len's voice was defensive. "Half of her is white."

Farley gave the matter some thought. "I'll admit, I kind of liked lookin' at her."

After breakfast McCawley led them back out to the corrals. A dozen horses stirred in a single pen, warily watching the men who entered the gate. He said, "Take your pick, Farley."

Andy had always known that despite his faults Farley was a good judge of horses. He strode among them, making them walk, watching how they moved. He soon made his choice. "I like that stockin'-legged red." He had always shown a partiality to sorrels.

McCawley said, "You've got a good eye. He'll take you there and bring you back."

The Rangers saddled up. Andy shook McCawley's hand. "Please tell the womenfolks again how much we enjoyed their good cookin'."

"And you-all watch out that the next

time you run into bandits, it's of your own choice and not theirs."

The Ranger camp was similar to one Andy had known on the San Saba River. It was a row of pyramid-shaped canvas tents and a set of crude but effective corrals built of tree branches tied together with rawhide. The tents could be moved on short notice as the need arose and the corrals quickly put together at the new site with whatever materials happened to be at hand.

A broad-shouldered man emerged from a tent and stood with big hands placed solidly on his hips as he watched the three riders approach. He gave Andy and Farley a critical study, then shifted his attention to Len. He said, "Look what the north wind just blew in. I figured you liked San Antonio so much that you wasn't comin' back."

Andy could not be sure whether the man was joking or not. He sounded serious, even disappointed that Len *had* come back.

Len took no offense. "I left as quick as I could, Sergeant. Brought you two men."

"Prisoners?"

"No, Rangers."

The sergeant squinted, one eye almost closed. "It's hard to tell. They got an outlaw look about them."

This time Andy was seventy-five percent certain that the sergeant was not joking.

Len said, "Sergeant Donahue, this is Farley Brackett and Andy Pickard. They been transferred here from out in West Texas."

Donahue studied Farley with suspicious eyes. "Brackett? Seems to me like I've heard that name."

Len said, "He's got a considerable reputation up yonder where he comes from."

"Good or bad?"

"Depends on who you ask."

Farley gave Len a cautioning look.

Donahue nodded. "Well and good, but we judge men by what they do here and not by their reputation somewheres else." He spoke to Andy. "You appear too young to have much of a reputation as yet. Are you here lookin' to get one?"

"I'm just here to do my job, whatever that is."

"Well, boy, you better watch these border Meskins. They'll grind you up and make tamales out of you. I just got one rule when it comes to them. If you're in doubt, shoot." He punctuated that statement by jerking his head. "Come on, you'd best report to Lieutenant Buckalew and get on the pay roster. That don't guarantee you'll get any pay, of course." He did not look back. He had the air of a man who has no doubt that his order will be obeyed. The three Rangers followed him, leading their horses.

Entering the headquarters tent, the sergeant introduced Andy, Len, and Farley to the lieutenant. Buckalew welcomed the newcomers with more enthusiasm than Donahue had shown. He said, "You men are a welcome sight. As you will soon discover, this company is somewhat under strength. There's been a dearth of state appropriations. I see you brought your blankets. I hope you brought lanterns as well. You will have more use for them than for a bed."

Len put in, "They're good men, Lieutenant. You tell them what to do and they'll get it done or bust a gut."

The lieutenant smiled. "They don't have to go that far. All I'll ask is that they work thirty hours a day and eight days a week."

Len reported on their confrontation with Hatton and his bunch. The lieutenant listened intently, glancing at Andy and Farley from time to time for confirmation.

The sergeant demanded, "Are you sure they wasn't Meskins?"

Len said, "They was blue-eyed gringos, every one."

Andy had not noticed the color of their eyes, but he nodded agreement with Len. "They were white men."

The lieutenant said, "You think they were part of the Jericho outfit?"

Len said, "I can't say for sure that they belonged to Jericho, but I'm pretty certain they're part of a bunch we swapped shells with some time back. You was there that day, Lieutenant. Remember, they was tryin' to get away with some of Big Jim McCawley's horses."

"I remember. Think you killed anybody?" He asked the question hopefully.

"Somebody hollered like he was hurt."

"I wish we could shoot them all, Jericho's bunch and the Chavez gang too."

Sergeant Donahue interjected, "Or euchre them into shootin' one another without costin' us anything."

Once the formalities were taken care of, Len headed for the mess tent. A dark-faced Mexican cook used a wicked-looking butcher knife to cut a quarter of beef hanging from a tree branch. He dropped the slices one by one into a tin pan. Finishing, he chased the flies away and wrapped a bloodstained tarp around what remained.

Len said, "Pablo, we're hungry."

Pablo had a long, drooping mustache and a pitted face that showed he had survived a long-ago bout with smallpox. He looked westward to gauge the position of the afternoon sun. "Always, Tanner, you are hungry. You will wait like everybody."

Keeping an eye on the butcher knife, Len lifted the lid from a cold Dutch oven and found leftover flat-baked bread. He tore off a chunk. "Try it, Andy. It ain't bad when you get used to it. Mexicans don't know about bakin' biscuits."

Andy gave Pablo a questioning glance before accepting. He knew that getting crossways with the cook was about the worst mistake a man could make in camp. He saw that Pablo was awaiting his verdict on the bread. He took a bite and nodded. "Tastes mighty fine to me."

Pablo grinned. "Any time you are hungry, you come see me. We find you somethin' to eat." He shook the knife at Len. "You got enough. You wait for supper."

Len broke off another piece of bread. He said, "Another good thing about camp

cooks is they've always got a givin' disposition."

The sergeant came looking for him.
"Tanner, the lieutenant says we need to get
the new men off to a quick start. In the
mornin' you'll take Brackett and Pickard
and patrol up the river. They need to get
acquainted with the lay of the land."

Len asked, "We got to take Farley?"

"He needs to learn the country."
Donahue frowned. "What's the matter?
Don't you and Brackett get along?"

"I get along with Farley just fine. As long
as I don't pay any attention to him."

Donahue grunted. "Just be damned sure
you pay attention to *me*."

5

Burt Hatton came to a fork in the road and glanced with foreboding at a sign which stood on the left. It said: THIS IS JERICHO'S ROAD. TAKE THE OTHER.

He wished he could take the other and keep going. Facing Jericho was always unpleasant when things did not go as Jericho wanted. Hatton turned in the saddle and looked at the men who followed. One led a riderless horse. He said, "Don't none of you forget what we've agreed to say. We got jumped by Lupe Chavez's bandits. The kid got shot before we could reach cover."

He hoped Jericho would be mollified at least somewhat by the fact that they did not lose the cattle money.

Jesse Wilkes always looked as if he had sucked on a sour persimmon, and he had more complaints than a dissatisfied mother-in-law. He argued, "I still say you can't lie to Jericho. He reads faces like me and you read a paper."

"Let me do the tellin'. You-all just nod. Maybe he won't ask many questions. He'll be busy figurin' out some way to get even with Chavez."

"Whatever he comes up with, it'll be us that get sent to do the job. He don't do anything the law can grab him for."

Hatton's voice sharpened. "You've got nothin' to bellyache about. You get your share."

"Money's hard to spend in the grave-yard."

"You can always leave if you're a mind to. Go back to East Texas. Maybe they've forgot about that murder charge they had out on you."

Wilkes seemed to shrivel. "They don't ever forget."

"And neither does Jericho, so keep your mouth shut and let me talk to him."

Wilkes went quiet, but his eyes still reflected his anxiety. Hatton had not chosen him as a member of the bunch; Jericho had done that. Hatton often found it hard to fathom Jericho's thinking. It was too bad Wilkes didn't catch that bullet instead of the kid. If it ever became necessary for Hatton to sacrifice somebody to save the rest, Wilkes would be his first pick.

Hatton's eyes kept searching the crooked wagon track ahead. Jericho kept a guard on this road in case some stranger came along who couldn't read the sign or chose not to heed it. The guard moved around often, so Hatton could never predict just where he would be. The regular guards knew Hatton and his riders, but sometimes Jericho put a new man on the job. Sooner or later he might assign somebody who was too slow on recognition and too fast on the trigger.

A horseman casually rode out from behind the leafy green cover of a mesquite tree and stopped in the center of the road, waiting. He had a rifle in a scabbard and a pistol on his hip but nothing in his hands except his bridle reins. A telescope hung from a leather string around his neck. He said, "Been watchin' you-all with the spyglass, so I knowed it was you. Been a long time on this trip, ain't you?"

Hatton wondered if the guard was being subtly critical. "It takes a while to drive a herd all the way up to San Antonio."

"Jericho's been gettin' a little nervous, wonderin' if maybe you-all decided to take the cattle money and look for greener slopes."

Curtly Hatton replied, "He knows me better than that." Should he ever succumb to that ambition he knew he had better travel a long way, for Jericho would send somebody to track him down. Jericho would not care how long it took. Forgiveness was alien to Jericho's nature. He never forgot, nor did he ever fully trust. Hatton harbored a suspicion that Jericho might have assigned one of the men riding with him to watch the rest. If there was such a spy in his midst — and Wilkes seemed the most likely candidate — Jericho would not be long in learning what really happened to his nephew.

Hatton tried to reason that he was wrong, that he was just being paranoid. A man was apt to get that way, working for Jericho.

The guard said, "I hope you'll tell him you saw me and that I was right on the job."

"Sure, I'll do that." But Hatton knew he would not. He had more important things on his mind than accommodating a lowly gun toter worried about staying on the payroll or hoping to be promoted to a more profitable position.

The nucleus of Jericho's headquarters had been built long ago in Spanish times when Indian raids were a periodic threat. The stone walls of the long main house were thick enough that no bullet would penetrate them. Narrow rifle ports allowed shooters inside to fire at an approaching enemy with minimum exposure. Beyond the outer walls that enclosed the major ranch buildings, the ground had been cleared of brush for two to three hundred yards to expose attackers as they came into good rifle range. The first brush removal had been done by the Spaniards. Jericho had maintained it for his own protection.

Most visitors were unwelcome, whether they were Mexican bandits or lawmen such as the Texas Rangers. He could stand them off if they ever came at him here in his stronghold. So far, none had tried. Even Guadalupe Chavez, who took pleasure in rustling the outfit's cattle, had never attempted to overrun the headquarters. Outlaws were welcome so long as they were white and were willing to operate under orders, though their stay was short unless they proved themselves.

Hatton hoped by riding directly to the barn that nobody would notice the riderless horse. That would give him time to present the money and put the boss in a good humor before delivering the bad news. But Jericho was at the barn, watching a hired hand shoe his favorite mount, a big gray capable of carrying a large rider. He watched the riders' approach, and his flinty gaze fastened hawk-like on the lead horse.

Jericho stood more than six feet tall, broad-shouldered and muscular. Women were drawn to him and considered him handsome, but they didn't see him as Hatton saw him now, coiled tight and dangerous like the spring on a trigger. Hatton wondered if even Jericho's Missouri-raised wife had ever seen him that way.

Hatton tried to head off the question by dismounting and immediately unbuckling his saddlebags. "The cattle brought a little more than we expected, boss. Got the money right here. I think you'll be tickled."

The big man was not to be distracted. "Where's the boy?"

Hatton swallowed. "It's a long story."

"Give me the short of it. Where's he at?"

Hatton stammered. "It's like this . . . we run into some of them Chavez bandits . . ."

Jericho seemed to tower over Hatton, his eyes cutting like blades. "You tryin' to tell me you got him shot?"

"It was . . . there wasn't nothin' we could do. They was on us so fast . . . we tried to shield the boy . . . but he was hit before we could . . . honest to God."

"Damn you!" Jericho's hard fist struck so quickly that Hatton did not see it coming. He fell backward, dropping the saddlebags and startling his horse into breaking free. The animal ran off a little way and turned warily to watch. Hatton shook his head and raised one hand to his aching jaw. He felt as if a mule had kicked him.

Jericho stormed, "I told you I didn't want him goin'. I told you to leave him at home."

Hatton found it difficult to speak. He had bitten his tongue hard enough that he tasted blood. He wanted to explain that the boy had trailed after them and had not let himself be seen until the second day out on the trail. He had declared that he would continue to follow even if not given permission. A reluctant Hatton had told him, "All right, stay, but make a hand."

One of these days, he thought, his soft heart was going to get him killed.

Hatton had seen many times how mercurial Jericho's moods could be. He could laugh one moment and roar in anger the next. His initial rage slowly cooled, and he took on a look of genuine sorrow. "He was a good kid. Didn't listen to advice worth a damn, but he was my wife's only nephew. Like a son to her, he was."

"I'm sorry. I wish it had been me." That

was an exaggeration. Hatton was glad it had not been him. He wished it might have been Wilkes. If not him, any of the others. He got up hesitantly, afraid he might get hit again.

Jericho said, "Why didn't you bring him home?"

"It was too far, and the weather was too warm. But we found a churchyard and buried him in hallowed ground. I just wisht we'd had a preacher to read over him."

"What kind of a church was it?"

"I don't know. Always thought one church was like another."

"They ain't. I'll bet you buried him in a Mexican graveyard."

Hatton could not look into Jericho's accusing eyes.

Jericho asked, "Can you find that church again? My wife'll want to go there and see where the boy is restin'. Maybe even bring him home. He don't belong amongst a bunch of Mexicans, especially seein' as it was Mexicans that killed him."

"Remember the village where that Ranger got killed a year or so back? He's buried in the same churchyard."

"Damned poor company for the boy. We'll move him."

Jericho looked toward the house, his visage grave. "I sure dread tellin' Thelma. This'll just about kill her."

His wife was the only person for whom Jericho showed any real affection. He catered to her as if he were deathly afraid she might leave him. Hatton could not understand how such a strong man could allow himself to be so much at the mercy of a woman, any woman. It was the only weakness he had ever seen Jericho display.

Hatton had seen very little of Thelma Jackson. Neither he nor any of the other hands were allowed in the big house except for Jericho's office, to which there was an outside door. To Hatton she was a shadowy figure, more mystery than reality. Jericho was strict about shielding her from the unpleasant aspects of his business and the men with whom he had to deal.

Jericho's grieving gave way to a dark and brooding anger that would simmer beneath the surface until some resolution was reached. "Chavez." He spoke the name as if it were a curse. "He'll pay if I have to follow him all the way into hell." His voice dropped so low that Hatton could barely hear it. "Has Chavez got any kids?"

Hatton felt a measure of relief. Maybe things were going to work out. "I never heard nobody say. I know he's got a woman or two. You know them Meskins . . . they shell out like rabbits. Stands to reason he's got kids."

"Even if he doesn't, that stepson of McCawley's is ridin' with him, ain't he?"

"So I hear."

"That boy is Lupe's nephew. You know what the Book says: an eye for an eye. A nephew for a nephew."

Hatton wondered where Jericho had learned about the Book. He had never seen him read from it.

Andy's horse lowered its head to drink from the Rio Grande. The other horses and the little pack mule followed suit. The river was less impressive than Andy had expected. It appeared no wider and certainly less deep than the Colorado or the Brazos. It had passed through a lot of desert country before it reached this point on its long journey to the Gulf.

Len said, "Depends on where you look at it from. Some places it gets wide and shallow. Mexicans can ride a burro across it. Other places it gets narrow and deep enough to drown an elephant. It's them wide, shallow places where we got to watch for signs of border jumpers. It's hard to hide tracks where a bunch of cattle or horses have crossed."

Andy asked, "If we find such a place, what're we supposed to do?"

"If they're headed south into Mexico, ain't much we can do. It's too late to help the owners. Their stock is gone unless they want to cross the border and try to take them back. The law don't allow us to do it for them. If the tracks head north, we may follow. Lieutenant Buckalew does. When Sergeant Donahue is in charge he usually tells us to leave well enough alone. He says Mexicans deserve to get robbed because they're all thieves anyway."

"Do we ever catch anybody?"

"Awful seldom."

"What could three of us do against a big bunch of bandits anyway?"

"Surround them. Give them to understand that we don't take kindly to their thievin' ways."

Ever since Andy had known him, Len had welcomed a vigorous scrap. He always maintained that an occasional good waking-up was healthful for the constitution, that it stirred the blood and loosened the bowels. As for Farley, he had been looking for a fight the first time Andy ever saw him, and he had not changed.

It could get dangerous, riding with two reckless companions.

Andy studied the land on the other side of the river. It looked no different from the north bank, though it was another nation. Over there he would be an alien and an enemy to most people. The thought was disquieting.

He had enjoyed the limestone hills and the fertile valleys of the San Saba River country. He found this region flatter and more desertlike, without the evident amenities he had found to the north. As someone had warned, most of the plants here had thorns, the animals had horns or tusks, and the insects had stingers. He remembered the homesickness that had afflicted him when he first fell back into the white man's world after his years with the Indians. Some of that emotion came over him now.

He supposed he might get used to it when he had been here awhile, but he was not sure he wanted to stay that long.

He expressed his feelings. Len said, "I felt the same way when they first sent me here, but you can find somethin' to like just about anyplace if you look for it. Else why would the devil live in hell?"

"I've never had a chance to ask him."

"You may run into him down here one

123

of these days. He's got family by the name of Jericho and Chavez."

Farley growled, "This looks like the kind of country the devil would pick for his home. Anything you touch or that touches you is apt to bring blood."

Len said, "But there's pretty places too. I've been plumb out to where the Rio Grande pours into the Gulf. They got palm trees out there, just like in the Bible. I kept thinkin' I ought to see a camel someplace, but I didn't."

They came upon a small field irrigated by a ditch extending from the river. Up the slope stood a small picket house. A few spotted goats nibbled at brush and watched the Rangers approach. When the horsemen came close they clattered away, then turned to look again.

Len said, "These folks keep chickens. Sometimes when I come by here I buy a few eggs. Sure makes fat bacon taste better. Even beef jerky."

Andy saw a family working in a garden. At the Rangers' approach the woman shouted at two girls. All three retreated into the house. Andy heard a wooden bar dropped into place to secure the door. Len said, "They've had experience with gringos before."

The man stood at the brush fence, waiting to meet the riders alone. He bowed slightly and said a few Spanish words that Andy took to be a greeting, though his dark eyes conveyed a different message. He could not hide his dislike and his dread.

Len said, "Most of these people can tell a Ranger as far as they can see him. They don't like us and they don't trust us, but they'll accept our money." He spoke to the man. "*Huevos.*"

"*Tiene dinero?*"

Len said, "He wants to see the money first."

Andy dug into his pocket and came up with two bits. "Reckon that's enough?"

"Two bits'll buy you the hen."

The man went into the house, returning shortly with several eggs in a small, crude basket woven of green willow stems. Len asked him something Andy did not understand. The man shook his head and replied with a shrug of his shoulders.

Len thanked him. "Says he ain't seen anybody cross the river in either direction except people who live close by. No bandits."

Farley said, "He wouldn't tell us anyway."

"If it's gringo bandits they'll tell you. If

it's Mexicans they won't. Ask most white people along the river and they'll do the same except the opposite."

Riding away, Andy looked back. He saw the woman hastily hanging clothing on a line.

Len observed, "Them clothes ain't wet. That's a signal that Rangers are about. Anybody waitin' on the other side knows he'd best keep his feet dry."

Farley said, "I'll go back and yank them clothes down."

"No, folks behave better when they know we're around. The lieutenant had rather keep them out of mischief in the first place than to chase them afterwards."

At sunset they stopped to make camp. Andy removed the pack from the mule while Len scooped out a shallow hole in the dirt and filled it with dry leaves and small sticks. He lighted it with a match, blowing into the first weak, flickering flames to make them lick into the dry wood. He said, "We'll fix our supper, then we'll build this fire up to where they can see it. There won't be no cattle run across here tonight."

Andy pondered. "What's to stop them from goin' up the river to the next shallow place?"

"Us. This fire'll be here, but we'll be there. With another fire."

Farley argued, "Three of us can't be everywhere up and down the whole Rio Grande."

"No, but we can keep them wonderin' where we'll turn up next. It'll be as aggravatin' as a tick in the ear."

Farley dragged up more dry brush to keep the fire going. "I'd rather aggravate them with a bullet in the gut."

The fire went out during the night. Next morning after their meager breakfast Andy heard cattle bawling and determined that the sound came from the other side. Farley said, "Looks like somebody is fixin' to cross over."

Len agreed. "Let's ride to the bank of the river and show ourselves. It'll give them somethin' to fret about."

Len took a position at the edge of the water. Andy and Farley followed his lead. Andy asked, "How'll they know we're Rangers?"

"They won't know for sure, but they'll have to think hard about takin' the chance."

"Looks like they've got us considerable outnumbered."

"But they know they'd be easy targets in

the water. Most of them would never make it all the way across if we set our minds to stoppin' them."

Andy could see the men milling about, several gathering as if in conference.

After a while he heard distant shots.

Len grinned. "Looks like they've got theirselves in a fix. Somebody's caught up with them."

The gunfire increased. Andy watched several riders plunge into the shallow water, making for the north bank. "They're leavin' the cattle behind."

"Wouldn't you?" Len slapped his leg and laughed. "Look at them run. If they could fly, they'd do it."

Andy saw a man fall from the saddle just as his horse entered the river. Another made it partway across before he slid into the water and began floundering. A companion grabbed him and pulled him against his horse's shoulder.

Farley drew his pistol. "They'll blame us for this."

Len drew his rifle from its scabbard and laid it across his lap. "Ain't it a shame." He appeared to welcome the prospect of a confrontation.

Andy cautioned, "Have you forgotten how to count?"

"They'll be stringin' out of the river one and two at a time. They're tired and pretty well boogered. Us three can take them all on."

Andy had his doubts but decided to put his faith in Len's prior experience and Farley's fighting nature. The Rangers met the riders as they straggled onto the bank, their horses dripping. Len pointed his rifle in their direction and ordered each in turn to shuck his weapons. Two seemed prepared to argue, but Farley cut them short: "Don't make us finish what them Mexicans started."

Andy had thought some of these might be men who had attacked him and Len and Farley several nights ago, but he recognized none of them.

Len said, "Well, looks like you boys bit off a bigger chunk than you could chew."

One growled, "All we done was buy a herd of cattle across the river. Bunch of Mexican bandits jumped us and took them over. You seen it yourselves, didn't you?"

Farley was openly skeptical. "How about showin' us a bill of sale?"

"Mexicans don't put much store in such as that. Most of them can't read or write."

"I'll bet they can read brands."

The raider complained, "We lost a man over on the other side, and we've got another with a slug in him."

Andy turned his attention southward. "Looks like those Mexicans are comin' across to finish the job."

The man's eyes widened as he saw riders moving into the river. "Let us have our guns back."

Len shook his head. "No, the best thing you-all can do is see if them horses of yours are faster than what the Mexicans are ridin'." He waved the muzzle of the rifle, pointing it northward.

The man protested, "Them guns cost us good money."

"If you don't hightail it you ain't goin' to have no use for money. And tell Jericho the Rangers said howdy."

The raiders' reluctance to leave without weapons was quickly surpassed by their fear of the angry-looking Mexicans coming across the river. Andy watched the men move away in a lope. He said, "We ought to've arrested them and taken them back to camp."

Len said, "We'd've lost half of them between here and there. Anyway, whatever they done on the other side, that's Mexico's business. They didn't break no Texas law. Wasn't nothin' we could charge them for."

Andy asked, "How do you know they're Jericho's men?"

"I'm just guessin'. Jericho runs most of the contraband business along this stretch of the river, just like Lupe Chavez runs it on the other side." Len dismounted and began picking up the weapons. "Let's wrap these in a blanket and tie them on the pack mule. Them Mexicans have got guns enough already."

Andy unrolled his blanket on the ground. "Do you think you can bluff them like you bluffed the others?"

"What makes you think I was bluffin'?"

Andy counted ten horsemen coming across the river. Several more had remained with the cattle. Len squinted, studying them. "I don't see Lupe Chavez, but you can lay odds that these are some of his men." He remounted and again brandished his rifle. Andy and Farley followed his example. As the riders came up to face them Len said, "You boys are on the wrong side of the river."

A lean young man pushed forward, a challenge in his dark eyes and the set of his shoulders. "There was a time when the river didn't mean nothin'. South side,

131

north side, it was all part of Mexico." He was dressed like a Mexican vaquero, but he spoke with little or no Mexican accent that Andy could discern.

Len said, "There's been two wars fought over that. If you ain't careful you'll start another." He softened. "I'm bettin' you'd be Big Jim McCawley's boy Tony. I heard you was ridin' with Lupe Chavez. Where's he at?"

The young man ignored the question. "I'm Antonio Villarreal. I'm Lupe Chavez's nephew, but I'm not McCawley's boy. Who are you to be blockin' the way?"

"We're Rangers." Len pointed to the handmade badge on his shirt.

The young man's face twisted. "Damned *rinches.*"

Andy had learned that *rinches* was a term the Mexicans applied to the Rangers, and not in a complimentary manner.

Villarreal said, "If you'll give us the road we'll take care of your job for you. We'll fix them so they'll never come again."

"Like you said, that's *our* job. You did yours when you saved your cattle."

"I know you Rangers won't do anything about those thieves. If *we* don't, they'll be back."

"Catch them on your side of the river

and you can feel free to shoot them all."

The young man's voice bespoke contempt. "Maybe someday we'll catch you *rinches* on the other side."

Andy studied the face. He thought he saw some resemblance to Tony's mother and half sister. He said, "We met your folks."

That seemed to pique Tony's interest in a negative way. "I guess they told you all about me?"

"They said mighty little, just enough to give us a notion you jumped the traces."

"My stepfather is a gringo."

"Everybody says he is a good man."

"He is still a gringo. When I was a boy I had to accept him as a father. Now I am a man, and he is not my father anymore."

Andy did not know whether to feel sorry for the young rebel or to be angry at him. He said, "I'd give anything I own to have a father."

"You can have mine. And next time you side with Jericho's thieves we'll run over you like a freight train."

Farley spoke up. "You'll find the Rangers harder to bring down than that man you killed over there."

"He was a bandit. Anyway, he was just wounded. He's not dead yet."

Andy heard two shots echo from across the river. He winced. "I guess he is now."

Tony said coldly, "One less gringo bandit. The world is better off." He jerked his head as a signal and rode back into the river. The other men followed him.

Andy said, "He doesn't know how lucky he is. At least he's *got* a father. Stepfather, anyway."

Len said, "Too bad, but that's how it is down here. Most people choose sides accordin' to whether they're light-skinned or dark. That boy has set his eggs down on the Mexican side."

Andy pointed northward. The raiders had faded into the distance, swallowed up by the mesquite and other brush. "We could follow them and find out where they came from."

Len said, "They came from Jericho's little kingdom. Ain't much doubt about that."

Andy was intrigued. "Kingdom?"

"He runs it like he was a king. Nothin' happens in there without his say-so. Nobody pokes his nose onto Jericho's ranch unless he says it's all right."

"Not even the Rangers?"

"We go now and again, but he sees to it that we don't find anything or anybody we're lookin' for. If an outlaw needs a hidin' place, Jericho gives him one. They go out and do their devilment, then come back and give him a cut. He's built him a bank with stolen money, but he's managed to keep his hands clean. Even if the law was to bring him to trial, you couldn't gather up twelve men with guts enough to convict him."

Andy declared, "I'd like to see what he looks like. Have you ever met him?"

"Yep. And I'd pay money to buy back my introduction."

"What about that man they killed? Are we just goin' to go off and leave him over there?"

Farley said, "His friends did," and started north, following the raiders.

6

Following the trail was easy. The raiders made no effort to hide it. Though crossing with Mexican cattle was illegal unless properly cleared through customs, they had returned without contraband. They had little reason to fear the law once they were north of the Rio Grande. Andy carried the blanket into which the men's weapons had been piled. He had to tie the ends together and lash the bundle onto the mule. It was an unwieldy load.

He said, "These guns may not ride this way very long."

Farley grabbed a handful of the blanket and tugged to get a sense of the weight. "I don't see where we owe it to them renegades to deliver their weaponry back to them. We ought to've thrown it all in the river."

Len said, "Jericho's got lawyers up in San Antonio that raise hell every time we even wink in his direction. There's a little store at the crossroads. We'll leave the guns there."

Andy asked, "You think they'll come back and get them?"

"I would if the guns was mine. A man appreciates things when he has to pay out his own good money for them."

They came to a plain-looking building, a nondescript mix of stone and picket construction. Len said, "That's the store. The owner sells stuff to Jericho's men and buys their stolen goods. He'll treat us friendly enough, but don't believe his smile. It's all show."

Farley said, "If he deals with Jericho's thieves, why don't we arrest him?"

"A jury that won't convict Jericho won't convict his friends either. I'd about as soon stand in front of a Mexican firin' squad as face Jericho's lawyers."

Andy grinned at a sudden thought. "If we can't put those border jumpers in jail, we can at least aggravate them a little."

Len brightened with curiosity. "How?"

"Let's stop in the shade of that tree yonder." Andy dismounted and lifted the heavy bundle from the mule. He laid it in the shade and untied the corners that held it together. The rifles and pistols slipped and slid, clattering against one another. "Let's take these guns apart. Puttin' them back together will give those boys some-

137

thin' to do besides play cards and drink whiskey."

Len was always enthusiastic over a chance for harmless mischief. "I'd love to stay and listen to them cuss a blue streak."

Farley was not smiling. "I still wish we'd dumped the whole shebang in the river and let them swim for it."

They removed barrels and cylinders from the pistols and field-stripped the rifles. It took a while, but Len never stopped talking, laughing as he pictured their reaction. When they were done Andy mixed the pieces as if he were shuffling dominoes.

Len said, "I'd give a pretty penny to watch them sort out all this mess. By the time they put everything back together, they'll be wantin' to use them on us."

Farley said, "Let them come."

Andy retied the bundle and attached it to his saddle horn. It still weighed the same but seemed less of a burden now. A middle-aged man came to the door, a smudged apron tied around his dough belly. He recognized Len. "Howdy, Ranger. Somethin' you-all need?"

"A little smokin' tobacco for me and Farley. Maybe a little *pan dulce* for the young'un here if you got any."

"Tobacco I got. He'll have to find the

sweetenin' someplace else. I don't cater to the Mexican trade. Let them people in here and they'll be pilferin' stuff when I ain't watchin'."

Andy said, "Speakin' of pilferin', did you see a bunch of riders pass by a little while ago?"

The tracks indicated that the men had stopped here, but the storekeeper claimed no knowledge of them. "Ain't seen hardly anybody all day."

"They were tryin' to get away with some cattle on the other side of the river, but the owners caught up with them. They came back to this side in a considerable hurry."

"You don't say!"

Len said, "Anyhow, we've got some stuff that belongs to them. Reckon you can keep it till they come back?"

"Sure enough."

Andy brought the blanket inside and spilled its contents on the floor. A couple of cylinders rolled across the room. One disappeared behind some heavy-looking boxes. The storekeeper started to object but choked it off.

Andy said, "I hope you've got an empty box to put all this stuff in. I'll be needin' my blanket." He folded it and laid it across his arm.

The storekeeper grunted. "You won't want to be here when they see you've took their guns apart."

Cheerfully Len said, "They're welcome to come callin' at their convenience."

Farley said, "Tell them my name's Farley Brackett, and they can come see me if they ain't satisfied. I ain't had a decent fight since I left Austin."

The storekeeper gave Farley a quizzical look. "Brackett? Seems to me like I've heard that name."

"Lots of people have. Be sure you give it to them."

The three rode on. After a time Andy inquired, "Where does Jericho's land start?"

Len said, "We're already on it. He's got a six-shooter claim, at least. He says he bought out a bunch of Mexican owners. Ran them off is more like it, or he got a court to throw out the old grants like he tried to do with the Chavez family. Then he bought the land dirt cheap off of the county tax office."

The tracks led them eventually to a point where the trail forked. Andy saw a sign: THIS IS JERICHO'S ROAD. TAKE THE OTHER. "You ever been up this road?"

Len nodded. "Me and some other Rangers was trailin' stock headin' north.

Jericho came out to meet us. Claimed the cattle belonged to him, and his men had just got them back from Lupe Chavez's ranch across the river. Even showed us some cattle with his brand on them. They wasn't the same ones we'd been followin', but we couldn't prove he'd pulled a switch on us. Sergeant Donahue wasn't anxious about it anyway. He said the more cattle that get stole out of Mexico, the better."

"In other words, just knowin' ain't enough. The only thing that counts is what you can prove."

Farley grumbled, "You get a little smarter every day, Badger Boy. But you still got a long ways to go."

Andy saw a dozen or so cattle grazing nearby. He rode over to look at them, moving slowly so they would not spook and run. "I see at least three different brands."

Len watched the cattle drift away. "And all Mexican. Most of Jericho's cattle are natural swimmers. Show them a river and they'll jump right in."

The horse tracks split at the fork. Some riders had gone on northward. Others had swung to the west, following the trail marked as Jericho's.

Len said, "I've already seen Jericho's

headquarters. The outside of it, anyway. If we stay with the other bunch we might find a new hangout. Someday that could be a handy thing to know."

Farley said, "I'll follow that bunch west. I'd like to know what Jericho's place looks like."

Len cautioned, "You're liable to learn more than you intended to. But I don't reckon it's my place to try and tell you what to do."

"Wouldn't matter none if you did." Farley rode off.

Len hollered after him, "Chances are we won't find one another again. We'll meet back at the camp." In a quieter voice he said, "And that'll be plenty soon enough."

If Farley attempted an answer, Andy did not hear it.

Andy and Len followed the northbound tracks until eventually the trail split again. Len said, "Ain't but one thing to do. You take the right hand and I'll take the left. When we've seen whatever there is to see, we'll backtrack and meet right here."

Andy felt concern. "If you bump into somebody, you won't try to tackle them by yourself, will you?"

Len shook his head. "You know me. I ain't one to go lookin' for a fight."

"I don't remember you ever duckin' out on one."

"I'm just goin' to see what I can learn. I ain't got my fightin' britches on."

Andy knew Len's propensity for getting himself into trouble. He had that much in common with Farley. However, Farley met his challenges with a growl and Len met them with a laugh. Andy conceded that Len had a point. Sooner or later Jericho was likely to make a mistake, and it behooved the Rangers to know as much as possible about his ranch and what went on there.

He told Len, "You take the pack mule." The mule had more or less attached itself to Len's horse. It would not so readily follow Andy's.

Len said, "You won't have anything to eat."

"We'll be back together before time for that."

The sun bore heavily on Andy's shoulders. The back of his shirt and the underarms were soaked in sweat. Ahead he saw a windmill tower. That meant water. He was pleased that the tracks he followed veered in that direction.

Windmills were relatively new on Texas ranges. Railroads were first to try the idea, then farmers and ranchers had quickly adopted them to allow use of neglected lands that lacked living water in the form of springs, creeks, and rivers. Andy had seen a few windmills, but they remained strange and exotic to him. He was fascinated by the notion of a mechanical device that could harness the wind to pump water from unseen storage deep in the ground. He wondered how much longer people could keep coming up with such ingenious inventions. Surely they must be nearing their limit.

This mill had a tower built of lumber that still looked new except that it was already darkly stained by lubricating oil spilled from its gears. The cypress fan looked to be twelve or fourteen feet across. The sucker rod clanked as it rode up and down, striking the walls of the steel tube that enveloped it.

Water poured into a surface tank hollowed out of the level ground. A few cattle turned and warily trotted away as Andy approached. He imagined the pleasant taste of cool water gushing from the end of the outlet pipe.

He failed for a moment to recognize an angry buzzing sound. By the time he realized he had disturbed a nest of wasps, they were attacking him and the horse. He tried swatting them away but seemed to make them angrier. The black horse squealed and kicked, then broke into pitching. Already off balance from fighting the wasps, Andy lasted only two jumps before he was jolted out of the saddle. Instinctively he tried to break the fall by extending his arm. He hit the ground hard. The arm twisted beneath him.

His left boot was caught in the stirrup. He felt himself jerked violently, then dragged as the horse pitched, squealed, and broke wind. He bounced on the rough ground. He tried to shield his face, but one arm felt numb and useless. His foot pulled free of the boot. The dragging stopped. The horse continued to run and pitch without him. A few more wasps stung Andy before they began returning to the nest. They swarmed around it noisily as if awaiting another target.

Finding himself lying awkwardly on the arm that had taken the first impact, he rolled onto his back. The arm began to ache as feeling returned. He examined it gingerly, fearing it might be broken. He satisfied himself that it was not, though it was badly scratched and bruised. The sleeve hung in strips, as did the rest of his shirt.

His face and hands burned in more than a dozen places where the wasps had stung. He felt his cheeks beginning to puff. His eyes pinched. He tried to push to his feet, but his whole body hurt. He managed to sit up and take stock of his situation as the swelling almost closed his eyes.

It had not occurred to him that the windmill and open tank provided a hospitable breeding ground for wasps in a region where water was scarce.

He began feeling nauseated as the venom took hold. Vision blurring, he was unable to see his horse. He did not know how far the animal might have run. He crawled on hands and knees to where his boot had fallen from the stirrup. Painfully he pulled it on. Thirst began to plague him, but he did not want to try for the windmill again. He could still hear the angry wasps.

He wished he and Len had not split up. He had no idea how far Len might go in following those other tracks. When he returned to the rendezvous point Len was likely to wait awhile before deciding to follow Andy and see what had delayed him. By then it would probably be dark, and he would be unable to see tracks until daylight.

No telling how long I'll be here by myself, he thought.

His canteen was empty, and Len had the pack mule with all their provisions. At the moment Andy was too ill to eat, but sooner or later he would be hungry as well as thirsty.

Damn wasps, he thought. They say the Lord had a purpose for everything He made, but I don't see any reason for wasps.

He crawled into the thin shade of a mesquite tree and wished it were as solid as an oak.

Dusk came. He knew he would be by himself at least until morning. His blanket had been tied to his saddle, and the saddle was still on the horse. He resigned himself to sleeping on the bare ground, hungry and thirsty.

As darkness closed in, he heard something moving about. He paid little attention at first, for cattle had been coming up for water. Most seemed not to notice him. Those that saw or smelled him kept an uneasy distance. His blurry eyes made out the shape of a horse, his horse. It looked strange until he realized that the saddle had turned under its belly. He pushed himself to his feet, his legs aching. He spoke in a soft voice as he moved slowly and painfully toward the horse.

"Whoa, son. Gentle now. Whoa."

Grasping for the reins, he found one had broken off just below the bits. Holding the other, he patted the horse on the neck and rubbed his hand down its shoulder, then felt for the girth's buckle. The horse almost jerked away from him as the saddle dropped between its feet.

"Easy, boy. Ain't nothin' goin' to hurt you now."

Andy figured the wasps had become inactive for the night. Deciding to take a chance, he led the horse to the farthest end of the surface tank. There he let it drink. Hearing no buzzing, he took an even larger chance and walked to the end of the outlet pipe. Cupping his hand beneath the flow, he drank until his stomach ached.

He disliked tying the horse up short, but his rope had been lost. He had nothing to lengthen the one remaining rein. He tied it to a mesquite limb. He was disappointed to find that his blanket was gone. It had probably snagged on a bush and pulled loose.

He had already made up his mind he would be sleeping on the bare ground, so he was no worse off than before.

Andy spent a long and fitful night trying

in vain to find a comfortable position. The itching was so intense that he could not help scratching the bites. That made them burn worse than before. He knew there were ointments that might help, but they had just as well be on the far side of the moon. He tried to remember if the Comanches had any remedy. Nothing came to mind.

Thirst told him he was running a slight fever. He drank his fill before dawn set the wasps to stirring again. He could see better than the evening before, but he still felt as if he were peering through a slit in a wall.

"Damn you, Len, hurry up."

Andy figured it must be around noon when Len finally appeared, following tracks from the south. He reined up and stared at Andy as if he were an apparition. He declared, "You look like wild horses have stomped on you."

Andy warned, "Don't get too close to that windmill. There's a jillion wasps in there, and every one of them is mad."

"You let a few little old wasps do all that to you?"

"When they hit you, you'll think they're the size of a cow." He told how his horse had thrown him and run away, losing his blanket and rope.

Len said, "I'll see if I can find them."

He came back in a while, carrying both items. The blanket was dirty and torn. He said, "Bet you ain't had nothin' to eat. I'll fix you some dinner."

Andy had begun to feel strong hunger pangs, a sign of improvement. Len roasted bacon on a stick. Andy eagerly bit in without waiting for it to cool.

Len said, "I'm fixin' to do somethin' about that wasps' nest." He pulled several handfuls of dry grass and wrapped them around the end of a thin dead branch from a mesquite. He dipped the grass into the fire, then carried the blazing stick to the windmill tower. He shoved it under the nest. A few wasps came buzzing out, but most were consumed by the fire.

Andy heard Len exclaim, "Uh-oh!" The flames licked upward along the tower's wooden leg, burning the oil spilled from the top. Len stepped back, swatting at a couple of wasps that had focused upon him as a target. "Looks like I've just played hell."

Andy said, "Throw some water on it."

"Too late for that, even if I had a bucket."

The flames intensified. Len backed away from the heat. "I think me and you had better mosey along. Jericho is apt to be a little put out about his windmill."

He saddled Andy's horse and shook out the dusty blanket, folded it, and tied it behind the cantle. Andy felt stiff. Swinging up onto the horse reawakened all of yesterday's soreness. The two horses and the mule danced uneasily, fearing the fire.

Len kicked sand over the small blaze on which he had fixed Andy's meager breakfast. "If they saw this," he said, "they'd know somebody camped here and set fire to the windmill."

"How else would it have burned?"

"Lightnin'."

Squinty-eyed, Andy looked up but saw no clouds. "Yeah, they'll sure be fooled, all right."

Riding south, Andy asked, "Did you find anything?"

"A few miles from where I left you, the bunch I followed stopped at an old Mexican ranch house. Jericho probably uses it as a line camp. Remind me to put it on the map when we get back to the company. What did you find?"

"A jillion wasps." Andy looked back. The fire had climbed up to the tower's platform. Once it burned all the wooden support and the cypress, the metal parts would crash to the ground. He said, "I'll bet that mill cost a hundred dollars."

"Jericho can afford it. His crew'll steal more than that between dinner and supper."

They had traveled a couple of miles when Len said, "Four riders comin' our way." Andy's vision had not improved enough for him to see them. Len said, "It's too late to hide. Let's just play innocent."

Len always had an innocent look about him, even when he was guiltiest.

As the horsemen came near enough for Andy to see them, he noted that a large man rode half a length ahead of the others. He said, "I'll bet that's Jericho."

"Yep, you're about to meet the big stud his own self. Don't act like you give a damn. He's built himself a little empire by makin' people afraid of him."

"From what I've heard, they've got a right to be afraid."

"Me and you can't afford to be. Show him the feather and he'll ride plumb over you."

Jericho Jackson looked to be more than six feet tall and stocky enough to weigh considerably over two hundred pounds. He was not fat, simply large. He rode a gray horse bigger than those of the three cowboys beside him. He had a reddish complexion and hair and beard of a strong rust color, not unlike Rusty Shannon's. His dark brown eyes fastened first on Andy, then on Len with a startling intensity. He recognized Len, though he probably could not have called him by name.

"Ranger, ain't you strayed a long ways from where you belong?"

"Rangers go anywhere they want to."

"Anyplace but my ranch. You lookin' for somebody?"

"Maybe. Who you got?" Len's voice had an insolent tone, one Andy was sure he had to work at. It was not his normal style. It would have been Farley's.

Andy recognized two of the riders. They had been with the men the Mexicans had chased back across the river. One leaned to Jericho and said something Andy could not hear.

Jericho said, "Seems like you've already made the acquaintance of my boys. They say you took somethin' that belongs to them."

Len said, "The guns? If they'll stop at that little gyp joint of a store they can get their property back."

Jericho switched his attention again to Andy. "You look like you been run through

153

a coffee grinder, boy. You a Ranger too?"

"Private Andy Pickard. My horse drug me a ways."

"Probably because you took him where you and him wasn't supposed to be." Jericho leaned forward, his manner challenging. "You Rangers are always pokin' into my business, comin' on my land without so much as a by-your-leave. But when you're needed you ain't nowhere around."

Len said, "When did you ever need us?"

"Mexican outlaws murdered my wife's nephew. Never gave him a chance. It was one time we could've used your help, and you wasn't there."

Len and Andy looked at each other. Andy said, "That's the first we've heard about it."

"It won't be the last. I'm sendin' a protest to Austin."

Len said sarcastically, "They'll be tickled to hear from you."

"He was an orphan boy. My poor wife set a lot of store by him. I'll see that Lupe Chavez pays for what they done. When I do, you Rangers had better stay out of my way."

Andy said, "We can't, not if you break the law."

"It's a damned poor law that says you can't kill a Mexican when he needs it. As far as I'm concerned it's open season the year around on every saddle-colored son of a bitch this side of the river."

Jericho's red mustache seemed to bristle. Studying him, Andy was reminded of a book he had read about pirates. He seemed to remember that the character's name was Red Beard, or something like that. The longer Andy looked at Jericho, the larger he seemed to get. He doubted that he and Len could handle him in a fistfight even if the three cowboys stayed out of it.

Jericho's voice deepened. "You men are trespassin'. By rights I could shoot both of you."

Andy said, "Those who try to keep the Rangers away have usually got somethin' they don't want us to see."

Jericho glowered. "You-all are startin' to aggravate me. People with any sense are careful not to get my blood stirred up. Next time, stay off of Jericho's road." He looked past the two Rangers. "We been watchin' some smoke yonder. Know anything about it?"

Len turned to see. "We noticed it too. Grass fire, more than likely. You ought to caution your boys not to be careless with their smokin'. They could burn up the whole country."

Rusty had once said Len could talk the devil into joining the church.

Jericho pointed eastward. His manner was stern. "That's the shortest way off of my land."

Len pointed south. His manner was stubborn. "We're headed back to the river." He started, and Andy followed.

Jericho shouted after them, but Len did not acknowledge him. Softly he told Andy, "Act like you don't even hear him. He's a land grabber and a thief, but he's too much of a man to shoot us in the back."

They rode about a mile. Len abruptly turned to the east. Andy said, "Thought we were goin' to the river."

"That was just to show Jericho we wasn't afraid of him. It's a long way back to Ranger camp. You've got some bad cuts, and them wasp bites need attention. I'm takin' you over to the McCawleys'. Like Jericho said, you look like you been run through a coffee grinder."

7

Andy was uneasy about baring his upper body to the McCawley women, but they brooked no argument. He had bathed in a stock tank to wash off the dirt, grass, and other debris left by the dragging. He had also rinsed his clothing. His shirt and the upper part of his long underwear had been shredded beyond repair, but they still covered enough to meet the requirements of modesty.

The older woman dug out several thorns with a needle, then rubbed him with alcohol that set him afire. He ground his teeth and tried not to groan.

She said, "The more it burns, the more good it does. You lost some hide."

Andy feared the alcohol was burning away whatever skin the dragging had left him. He drew his arms in tightly against his ribs and squeezed his eyes shut until the worst had passed.

Juana McCawley said, "You have more thorns, but they are in too deep. They'll have to fester out in their own good time."

He was glad she did not intend to poke around anymore with the needle. He said, "I'm obliged to you, ma'am."

The daughter, Teresa, rubbed a soothing salve over the wasp stings. He enjoyed the careful touch of her fingers, a contrast to her mother's less than gentle treatment with the needle and disinfectant.

Big Jim McCawley fetched him a shirt and a suit of underwear. "Our Tony left these behind. They'll fit you better than mine would."

"Many thanks."

McCawley said, "Len tells me you talked to Jericho."

"Mostly it was him that did the talkin'."

"That's his way. He's not interested in what anybody else says. He'll either scare you to death or make you mad enough to chew up a horseshoe and spit it at him."

Andy could understand that Jericho's physical size would intimidate many, but he doubted that McCawley had any fear of him. McCawley was about as large as Jericho, and like Jericho he was all muscle. Either man looked capable of wrestling a bull to a standstill. If they ever came to blows they might tear up enough ground to plant a garden.

From what he had heard of Lupe

Chavez, Andy thought he must be a large man too. He had to be if he lived up to the stories.

Neither Andy nor Len mentioned seeing McCawley's stepson with the Mexicans who had crossed the river in hot pursuit of Jericho's raiders. They had decided it might upset his mother and sister to know he was putting himself in harm's way.

Teresa asked Andy, "Where is the other Ranger, the one who was with you last time?"

"Farley Brackett? He broke off from us to follow a different set of tracks."

Self-consciously she said, "He seemed rather nice."

Andy blinked. "You sure you haven't got him mixed up with somebody else?" *Nice* was not a term he had ever considered in relation to Farley.

She said, "He's not exactly handsome, but he's not ugly either, even with that scar on his face. How did he get it?"

"He brought it home from the war. Somebody told me it came from a Yankee saber. I never asked him." Farley would probably have turned on him like a biting dog and told him to mind his own business.

She said, "I think he is a lonely man."

For good reason, Andy thought. Farley

never let anybody get close to him.

She asked, "Has he ever been married?"

"I doubt he ever considered it."

She suggested, "Maybe he never met the right woman. Or maybe he doesn't like women." She phrased that more like a question than a statement.

Andy knew Farley liked women, though on his own terms. He had bought and paid for commercial affection in San Antonio, but this was not something Teresa would want to hear. Andy said, "He's just been too busy bein' a Ranger."

"Most Rangers do not remain Rangers forever, do they?"

Sooner or later Farley was sure to provoke the wrath of some officer and find himself dismissed from the force. But she would not want to hear that either. "Who knows what any of us are liable to do?"

She said, "I've never seen a really *old* Ranger."

That would be easy to explain, though he did not. Most eventually became too stove up, or they wearied of endless horseback travel and wanted to settle in one place. Or, as occasionally happened, they died in the line of duty.

He said, "I'll tell him you asked about him."

She reddened. "Oh no. Please don't do that." She left her chair and hurried from the room.

Her mother watched her go, then said, "It is not seemly for a young lady to express interest in a man."

Embarrassed, Andy said, "I was just tryin' to help. Ain't had much experience in matters such as this." Perhaps a good woman might smooth Farley's rough edges and make him easier to get along with. The Lord knew he needed help of some kind. On the other hand, any woman who would give Farley more than a minute's consideration was probably not in her right mind.

Mrs. McCawley smiled. "Some things you must leave alone. They will work themselves out if the Lord wishes them to."

Because it was late in the day, the McCawleys had little difficulty in persuading Andy and Len to spend the night before they started back to camp. Andy looked forward to a couple of kitchen-cooked meals. And he found it easy to look at Teresa McCawley, though the memory of Farley's sister Bethel intruded, giving him a disquieting sense of guilt.

After supper the three men sat on the

front porch of the rock house. McCawley smoked a pipe in silence. Silence was one thing Len could not long abide. He asked, "How come you and Jericho to get crossways in the first place?"

McCawley took the pipe from his mouth and stared at its glowing bowl. "There was a time long before the big war that me and him rode together. We didn't have nothin'. We were both ambitious, wantin' to make somethin' of ourselves. But Jericho had a different notion of how to go about it. He saw people pushin' Mexicans off of their land and decided he could too. It was easy to say it was a patriotic thing to do since there'd been two wars with Mexico.

"I'd gone to work for Don Cipriano Chavez. He treated me good, and I took a likin' to him. Jericho tried to run him off and grab his property like he'd done with some others, but the old man fought back. So Jericho had him killed. Juana's first husband too. He hounded the son, Lupe, till Lupe took refuge in Mexico. That's when I married Juana. Puttin' an American name on the land kept Jericho from pullin' his shenanigans at the courthouse. He's been a thorn in my side ever since. And me in his."

Andy said, "Looks like the law ought to do somethin'."

McCawley nodded. "It does. For the most part it looks away, or it sides with Jericho and them that think like him. It doesn't pay to lose a war, and the Mexicans have lost two."

Andy asked, "What about the Mexicans that were livin' here in Texas? Did they take a hand in the wars?"

"Maybe not directly, but most of them sympathized with Mexico. A lot of Americans claim that justifies takin' away their property. Many Mexicans still claim that everything south of the Nueces River belongs to Mexico. That makes Americans and their property fair game. People like Lupe Chavez figure they're only takin' back what belonged to them in the first place. Both sides believe they're in the right. Those of us who try to sit on the fence take fire from both directions."

Andy asked, "Do you see any answer?"

"Maybe someday, but wars last a long time. They're not over just because the cannons quit. They're over when nobody is left who remembers what the trouble was all about."

The bullet sounded like an angry wasp as it passed between Andy and Len. The crack of a rifle shot followed in an instant.

By instinct Andy ducked low on his horse's left side, opposite the source of the fire. Len shouted and set his mount into a hard run toward a little puff of white smoke rising behind a bush. Andy spurred hard to catch up with him.

They caught a Mexican trying desperately to reload a rifle. Andy leaped from the saddle and knocked him off his feet. The shooter fought, struggling to bring the rifle into position. Its bolt was jammed open. Andy wrested the weapon from his hands and hurled it away.

Mouth half full of dirt, the man shouted an angry string of muffled words. The only one Andy knew was *gringo*.

Len said, "Turn him over." He pulled the Mexican's hands together in front of him and snapped a pair of handcuffs on his wrists. The man saw the silver peso badge on Len's shirt and launched into another spasm of cursing. Andy caught the word *rinches*.

He asked, "Do you know what he's talkin' about?"

Len said, "Us, mainly. And he's upset over bein' a poor shot."

"What'll we do with him?"

"Take him to camp. The lieutenant'll have some questions for him."

"Reckon he's part of Lupe Chavez's bunch?"

"Could be. But there's oodles and gobs of bandits that don't belong to Lupe, just like there's a lot of Texas border jumpers that don't ride for Jericho. He may be one of those that got pushed off of their land. Killin' gringos helps them sleep better."

Andy looked around with some apprehension. "He might not be by himself."

Len said, "It's kind of like with rattlesnakes. Where there's one you'll sometimes find more."

Andy said, "I'll make a quick circle and find out." He rode out a little way while Len shouted at him to be careful. He saw no sign that anyone had been with the shooter, though he found the man's horse tied a short distance away. He led it back.

He motioned for the prisoner to mount. He cut a leather string from the man's saddle and tied the handcuffs to the big flat Mexican saddle horn. Anger in the prisoner's eyes began giving way to fear. He said something Andy did not understand.

Len said, "He's askin' what we're fixin' to do to him. I can't talk enough Mexican to give him an answer. About all I can say is *'Quién sabe?'* Who knows?"

165

Andy added that to his vocabulary. By now he had learned at least half a dozen usable words, not counting a few curses picked up here and there.

Riding alongside the Mexican, Andy was aware of the man's growing anxiety. His own initial resentment ebbed. He even began to feel a twinge of sympathy. "I believe he thinks we're goin' to shoot him."

Len said, "We ought to, but it's probably against some law or other. There's so many laws nowadays that a man can't do nothin', hardly."

By the time they approached the row of tents that made up the camp, the prisoner's head was bowed, his eyes closed. He mumbled to himself. Andy suspected he was saying a prayer.

They rode to the headquarters tent. The camp looked to be almost deserted except for the cook and a couple of Rangers standing at the mess tent. Sergeant Donahue emerged, gravely eyeing the prisoner. He asked, "What you got here?"

Len said, "He taken a shot at us. I swear I felt that bullet tickle the hairs growin' out of my ear."

Andy said, "We thought the lieutenant would have some questions for him."

"The lieutenant's been called to Austin.

I'm in charge." Donahue motioned toward the headquarters tent. "Bring your prisoner in. I'll question him." The two Rangers had left the kitchen and ambled up to see what was going on. One of them was Mexican. The sergeant said, "Tanner, Pickard, you-all go on down to the mess and have Pablo fix you somethin' to eat. Me and Manuel will talk to your prisoner."

Manuel was the only Mexican Ranger in camp and one of only two or three Andy had seen anywhere. Manuel untied the leather string that bound the prisoner's handcuffs to the horn, then spoke sharply in Spanish. The man dismounted, casting a fearful look at the sergeant.

Donahue said, "I ain't real good at Mexican lingo. Manuel knows how to question a bandit."

It struck Andy that Manuel should have compassion because he and the prisoner were of the same blood, but Donahue dispelled that idea. He said, "Manuel hates bandits even worse than the rest of us do. He lost his family to them."

Andy turned that over in his mind. "Maybe he's *too* hostile."

"They may lie to him once, but they don't do it a second time. You-all go on like I said, and get you somethin' to eat.

We'll take care of this, me and Manuel."

Manuel grasped the prisoner's shoulder and roughly pushed him into the tent. Donahue followed, closing the flap's opening behind him. Andy heard a clatter, then a solid thump, like a chair falling over and someone hitting the ground.

Len motioned. "It's none of our business from here on. Let's go eat."

"Sounds like they're knockin' him around."

"They're not treatin' him as rough as what he had in mind for us. He meant to see us both dead, remember?"

"I hate to see anybody mishandled."

"If you was to get caught by Mexican bandits, you figure they'd treat you like a pet? You know what your Comanche brothers did to people they captured. Like for instance your —"

Len broke off. Andy knew what he had been about to say — *like your mother.* The unexpected thought left him feeling cold.

He said, "I guess you're right. We'd better go eat." But he wondered if he would be able to.

Pablo saw them coming and lifted a blackened Dutch oven onto a bed of glowing coals. He dropped a generous quantity of lard in to melt as the bottom heated. "Pretty soon I fix you a good supper. You hungry, Andy?" He ignored Len.

Andy had lost his appetite, but it gradually returned as he smelled the aroma and listened to steaks sizzling in the boiling grease. Beef was plentiful. The Rangers had no compunctions about slaughtering cattle that strayed across the river from Mexico, even if sometimes they had to encourage the move.

Beans cooked for the noon meal had been reheated for supper and kept hot for anybody riding in late like Andy and Len. Andy sipped steaming coffee and tried to concentrate on the coming meal rather than what might be going on in the headquarters tent.

Len told Pablo about their trip, including their meeting with Jericho. He did not mention burning the windmill.

Pablo's mustache drooped more than usual. "That Jericho is *un mal hombre*. Very bad fellow."

Len shook his head. "I think me and Andy could've whipped him. But he ain't on the fugitive list, so there wasn't no use."

Andy pictured Jericho in his mind. "I'm not all that sure we could've done it. He looked as big as a horse."

Len said, "The big ones take longer but fall harder."

Pablo announced that the steaks were done. *"Comida."* Andy and Len each got tin plates and dipped the meat from the boiling lard. They added a generous helping of beans and broke off chunks of cold flat bread left from the company's supper. Pablo pointed to a can of molasses. "Got plenty lick. Good with the bread."

Len said, "We'll finish up with that for *de*ssert." He lit into his supper with a vengeance. "The Ranger service feeds good when you're in camp. The hell of it is that we're gone most of the time and have to fix our own. Old Pablo's hard to beat." He looked up at Pablo. "Where'd you learn to cook so good?"

Pablo wiped his dark hands on a cloth apron that once had been a sugar sack. "I was one time a soldier. The officer, he gives me a pot and says I must cook. I know nothing of such things, but when an officer says do, you do."

Len asked, "When was that?"

"In the war against the *americanos*. Once I fight you. Now I cook your supper. Pretty good joke."

"As long as you don't put rat poison in the beans."

"I would not do that for such a good boy as Andy. But you?" Pablo shrugged as if in some doubt.

Andy carried his plate and utensils to a washtub and dropped them in. He had just poured a fresh cup of coffee when he heard a shout from the direction of the head-quarters tent. Turning, he saw the Mexican prisoner running. The interrogator Manuel calmly stepped outside, leveled a rifle, and fired. The prisoner staggered and pitched forward on his face.

Andy spilled most of his coffee. Len simply stared, his mouth open.

Pablo did not appear surprised. He said, "He was dead already when he came. When Manuel finishes with the talking, it is left only to bury them. It is an old Mexican way, the *ley de fuga*."

Andy had heard the expression. It referred to shooting a prisoner trying to escape.

Len broke his silence. "Lieutenant Buckalew don't hold with such as that."

Andy said, "But he's not here. I'm bettin' they pushed the prisoner out of the tent and told him to run."

Len frowned. "Whatever you think, you'd best keep it to yourself. Donahue can make life tougher than a boot for them that ask questions. Anyway, you didn't see the prisoner start. You just saw him fall."

"Call it a Comanche hunch."

"It ain't somethin' you could swear to in front of a jury."

Andy had seen death before, but it still shook him to look it in the face, especially when it was sudden and unexpected. He walked up as Donahue knelt beside the dead man and examined a blood-rimmed hole in the back of his shirt.

Donahue said, "Caught him right between the shoulder blades. Damned if I'd want Manuel aimin' at me."

Andy felt a troublesome responsibility inasmuch as he and Len had brought the prisoner in. "Did you-all have to kill him?"

Donahue was surprised at being challenged. "Look, Private, he was runnin' away. He was just another Mexican bandit. There's plenty of them left, so it's a small loss to the world." He started to leave but turned for a few more words. "Since you're so concerned, you can take a shovel and dig a hole for him. You and Tanner." He pointed. "He ain't the first. You'll find a bandit graveyard yonderway about a hundred yards."

"Anybody goin' to read over him?"

"Hell no. It was the devil that sent him.

The Lord doesn't want him."

Andy wondered how so many people seemed to know what the Lord wanted.

Len walked up in time to hear most of it. When Donahue was gone he said, "Looks like you talked us into a diggin' job."

Andy knew who would do most of the work.

Mounds indicated half a dozen unmarked graves. Whoever was buried there had simply vanished from the earth. Andy guessed that friends and kin still wondered what had become of them. He and Len took turns with the shovel, though Len's turns were shorter than Andy's. When the hole was dug they buried the blanket-wrapped prisoner without witnesses and without ceremony. Andy doubted that a minister or priest had ever visited this burying place or given it the sanction of a church.

He said, "Wonder what his name was?"

Len wiped his dirty hands on his trousers. "You probably couldn't spell it even if you had a board to carve it on."

They returned to the mess tent for coffee. Manuel stood at the edge of camp, smoking a cigarette and staring off into the gloom. Pablo saw Andy looking in Manuel's direction. He said, "He has much hate in his heart."

"The sergeant said bandits killed his family."

"His papa had a farm. Not big, you know, just a little farm, but the Spanish king gave it to his great-papa long time ago. Banditos come. They shoot Manuel, they kill his papa, his mama, they carry his sister across the river. For a long time he looks, but never does he find her. So he kills bandits, and maybe sometimes he kills some who are not bandits. Many over there have tried to kill him, but some say he can never die. They say he is a son of the devil. The devil himself maybe."

Andy shivered. "Damned if he doesn't look like it."

Just before time for bed, Donahue came to the tent Andy shared with Len and others. He said, "Your horses need a day of rest. You and Tanner will stay around and stand horse guard tomorrow."

Andy noted that Donahue's concern was for the horses rather than the men. Guarding the company horses was usually easy duty but boresome. Most Rangers came to dread it. Andy had done his share on the San Saba.

Donahue added, "You can start tonight,

Pickard. You'll stand the after-midnight watch."

"Yes, sir." Andy knew he would get little sleep before going on duty and none the rest of the night. He was paying for having questioned the sergeant.

Donahue gave Andy a long study, one eye almost closed. "I hear you was raised by the Indians."

Andy felt belligerence on the sergeant's part. "Till I was maybe eleven or twelve years old."

"I got no more use for Indians than I have for Meskins. I hope you ain't still got a bunch of Indian ideas in your head."

Defensively Andy said, "I don't scalp people, if that's what you mean. And I don't shoot them in the back."

"You better walk a real straight line, Pickard. I'll be watchin' you."

As Donahue walked away, Len said, "Talkin' too much can lead to trouble. You'd better learn to keep quiet, like me."

A raid was more likely here near the border than it had been on the San Saba, so Andy fought the sleepiness that kept tugging at his eyelids after he went on duty. Out west it might not have mattered if he gave in to it so long as an officer did not catch him. Here it could lead to deadly consequences if either Texan or Mexican raiders decided to make a try for the Rangers' remuda. A man could get killed before he came fully awake. The ugly image of the dead prisoner kept rising before him.

He pictured what Rusty Shannon's reaction might have been had he seen what Andy had witnessed.

A vague figure moved in the night. A man walked among the horses, bridling one and saddling it. Andy challenged him. "Who are you?"

A voice said, "Manuel."

"What're you doin' out here afoot in the middle of the night?"

"I have business across the river. Sergeant Donahue, he knows."

Andy thought on what Pablo had told him. He shivered. "You already killed one today. Isn't that enough?"

"It will be enough when they are all dead." Manuel rode toward the river, disappearing like a malevolent ghost into the darkness.

Andy began to wonder if he had made a mistake in agreeing to come to this part of the country. Rangers — some, anyway — had a different view of duty here than they had to the north and the west. In retrospect, Rusty's farm looked better than he had realized when he left there.

8

Farley Brackett rode in about noon, hunched in weariness. Andy was standing horse guard. Farley reined in beside him and declared with a tone of accusation, "You-all didn't wait for me."

"We figured you'd come on back to camp."

"I might've needed you if I'd had a little bad luck."

Andy suspected Farley had not returned to the appointed place either. This was his way of grabbing the offensive and keeping it. Andy refused to take the bait. "We figured you're man enough to take care of yourself."

"I am. Many a state policeman found that out to his regret." Farley frowned. "I wish you and Tanner hadn't rode off with the pack mule. I ain't et in two days. Damn a country where you can't stir up at least a squirrel or a prairie chicken. I came near shootin' a javelina hog."

A little spell of hunger might teach Farley humility, Andy thought. Farley had ridden away in his own direction without even mentioning that he might want the pack mule or at least some of what it carried. Andy saw no gain in pointing this out. Farley would come up with an answer.

Farley gave Andy's face closer attention. "You been in a fight?"

"Wasps. I lost." Most of the swelling had gone down. Andy had thought it might no longer be noticeable, but Farley didn't miss much.

Farley snorted. "The country's full of bandits, and you waste time doin' battle with wasps."

Andy asked, "Where you been all this time?"

"I followed them cowboys plumb to Jericho's headquarters. That place is like a fort. The Spaniards that built it must've been awful scared of Indians."

"Len and me, we saw Jericho himself."

"So did I. He came in just before dark. He was damned mad about somethin'. I couldn't sneak up close enough to hear what his trouble was."

It might have been about a burned windmill. Andy chose not to tell about that. Farley would harp on it for a week. He said, "We got so close we could've counted his red whiskers if we'd wanted to."

Gruffly Farley said, "I got close enough to see what I went for, and I didn't let a few little wasps booger me away, neither." He shook his head. "Wasps! What are the Rangers comin' to?"

Andy flirted with the idea of putting a nest of wasps in Farley's bed, but he saw no way to do it without being stung again. He realized the notion was childish. Even so, it was pleasant to contemplate.

Farley turned toward camp. "I've been about to start gnawin' on my saddle strings. Has that Mexican Pablo called dinner yet?"

"Not that I've noticed." At mealtime the cook hammered on an iron rod bent into the shape of a triangle. The sound could reach for a mile.

Andy wanted to hear more about Jericho's headquarters, but asking questions would subject him to continued unpleasantness from Farley. He saw that a couple of the company horses had grazed far enough to be almost out of his sight. He trotted his mount around them, gently hazing them back toward the main remuda. The horses not in use were loosely herded during the day to allow them to graze freely but not to stray far enough that they could be picked off by an opportunistic thief. Every remuda seemed to have a few bunch quitters that preferred to be off by themselves. They had that in common with Farley Brackett.

Andy heard the dinner triangle, but he had to wait until someone came to relieve him. After a time Len showed up. He said, "Better go eat before Farley takes it all. Acts like it's the first meal he ever had."

Len could put away a prodigious amount of grub himself.

Most of the men had finished eating by the time Andy got there. Pablo stood at an iron stove. Its black smoke pipe extended out through a slit in the side of the tent. A young Mexican boy washed tin plates, cups, and utensils in a tub of soapy water. The boy was a prisoner being treated as a trusty. He had stolen a sack of sugar out of a Mexican store. Most border Rangers paid little attention to crimes by Mexicans against other Mexicans so long as they stopped short of murder. Even minor crimes against whites, by contrast, were treated as serious because it was thought they might lead to something worse if they were tolerated.

Sergeant Donahue's motto was, "Let them steal a chicken one day and they'll steal a cow the next."

Farley had finally eaten his fill. He sat facing Andy and cradled a cup of coffee in his hands. Sergeant Donahue was questioning him. "You say you saw Jericho's men brandin' cattle?"

"A steer herd, it was. Looked to me like they was puttin' a trail brand on them. Probably gettin' ready to drive them north to the railroad. I wasn't close enough to read the original brands."

Donahue nodded. "That connects with the report Manuel brought back from Mexico. Our spies told him Jericho is puttin' together a big trail herd, and the Chavez gang plans to capture it. They want to get even for that last sashay Jericho's men made across the river."

It was not a private's place to ask unnecessary questions. Andy assumed the sergeant intended for the Rangers to set up an unpleasant reception for Chavez's men.

Len was never bashful. If he wanted to know, he asked. "What's the chance we'll get Lupe Chavez hisself?"

Donahue seemed a little annoyed at Len's impertinence. Privates were supposed to listen, not speak. "Not good. We've never been able to catch him on this side of the river, just like we've never caught Jericho at anything that would stick against him."

Cutting off a chance for more questions, the sergeant strode toward the headquarters tent. He returned in a short time and said, "I'm takin' eight men with me on a special detail. We start in half an hour." He pointed to Andy and Len first, then nodded at Farley.

Len said, "I thought me and Andy was goin' to rest a little."

"You can rest when you get old. If you live that long. Now roll your blankets, then saddle up. I don't abide laggards."

Sergeant Donahue dropped the men off singly at intervals. He said, "You'll each patrol your section along the river. Watch for Meskin raiders, but don't challenge them. When they cross, get word to the men on either side of you. That word will work its way up to me. We'll all join together and quietly follow them to Jericho's herd."

Len asked, "Hadn't we ought to stop them before they get there?"

The sergeant cut him a hard look. "Damn it, Tanner, you ask more questions than an old maid schoolteacher. Can't you just follow orders?"

"Always did. I like to know the reasons, is all."

"We're not doin' this to save Jericho's cattle. We're doin' it to cripple Lupe Chavez. I figure Jericho's men will whittle them Meskins down a right smart before we have to step in and pick up the leavin's."

"Jericho's apt to lose some men."

"If so, we can mark them off of the wanted list."

Donahue dropped Andy a few miles after he dropped Len. He left Andy with an admonition: "You'll ride downriver far enough to meet Tanner, then you'll turn and go back upriver till you meet Brackett. The bandits'll likely cross over in the dark, so hit the saddle as soon as it's light enough to see tracks. And don't let Tanner drag you into any long-winded conversations, or you're liable to miss somethin'."

Donahue had said no bandits were likely to cross the river in daylight, so Andy saw no harm in resting awhile. The sergeant might not approve, but what he did not know would not hurt him. Andy had raw bacon and jerked beef as well as some of Pablo's leftover biscuits. He ate a little, then stretched out beneath a mesquite.

He awakened to see the sun going down.

184

He chewed a little more tough jerky while he took his time saddling his horse. Watching the riverbank for tracks, he moved downriver in an easy trot. Eventually he met Len coming toward him. Len dismounted and stretched his long legs.

Andy said, "I see that no outlaws have shot you yet."

"It's so quiet I could hear the sun bump as it went down. I think Donahue saved the most likely stretch of the river for himself."

"Are you spoilin' for a fight?"

"Jericho's men may not leave enough of them to give us a decent scrap."

Andy said, "It doesn't matter who gets them so long as they're got. It'll be justice if some of Jericho's bunch are got too. There's no saints on either side."

Riding back the way he had come, Andy could see little by the scant light of a quarter moon. He wished for bright moonlight but knew this kind of night would be a border jumper's preference. The darker the better.

He heard water splash and stopped abruptly. He made out the vague form of a man riding a burro across a wide, shallow stretch of the river. He drew his rifle but soon slipped it back into its scabbard. One man on a burro hardly constituted a raiding party. He could imagine many reasons for the crossing. The rider could be going to or from a sweetheart. He could have family on both sides. Or maybe he was just stealing a burro. Whatever his mission, it was not likely to be of concern to the Rangers. But seeing the lone man reminded Andy how easy it was to pass between the two nations. The boundary was too flimsy to be a challenge to anyone determined to cross over.

He rested again. Just before daybreak he heard a horse walking toward him from the west. He stepped quickly to where he had his mount staked and put his hand over its nose to prevent it from nickering. Not until the rider was almost upon him did he see clearly enough to recognize Farley from the way he sat in the saddle.

Andy said, "You're awful early. See anything?"

Farley exclaimed, "Damn. I didn't even see *you*. Don't you know you could get shot, surprisin' a man that way?"

"Shootin' me would've pleasured you, wouldn't it?" The question was not entirely in jest.

"It'd cause me a lot of aggravation, talkin' to all them lawyers. I'd rather just ignore you." Farley rolled and lighted a cigarette. "I take it you ain't seen anything either."

"Nothin' but a Mexican on a burro awhile after dark. Probably visitin' a woman."

"A good time of night for it. You ever had a sweetheart, Badger Boy?"

"Always been too busy."

"For a long while I've known you're sweet on my little sister. She could do better for herself." Farley turned his horse around and started back upriver. He shouted over his shoulder, "Go on back to sleep."

In early daylight Andy built a small fire. He impaled a chunk of fat bacon on the end of a stick and propped it securely over the low flames. He fetched river water in a tin can and added ground coffee. That he set atop the coals. It was a poor substitute for Pablo's cooking, but it would sustain him. He doubted that the sergeant had anything better. Few Rangers ran to fat.

The sergeant showed up about the middle of the afternoon, checking each man's position. He said gruffly, "I hope you ain't been asleep and let somethin' go by you."

Andy's answer was curt. "I've had my eyes open."

"Some people have their eyes open and still don't see past their shadow."

"Nothin' has crossed over except a couple of buzzards and a man on a burro."

Donahue gave him a hard study. "Maybe. I suppose if that loudmouth Tanner had found anything he'd be up here by now to tell you about it."

"I expect so."

"Tonight'll be another dark one. Get an early start in the mornin'. If you find that they crossed in your sector, fetch Tanner, then send word up the line to me. Each man will relay the message and then ride down to where you're waitin'."

"You don't want me and Len to start followin' the tracks?"

"No. Tanner'd be faunchin' around wantin' to fight. He'd likely spring the trap too early."

Andy's impatience got the best of him. He declared, "I can see that you don't think me and Tanner can do the job. Why did you bring us with you?"

"I can't always have my pick. I make do with what I've got. Sometimes it ain't much."

Andy's face warmed. Watching the sergeant ride away, he began thinking of comments he should have made in rebuttal.

Such ideas usually came too late.

He rode downriver toward Len's solitary camp. Len was at the halfway point, waiting. He lay in the meager shade of a mesquite. Andy told him what the sergeant had said. "He said me and you aren't supposed to follow the tracks, just wait till everybody else gets there. He doesn't want us gettin' in a fight till everybody's ready."

Len said, "He doesn't know how good a fight we can put up by ourselves, me and you. We're as good as any he's got."

Andy voiced his doubt. "Donahue doesn't seem to like me much. I don't know why. He makes me wonder if I ought to be a Ranger at all."

"Leavin' the Rangers wouldn't get you away from people like him. You'll run into his kind wherever you go."

"I guess. I remember a Comanche warrior —" Andy stopped himself before he spoke the name. He had never gotten past his Indian-taught reticence about using names of the deceased, at least those who were Comanche. For some reason that he did not understand, he had no such reservation in regard to white names.

Len asked, "You hungry?"

"I fixed a little breakfast, such as it was."

"I happened onto a fat young kid goat

runnin' loose. He looked lost, so I declared him the property of the Rangers. Us two Rangers, anyway."

"Some people would call that stealin'."

"Looked like a stray to me. I didn't see nobody claimin' to own him. He probably swam across the river."

Andy doubted that. He also doubted that Len had made much of a search for the owner. But the goat had already been butchered. It hung by its hind legs from a tree limb. He said, "Whoever it belonged to, he'd probably call it a shameful waste to let that meat spoil."

After helping Len put away a good part of the kid, Andy made his way back to his own camp, then beyond to the point where he expected to meet Farley. Farley showed up after a time. He had a jug tied to the horn of his saddle. Andy asked him about it.

Farley said, "I found a Mexican comin' across the river with a mule load of this contraband. Ain't been no whiskey tax paid on it."

"Did you put him under arrest?"

"No, a workin' man has got to make a livin' whichever way he can. I just fined him one jug and let him go on his way."

"You're not a judge."

"He rode off happy as a pig in the sunshine. It was like I done him a favor by not shootin' him."

"Some favor. You swindled him out of that jug."

"He was breakin' the law. I had to do somethin'."

Trying to understand Farley's way of thinking could give Andy a headache. He said, "I'd best turn back. Sergeant says they're liable to come across tonight."

"See that you don't go to sleep in the saddle." Farley took a corncob stopper from the jug and tilted it over his arm without offering any to Andy.

Guadalupe Chavez took a long drink of pulque and wiped his bushy black mustache with the back of his hand. He passed the bottle to his nephew. He said, "It would be my wish that you not go tonight, nephew. I had a bad dream about this."

Tony Villarreal tipped the bottle upward and grimaced at the burn of the raw liquor. "I had a dream too, but it was a good one. I welcome a chance to poke Jericho in the eye. Besides, you are sending some good men with me. Why do you worry about me but not about them?"

"They are not of my flesh and blood. You are."

Tony stood nearly a head taller than his uncle. Despite his fierce reputation, Lupe Chavez was small in stature, not much over five feet tall but still as wiry as a half-grown boy. Some of his facial features resembled Tony's mother's, though the harsh demands of an outlaw life made him look older than his actual years. His hair remained black as a crow's wing despite the furrows time and hardship had carved into his dark brown skin.

Tony said, "If God smiles on us I will bring you Jericho's ears."

"Be careful that you do not lose your own. Jericho may have the *rinches* on his side. They are gringos, but they can be terrible when their blood is hot."

"Their blood spills as easily as other men's."

"How would you know? How many have you killed?"

"None so far, but I look forward to the chance."

"You know that your stepfather is a friend to the *rinches*."

Tony's face darkened. "I do not acknowledge any stepfather."

"But he is your mother's husband, and

half of your sister's blood is his. It is gringo blood."

"Hers, not mine. If it were mine I would be willing to see half of it spilled to rid me of the taint."

"That is easy to say when you have not bled. But I have, and I found no satisfaction in it. I am satisfied only when I see the gringo bleed. He has caused all the problems of our people. He has murdered our kin and stolen our land and raised his own flag over it. I wish we could call down a pestilence that would cause him and all his kind to die in slow agony. I thought we had it once, in the time of the rebel Cheno Cortina."

"Uncle, perhaps you are the new Cortina."

"I could not polish his boots, nor those of my father. But I do what I can."

"And it is my pleasure to help you."

Chavez smiled. "You are a good boy. We may yet see a day when not a gringo remains south of the Nueces. This country belongs to the Mexicans. We will take it back when the time is right. But not you, not today."

Tony did not answer. No matter what Tío Lupe said, he was going.

As the evening light faded, Jericho

Jackson held his fidgeting horse outside the corral and watched more than a dozen men saddling mounts. All were armed with a pistol and either a rifle or a shotgun.

Burt Hatton looked up at him, for Jericho stood taller and broader in the shoulders than any man who worked for him. Hatton asked, "You think Chavez will come tonight?"

"Tonight, tomorrow night, it don't matter. Gonzales told me they'll be comin', and we'll be layin' for them when they do."

Gonzales was a spy, useful because he would do anything for money. He played the role of a harmless, poverty-stricken *curandero*, a faith healer, and moved freely wherever information was to be gathered. His information was always for sale.

"I never trusted that sneakin' Meskin. He may be lyin' to you."

"He likes my money too much to take that chance. Besides, he knows I'd gut him like a catfish."

Hatton worried, "What about the boys holdin' the herd? They could get killed."

Jericho shrugged. "I've told them to hightail it at the first sign of trouble. Let the raiders have the cattle. They won't take them very far. Just when they think they're gettin' away, we'll hit them like a hailstorm. There'll be dead Mexicans layin' all over the place."

"And maybe a few of our boys."

"They're bein' paid to take the chance. If any of them lets some Mexican kill them it'll be because they wasn't good enough to earn their wages."

Hatton suspected that Jericho considered him as expendable as any of the other men. He resented that, though his loyalty to Jericho was equally shallow. It was simply bought and paid for like any other kind of merchandise. He said, "Maybe we'll be lucky and get Lupe Chavez."

Jericho shook his head. "He's too cagey to go out on these forays himself. He sends other people to take the risks. But maybe we'll catch his nephew, Jim McCawley's stepson. If we do, I don't want anybody killin' him. That's a pleasure I want to save for myself."

Jericho's grim eyes made Hatton feel cold. Jericho wanted to take revenge on Tony Villarreal for the death of his wife's nephew. Nobody had dared tell him the truth, that the boy had died in an abortive raid on a travelers' camp and not at the hands of Chavez's men. Hellfire and brimstone would rain down if Jericho ever found out.

Hatton made up his mind that he would not stay to see that day. At the first good opportunity he would gather up whatever belonged to him, and whatever else he could easily lay his hands on, then leave this part of the country. He could not escape into Mexico, for too many people knew him there and had knives sharpened and waiting for his throat. The word *California* had a nice ring to it.

Jericho said, "Let's try not to let none of them get away. I'd like to take a dozen dead Mexicans and pile them up for everybody to see, like McNelly done that time in Brownsville. Them people have got no respect for us, but they do respect force. I don't see why the Lord don't send down a plague to kill every one of them north of the Rio Grande, and maybe south for a hundred miles."

"They must've done somethin' awful to make you hate them so bad."

"They made me an orphan when I was just a barefooted kid. Left me to root hog or die. Damn right I hate them. I been payin' them back ever since, and I ain't half done yet. I hope I can live to see the last of them gone."

9

A distant crackle of gunfire made Andy's heartbeat quicken. It came from the north, but he was unable to judge how far. A Ranger named Bill Hewitt pushed his horse into a run. Sergeant Donahue called him back.

"Hold up there. Don't get in a rush."

Hewitt protested, "The fightin' has started and we ain't in it."

"We'll get there in our own good time. Let them have at one another awhile."

"There's white men in trouble up there."

"And not a Sunday school teacher amongst them. It's no great loss if some of Jericho's outfit get dirt shoveled in their faces. They ain't much better than Meskins."

Andy had found the tracks shortly after daybreak. A dozen or so horsemen had crossed the river in the night between Andy's station and Farley's. He had hurried to let Farley know, then had backtracked to fetch Len while Farley sent word up the line. It had taken a couple of hours for all the Rangers to gather. Donahue had led them in an easy trot, following a trail so plain that a tenderfoot could not have missed it.

Andy understood Donahue's lack of haste. The sergeant was letting Jericho's men administer the bulk of the punishment and take some themselves. The Rangers would arrive in time to sweep up any remnants of the raiding party. Jericho's losses would cause no regret except in Jericho's camp.

Farley said, "With any luck, the Rangers will get most of the credit without it costin' us anything except some shells."

Andy asked, "What does it matter who gets the credit?"

"Wake up and think, Badger Boy. Donahue would sell his mother to get promoted to lieutenant. If the papers in San Antonio and Galveston get wind of this, he's liable to make it. And I'd bet my saddle and fixin's that he'll make sure they hear about it."

Though Andy had reservations about Donahue, it had not occurred to him that the sergeant might have planned this little campaign more to advance his career than to punish outlaws.

Farley said, "There ain't many people do

things just from the goodness of their heart. Most of them look out for theirselves first. You'd better learn to do the same if you don't want to set your boots under a poor man's table all your life."

If this was true, Andy thought, perhaps headquarters in Austin would assign Donahue to some post where he would consider the adversaries to be worthy of his attention. He had only contempt for Mexican border jumpers.

Hewitt kept pushing out in front, eager to get into the fight. Len was but little behind him, pistol already in his hand. A growing cloud of dust indicated that gunfire had spooked the cattle into a stampede. Through the swirling of hoof-stirred earth Andy began to see horsemen circling about. They were too busy firing at one another to try to control the herd.

Donahue shouted, "Spread out. Shoot every Meskin you see."

Andy followed Len, wanting to keep him in sight because he feared the excitement might make Len careless. But in the dust and confusion he lost him.

A Mexican appeared, a white horseman in close pursuit. The fugitive's horse fell, spilling its rider. The man jumped to his feet and raised his hands, pleading. The pursuer rode within point-blank range and shot him between the eyes.

Andy felt choked. He blamed it on the dust.

Two hundred yards away he saw a white rider slump from the saddle, then struggle to rise from the ground. A Mexican leaned over the fallen man and put two more bullets into him. Before the Mexican could pull away, a Ranger shot him down.

Andy's stomach turned. Both sides were turning this into an orgy of killing.

Donahue was chasing a fugitive but pointed at another who was spurring eastward. He shouted, "There goes a Meskin. Don't just sit there, Pickard. Get the son of a bitch."

By reflex Andy set off in a long lope. Sensing someone behind him, he looked back and saw Farley twenty yards in the rear, trying to catch up. The runner's bay horse was long-legged and strong of wind. For a while it lengthened its lead. The chase stretched to one mile, then two. Andy began to doubt that he could overtake the raider. But gradually the bay weakened, its hide glistening with sweat, its mouth white with foam.

Someone else appeared behind Farley.

He was neither Mexican nor Ranger, so Andy figured he was a Jericho man. Farley pointed a pistol at him, and the rider turned back.

Andy tried to aim at the fugitive, but uneven ground made it impossible to hold the pistol steady. He shouted, "Stop or I'll shoot you."

The threat was hollow. Surely by this time the runner realized that if he was not shot now he would be shot soon after his capture. That was the fate of any raiders unfortunate enough to be run down.

The bay stumbled. Its rider tumbled to the ground, rolling up against a bush. Andy slid his horse to a stop and thrust the pistol toward the fugitive's face. "Raise your hands!"

He saw blood spread over the man's shirt front. As the raider looked toward him, recognition struck Andy like a fist to the jaw. This was Tony Villarreal.

The voice was weak but full of fight. "Go ahead, you damned *rinche*. If you're goin' to shoot me, do it."

Andy lowered the pistol, his mind in turmoil. He heard a horse coming up behind him. It was Farley's. He said, "Don't shoot him, Farley. This is Big Jim's stepson."

Farley said, "The hell you say. Looks to

me like you've already shot him."

"Not me. Somebody did it before I saw him. How bad are you hit, Tony?"

Tony touched a hand to his ribs and drew it away, covered with blood. "What difference does it make? If you don't kill me, Jericho will. They're killin' everybody."

Dismounting, Andy turned to Farley. "Let's see what we can do for him. At least stop the bleedin'."

Farley did not leave the saddle immediately. "Ain't much we can do. He's a Mexican. Jericho's crowd'll finish him off."

"Not if we get him away from here."

"Where to? Not to the river. We'd run into some of Jericho's men as sure as you're born. They might shoot him *and* us."

Andy jerked his head, motioning to the east. "We could take him to his folks. I don't think Jericho's outfit is apt to try for him if we can get him to Big Jim."

"Maybe not, but Donahue'll raise hell. Fire us both, more than likely."

"After what I've seen this mornin', bein' a Ranger doesn't shine all that bright anyhow."

Tony's face was pale from shock, but his raspy voice was still defiant. "I don't need help from no *rinches*. Catch my horse for me and I'll take care of myself."

Andy said, "You'd fall out of the saddle before you went two hundred yards. We ain't doin' this for you. We're doin' it for your folks. I don't see where we owe you a damned thing." He took off his neckerchief and wadded it. Sharply he said, "Hold that against the wound. Maybe it'll slow the bleedin' till we can get you out of Jericho's reach." He looked back, fearing he might see someone coming.

Farley brought up Tony's bay. "I doubt this horse has got many miles left in him."

Andy said, "If he quits, we'll ride double." He helped Tony up into the saddle. "Hang tight to the horn. I'll ride close by and try to catch you if you start to fall off."

Tony muttered, "I can take care of myself."

"You've done right poorly at it so far."

As Andy mounted, Farley moved around to the other side. He cautioned, "You must like trouble, Badger Boy. You're fixin' to get us into a mess of it."

"If you want to leave, go ahead. I can manage alone."

Farley shrugged. "It's always pleasured me to aggravate people I don't like. I don't like Donahue much, and I got no use at all for Jericho. Let's move before him or some of his gun toters come lookin' for this hot-headed idiot."

Tony rasped, "Go to hell."

Farley growled, "Some people have got no appreciation. They'd complain if they was hung with a brand-new rope."

Despite the risk that Tony's tired horse would give out completely, Andy held to a brisk pace for the first couple of miles. Then he slowed, for Tony was barely able to grasp the horn and stay in the saddle.

He said, "Maybe we'd better tie him on."

Farley said, "He could fall and get tangled in the rope. I seen a man drug to death once. It was a gut-grabbin' sight."

The mental image was disturbing. Andy said, "Tony, you'll just have to grit your teeth and hang on."

The young man made no response. Andy was not sure he was still able to comprehend.

Farley turned in the saddle and swore aloud. "I knew our luck wouldn't hold. Somebody's catchin' up to us."

Andy looked back, holding his breath. He saw two horsemen. "They're not Rangers. Must be some of Jericho's people."

Farley squinted. "People, hell, one of

them is Jericho hisself, big as a barn door."

Andy started looking for a defensive position but saw nothing except low thorny brush and almost flat ground. "Poor place to stop and put up a fight."

Farley grunted. "Most of the fights I ever had was in poor places. Best we get down and stand behind our horses."

Andy and Farley both struggled to get Tony to the ground without letting him fall. Andy drew his rifle and propped it across the saddle.

The red-bearded man seemed too large even for the tall horse he rode. Jericho and another rider reined their sweating mounts to a stop. The other man said, "Told you he looked like Big Jim McCawley's kid. We like to've lost him."

Jericho smiled coldly at the sight of Tony, leaning against his saddle and holding on to keep from falling. "Well, he's caught now." He seemed to recognize Andy. "Thanks for catchin' him for us. I'll take charge of him now."

Andy said, "No, you won't. We've got him under arrest."

"I don't see no badges on you."

"They never issued us any, but we're Rangers just the same."

Jericho's mouth twisted as he considered

the situation. Andy watched him warily. Jericho outweighed him by fifty or seventy-five pounds. He had an air like a bull ready to charge. If he had been one he would be pawing the ground.

Jericho said, "You've done your job. You can turn this renegade over to me and go on about your business."

"He *is* our business. He's our prisoner."

"You're a long ways from a jailhouse. Give him to me and he won't get away again, not now and not ever."

Andy said, "We've seen how you handled the others you've caught."

"There's just one way to treat a bandit: kill him where you find him. No judge, no lawyers, no jury that might turn him loose and let him do it again."

"Do you know who he is?"

"He's a nephew of Lupe Chavez."

"And he's Big Jim McCawley's stepson."

"Makes no difference. He's a bandit. It's open season on all of his kind."

Andy's rifle had been pointed upward, toward the sky. He lowered the muzzle so Jericho could look directly into it. Instinctively Jericho tried to draw to one side, but Andy let the front sight follow him. The rancher made a big target.

Andy said, "Now, sir, if you'll back off,

we'll be on our way."

Jericho showed no sign of retreat. He said, "I never seen a Ranger that had two dollars in his pocket. I'll pay you a good price for him. What'll you take?"

"They ain't buyin' and sellin' people anymore. Didn't you ever hear of Abraham Lincoln?"

Jericho glowered. "They shot *him*."

Andy held firm. "You ain't gettin' our prisoner."

Jericho's mouth made contortions without producing any sound. At last he said, "I don't know where you figure on takin' him, but wherever it is, I don't think you'll get there." He jerked his head. "Come on, Baldy, before I let my temper make me kill a couple of Rangers."

Nobody spoke until Jericho and his companion were a hundred yards away. Farley took a deep breath. "You sure put the Indian sign on him. I guess it's all that Comanche in you."

"You heard what he said. He ain't given up." Andy turned to Tony. "Let's move while he's tryin' to figure out what to do next."

Andy helped Tony into the saddle. Tony touched his hand against the wound in his side. It came away with fresh red color.

Andy said, "Still bleedin' a little. Keep pressin' my neckerchief against it."

Farley remarked, "That dirty neckerchief is liable to kill him if the bullet don't."

As they rode, Tony asked, "What he said about you bein' part Indian . . . is that a fact?"

"Depends on how you look at it. My folks were white, but the Comanches took me when I was a boy. Kept me a long time. Some of their teachin' has stuck with me."

"I've been raised white and Mexican both. I guess me and you have got somethin' in common."

Andy shook his head. "Damned little. I've never swum the Rio Grande to raid somebody's cattle."

"It's not just somebody, and it's not really about cattle. It's about Jericho Jackson. Tío Lupe and me, we won't stop till we've settled our score with him."

"Looks like he stopped you today. Most of the men who came with you appear to've got themselves killed."

"Too bad, but there's plenty more ready to rise up against him. He's already dead. He just don't know it yet."

Andy touched spurs to his horse's ribs. "He's about the livest-lookin' dead man I ever saw. And I'm bettin' he's trailin' behind us, just out of sight." He pointed in a northeasterly direction. "Seems to me that ought to be the right direction to Big Jim McCawley's."

Tony protested, "It's not his place. It's my mother's and Tío Lupe's. I don't want to go there."

"It's our only chance, poor as it is. Jericho would never let us get you to the river."

They traveled slowly because Tony had trouble staying astride. Andy had to reach across at times and hold him in the saddle. He kept looking back.

Farley said, "Ain't no use lookin' behind us. They ain't there anymore." He pointed. "They're alongside us, and it looks like Jericho has picked up a couple more men."

Jericho and three others were two hundred yards to the left and working their way around in a slow lope to position themselves in front.

Farley spoke with a touch of sarcasm. "Well, Badger Boy, you got any ideas?"

"I can't think of a one."

Tony said, "Give me a gun. At least let me take him with me."

Farley said, "You bluffed him once, Andy. Maybe you can do it again."

"I wasn't bluffin'. I'd have shot him if I

had to, and he knew it. I still will."

Jericho and his three riders stopped fifty yards away. They formed a line facing Andy, Farley, and Tony. Andy dismounted and helped Tony to the ground. He stood behind his horse, rifle again resting across the saddle.

Farley followed his lead. He said, "Maybe if we kill one or two, the others will figure out we're serious."

Andy said, "I don't like killin' a man if I don't have to." As the four began moving forward, he took careful aim and fired. A horse went down kicking.

Farley said ruefully, "But you've got no scruples against killin' a horse. I'd sooner kill a man."

"It's a poor choice either way." Andy levered another cartridge into the breech.

Jericho and his men stopped their advance. They appeared to be confused and quarreling. One rode away, his posture indicating that he had lost an argument. Jericho called after him angrily but to no avail. Jericho and the other remaining horseman dismounted.

Andy fired again, kicking up dirt between the two horses. Both jerked loose and ran. Farley took a shot, putting it just behind them. The horses broke into a full gallop, leaving the three men afoot. Andy could hear Jericho's voice, loud in rage.

He said, "They'll be a while runnin' those horses down. Let's circle around them and put some distance behind us."

Jericho fired a couple of futile shots as they cut to the south, then east again.

Farley muttered, "Keep shootin', Jericho. That'll just make the horses run faster."

Tony bent low over the saddle horn. Andy asked him, "You think you can make it the rest of the way?"

Tony ignored the question. He said accusingly, "You ought to've shot Jericho instead of the horse."

They had traveled most of a mile when Andy heard hoofbeats coming from the east. "Damn! I thought we'd left the trouble behind."

Shortly he saw two riders, one a large man on a big horse. Frustrated, he demanded, "How did Jericho get ahead of us again?"

Farley said, "Blink your eyes and take another look. That ain't Jericho, it's Big Jim McCawley."

Tony raised up, trying to see. "Tell that old gringo I don't need him."

Andy looked back. He saw Jericho and

one horseman catching up but still three hundred yards away. "You'll never need him worse. Let's get to him before Jericho can get to us." He took hold of Tony's shoulder. "Hang on tight. We're goin' to lope up."

McCawley reached them first. He had already recognized his stepson. His eyes were wide with concern. "What's happened to Tony?"

Andy said, "He's got a bullet in him. If you hadn't come along, it was startin' to look like he might get some more. And us too."

Jericho paused to watch from fifty yards behind.

McCawley dismounted and stood beside Tony's horse. "Let's take a look at you, son." Tony tried to pull away from him, declaring, "Don't call me son."

McCawley tore the bloody shirt open. He did not like what he saw. "We'd better get him to the house as quick as we can."

Andy said, "That's where we were tryin' to take him. Jericho had it in mind to stop us."

Tony argued, "I ain't goin' with you. I'm goin' to Tío Lupe."

Jericho moved closer, his hired man following with obvious reluctance. The Mexican who had arrived with McCawley pointed his rifle toward them. Jericho made a show of keeping his hands high. He halted a few feet from McCawley and his stepson.

"Jim," he said, "you came near losin' this boy of yours. If it hadn't been for these Rangers . . . You better break him of runnin' with your brother-in-law's renegades, or he's in for a damned short life."

Andy felt hair rise on the back of his neck. Animosity passed between the two big men like lightning coursing through stretched wire.

Jim McCawley spoke in the voice of a judge pronouncing a death sentence. "If you ever hurt any of my family again, you'd better have a grave dug and waitin' for you."

"There ain't no grave deep enough to hold Jericho Jackson." Jericho pulled his reins, backing his horse a couple of steps. "You keep that chili-eatin' kid away from everything that's mine. Else when I've taken care of the son, I'll come lookin' for the daddy."

"You'd better hope to God you don't find me."

Tony knotted a fist and leaned forward. "Kill him! Kill him while you've got the chance." He lost his balance. His father caught him and pushed him back into the saddle. "Easy, son, or you're liable to kill *yourself.*"

Tony tried again to pull away. "I ain't your son. I don't have no gringo daddy."

The blood on his shirt had dried. Now it glistened again, fresh and red.

McCawley spoke in Spanish to the Mexican who had come with him. The Mexican rode in close to support Tony while McCawley remounted.

Jericho and his rider had pulled back but stopped thirty yards away. Andy could read Jericho's intentions from the way he sat, poised like a cat waiting to pounce. He said, "Might be a good idea if me and Farley was to ride with you, Mr. McCawley. Just in case."

"I'd be obliged. Even Jericho respects the Rangers."

"Not these Rangers, I'm afraid. But he'll respect the guns we're carryin'."

Tony still acted as if he might pull free and go his own way. His stepfather forcefully took hold of the reins and said, "It'll be good to get you away from your uncle Lupe for a while. Looks to me like he's poisoned your mind."

"Don't you say nothin' against Tío Lupe."

Farley told Andy, "I'm thinkin' Big Jim ought to've worn out a quirt on that boy's butt when he was young enough for it to've done some good. It's probably too late now."

Andy offered no argument.

10

Only two men had returned so far to the stone house where Guadalupe Chavez waited south of the Rio Grande. They had come separately, one with a bullet in his shoulder, the other walking and leading a bleeding horse. Both said it was unlikely anyone else was coming.

"It was a trap, Don Lupe," the wounded man said. "We found but four men with the cattle. They ran away. But the Jericho, he had other men hidden. They came down on us like a whirlwind."

"What of my nephew?" Chavez demanded, eyes afire with accusation. "Did you run away and leave Antonio?"

"I did not see him, but the Jericho's men were everywhere. They were killing everybody. We had no chance."

Chavez was more inclined to shoot the wounded man than to treat him. "You should have watched out for him. He is but a boy."

"He is a man, a man who should not have gone with us." The black eyes held accusation of their own. Chavez flinched at a pang of guilt. He had tried to talk Antonio into staying behind but had yielded to the young man's insistence. He should have held tough.

Chavez pointed to a much larger stone house. "Go to the women. Let them tend your wound."

"Yes, *patrón.*" The man hesitated, holding a hand to the bad shoulder. "Good men have died today. What do we do now?"

"I will tell you when the time comes. First I want to know what happened to my nephew. Send Gonzales to me."

Gonzales was an efficient spy. He could move about freely, appearing to be a ragged wood-gathering old peasant and no threat to anyone. To the contemptuous gringos he seemed beneath their notice, almost invisible. This worked to his advantage, for his ears were always open for information and his palms open for coin.

Gonzales appeared, his clothing tattered, his dusty feet protected only by *guaraches* so old that the leather was dry and twisted and black. His long gray mustache drooped like his shoulders. "You have work for me, *patrón?*"

"I want you to go across the river and

see what has happened to my nephew. If he is dead, I want his body brought back here where he can be buried in hallowed ground with a priest to help his soul find its way to paradise. If he is alive I want to know where, so that I may send men to rescue him."

"This will be a dangerous business. The Jericho is killing every Mexican he sees."

"He will not waste a bullet on a worthless old man. He would not even stop to spit on you. I will pay well for the right information."

Gonzales nodded. Chavez had known he would respond to the prospect of liberal payment. His only concern was the man's greed. He suspected that Gonzales would be easily tempted. Should Chavez ever catch him dealing double, he would stake him down in an ant bed and let him consider the wages of perfidy while he died slowly, one bite at a time.

Gonzales said, "It is told on the other side that one of your men killed a nephew of the Jericho. For revenge he is resolved to kill a nephew of yours."

"Antonio?"

"Have you another?"

"Yes, but they are far away. Only Antonio has been with me. When were we said to have killed Jericho's nephew? I have heard nothing of this."

"I know nothing more, only what I have told you."

"Go then, and find Antonio. If he is alive, we must get him back. If he is dead . . . find out if Jericho has other nephews."

The lead slug clanked heavily as Farley dropped it into a tin pan. He pressed a clean, folded cloth over the wound. Bleeding had started afresh as he probed. "I've treated many a wound like this, a couple of them in myself. Now, let's hope he don't take blood poisonin'. Been as many died that way as of the bullet itself."

Andy asked McCawley, "Don't you think you'd better take him to a doctor now?"

"The nearest one is a two-day ride from here."

Tony's mother said, "He'll get better care from his own family than from a busy town doctor."

Few small towns had a hospital. A doctor might keep a patient or two in his own home. More likely he would lodge patients in a boardinghouse and visit them as necessary or as time permitted.

Teresa said, "You're tired, Farley. I'll

bandage him for you."

Andy noticed her use of Farley's first name. Propriety would call for her to say *Mr. Brackett*. He was aware that Farley had been watching the girl, trying not to be obvious about it. And several times Andy had noticed her dark eyes fixed on Farley until he looked her way. She would quickly transfer her attention elsewhere.

Farley stepped out onto the back porch to wash his hands in a basin. McCawley and Andy followed. The big man said, "I'm much obliged to you both. If it hadn't been for you, Tony would be dead."

Farley only grunted. Andy said, "We did what we could. I only wish we'd got to him sooner, before he was shot."

"You've made an enemy. Jericho doesn't forget, and he doesn't forgive. You bein' Rangers, he probably won't shoot you himself, but he may hire somebody that can't be connected to him."

Andy said, "I'm not sure we'll still be Rangers when we report back in. Sergeant Donahue doesn't forgive or forget much either."

"I'll go over his head. I know people in the Austin office."

Tony had resisted Farley's initial effort to treat him. He had insisted, "Get Tío

Lupe. I want him to do it."

McCawley had argued that by the time Lupe Chavez could reach here, Tony would be dead. And Chavez would probably not be able to come in any case. On the Texas side of the river he had a price on his head large enough to tempt even some who sympathized with him.

Now Tony lay half conscious, senses dulled by several liberal doses of whiskey before the surgery began. Andy knew it would be poor taste to ask McCawley why his stepson seemed to resent him so much.

Farley had no such inhibitions. He said, "There must've been a hell of a bust-up between him and you. What did you do to him?"

McCawley seemed jarred by the question. "Nothin' except to be white. We were havin' a right smart of trouble with bandits, so I sent my family down to his uncle. Figured they'd be safer at Lupe's place in Mexico. I didn't figure on Lupe fillin' his head with so much hate for everything gringo. Juana and Teresa came home after that spell of trouble died down, but Tony stayed."

Farley said, "Maybe you should've gone and brought him whether he wanted to come or not."

"I wouldn't have gotten back across the river alive." McCawley's eyes were sad. "Some folks complain about discrimination against Mexicans, but the knife cuts both ways. There's blind people aplenty on either side."

All the windows had shutters that could be closed and barred from the inside, a holdover from earlier Spanish times when Indian raids had been a recurring challenge. McCawley saw to it that the window in Tony's room was shuttered so no one could see in and perhaps get a shot at him. He said, "If Jericho's dead set on killin' him, an open window would be too much temptation."

Andy said, "Do you think he'd be bold enough to come here?"

"If Jericho sets his mind to somethin', he'll walk through hell's fire to get it done. I'll be puttin' men on guard tonight."

Andy said, "You can figure on me and Farley."

Farley gave Andy a cautioning look that said to speak only for himself, but he assured McCawley, "I'll stand my share."

McCawley said, "I'd be obliged if somebody would stay in Tony's room tonight and make sure nobody sneaks in."

Or out, Andy thought. He would not be

surprised if, despite his wound, Tony took a notion to slip out of the house and make for the border. He probably would not get far, but it would not be for lack of trying.

Tony's sister sat at his bedside when Andy and Farley returned to the room. Tony appeared to be asleep but restless. Teresa said quietly, "He's running some fever."

Farley laid his palm against the boy's forehead. "At least he won't be runnin' for the border tonight."

She said, "He wouldn't do that. Would he?"

"He might. He's got guts. Meanin' no offense, but it's too bad he ain't got good sense to match."

She said, "I'll admit he's a trial sometimes. But he is my brother. I'd hate to see more harm come to him."

Farley placed a hand on her shoulder. "It won't. Me and Badger Boy will see to that."

She reached up and touched his hand. "Badger Boy?"

"It's a long story. If you've got time maybe I'll tell it to you."

She smiled. "I have plenty of time."

Andy left the pair and walked out to the kitchen to see about getting a cup of coffee. He doubted that Farley's story would paint him in a good light.

Someone shouted outside, "Mr. McCawley. Riders comin'."

McCawley flung the door open and stepped out into the night. He shouted, "Don't anybody shoot unless we're shot at."

Rifle in hand, Andy joined McCawley at the front of the house. Farley came hurrying, pausing to blow out the lamp in the parlor. Andy said, "Don't seem likely that it'd be Jericho. Not bold and open like this."

McCawley said, "Anybody who can outguess Jericho ought to be able to outguess the weather and the cattle market too. I'd put him on my payroll." He shouted to the oncoming horsemen, "Who are you?"

The answer came in a familiar voice. "Sergeant Donahue, Texas Rangers. Is that you, Jim McCawley?"

"It is. You-all come in slow so I can get a look at you." McCawley lowered his rifle once he was satisfied that the visitors were indeed Rangers.

Andy counted five men including the sergeant. He was pleased to see that Len Tanner was among them. He had been concerned that Len might have charged into the fray with his usual recklessness and gotten himself hurt.

Donahue gave Andy and Farley a critical look. "Figured you two would be here. I talked to Jericho."

Andy acknowledged him with a nod.

Farley said, "I'd guess he hollered murder."

"Somethin' like that. Said you-all took a prisoner away from him."

Andy said, "It wasn't quite that way. He tried to take a prisoner away from us. We didn't let him."

Donahue's frown deepened. "You exceeded your authority."

"I always thought a Ranger is supposed to protect a prisoner and not let anybody take one from him."

"Jericho claimed you threatened to kill him."

Farley said, "All we done was tell him that if he didn't back away from our prisoner, we'd shoot out his liver and lights."

"You meant it, of course."

Farley replied, "It ain't my way to say somethin' unless I mean it." He glanced at Andy. "This Indian boy's neither. Folks don't always agree with us, but they seldom misunderstand what we tell them."

"Why did you bring your prisoner here

instead of deliverin' him to camp?"

Andy said, "That was too far. He could've bled to death. Besides, we figured Jericho would gather up more men and head us off. He had blood in his eye."

"It was still there when I talked to him." Donahue looked back at McCawley. "Jericho said it was your stepson. Have I your permission to go in and take a look at him?"

McCawley considered the question. "Just you. And understand that you're not takin' him when you go. He's too bad hurt to be moved."

Donahue stiffened. "I am an officer of the law. I do not accept conditions."

"You'll accept this one or you'll hear from my friends in Austin."

Donahue's mustache twitched in anger at this threat to go over his head. "Very well, but you should understand that I consider your boy a prisoner. I'll leave a guard. As soon as he's fit to travel, he'll be taken to jail."

McCawley yielded no ground. "We'll discuss that when the time comes." He motioned toward the door. "After you."

Len waited until Donahue and McCawley had gone inside. He moved up to Andy and said, "You-all have played hell with the sergeant's digestion. He wanted Jericho to get that boy. Said it would serve Big Jim McCawley right for marryin' a Mexican woman."

"I knew he had somethin' stuck in his craw."

"Ain't much he can do about the kid for now, but he'll chew on it. He'll have an awful stomachache by the time he gets back to camp."

Farley growled, "It'll be good for him."

Len shook his head. "But not for the rest of us."

Andy asked, "Were you with him when he talked to Jericho?"

"Yeah. Looks like Jericho's crew killed most of the Mexicans, but they took a pretty hard lickin' theirselves. He'll be shorthanded till he can rustle up some more men."

"So will Guadalupe Chavez. Maybe that'll put a stop to the raids around here for a while."

"Maybe." Len grinned. "But it was a pretty interestin' scrap while it lasted."

Donahue came out in no better mood than before. He was telling McCawley, "It wouldn't make no difference if you was the governor of Texas. An outlaw is an outlaw no matter who he belongs to."

McCawley asked, "Did anybody see him steal any cattle?"

"He was there."

"So were you. So were Jericho's men. Just bein' there doesn't prove anything."

"It'll be enough for a jury." Donahue jerked his bridle reins from the hands of a Ranger and jammed his foot into the stirrup. "I intend to see that he stands in front of a judge and jury that won't care about anything except him bein' Lupe Chavez's nephew."

Andy walked up as Donahue mounted. "Sergeant, you said you're leavin' a guard. Since he was our prisoner, I'd like to volunteer."

Donahue glared at him. "Permission denied. In fact, you and Brackett can consider yourselves unemployed. I am strikin' you from the roll as of now."

Farley protested. "On what grounds?"

"On the grounds that I don't trust either one of you any further than I can spit."

Farley said, "I got wages comin'."

"Take it up with Austin." Donahue pointed to the Ranger named Hewitt. "You'll stay here and be sure that boy doesn't set foot out of this house. Soon as he's able to ride, I'll send a detail to pick him up." Donahue looked back at Andy

and Farley. "If you two have any belong-
ings left in camp I'll send Private Tanner
back here with them. If I ever see either of
you again, I'll file charges on you for mal-
feasance."

Andy trembled with anger. He could not
bring out the words he wanted to say.

Farley said them for him, a burst of profanity that would have done credit to a
drunken mule skinner.

As the Rangers moved off, Len held
back for a moment. "Sorry, Andy."

Andy shrugged. Nothing was left to say.

Farley grunted. "It may be a good thing
anyhow. Have you ever seen an *old*
Ranger?"

McCawley put his big hand on Andy's
shoulder. It felt heavy as an anvil. "You've
both got a job here with me if you want it.
After a little coolin' off time . . . well, like I
said, I've got friends in Austin."

Ranger Hewitt seemed unsure what his
relationship with Andy and Farley should
be, so he kept it formal. He said, "I'm
sorry for what happened to you men, but I
don't want it happenin' to me."

Andy tried to set him at ease. "We don't
hold anything against you."

Farley added, "It ain't your fault you're

workin' for a son of a bitch."

Hewitt said, "I'd ask for a transfer, but Donahue would probably fire me instead."

"You could hire out somewhere as a deputy sheriff. I hear most county deputies are paid better than Rangers," Andy suggested.

"But my daddy was a Ranger before the war. Died fightin' Indians. All I ever really wanted was to be a Ranger like him."

Farley said, "Then stay with it. Sooner or later Donahue is liable to bite himself like a rattlesnake. I don't see why the main office puts up with the likes of him."

Hewitt said, "You have to admit that he's pretty good at what he does. The trouble is that he knows it."

Andy nodded. "I can see why he's got his sights set on Lupe Chavez. I just can't see why he cozies up to the likes of Jericho Jackson."

Hewitt said, "You can't see it because you don't have a devious mind like his. He wanted Jericho to kill the McCawley boy because he knew it'd make Chavez mad enough to come shootin'. He wants Chavez and Jericho to hit like two freight trains rammin' together. With any luck they'd wipe each other out. Then Donahue would get credit for cleanin' up the border.

He'd like to be known as another Leander McNelly."

Farley pointed out, "McNelly is dead, but Donahue looks so healthy it turns my stomach. I guess we shouldn't hope for too much in this world."

Next morning Andy watched as Jim McCawley prepared to walk out to the corrals. He said, "You haven't been in to see Tony this mornin'."

McCawley's expression was dark. "He talks to his mother and sister. He doesn't want to talk to me."

"I'm sorry."

"It's nothin' for you to trouble yourself about. It's between me and Tony . . . and Lupe Chavez."

Andy thought it best to change the subject. "I've been thinkin' about goin' back home to the Colorado River, but I'll stay awhile if you have a use for me. I don't know that I'm much of a cowboy, though. Never did much of that."

"I've already got enough cowboys. I'm afraid Jericho hasn't given up on the notion of killin' Tony. I'd like you to stay around close and help watch out for him. Farley too, if he's of a mind to stay."

"I don't think Farley is in any hurry to leave." Andy had seen Farley in intense conversation with Teresa after breakfast. He added, "Jericho might not stop with Tony if he saw a chance to get you too."

McCawley filled a pipe with tobacco, tamped and lighted it. "There's no enemy quite as bitter as a friend who's turned against you. Jericho wanted this ranch so bad he'd sell his soul to the devil to get it. Lupe Chavez couldn't stop him, but I did."

"What's to keep him from slippin' up and shootin' you while you're out on horseback, workin' cattle?"

"I have some good men with me, white and Mexican both. And I've got eyes in the back of my head when it comes to Jericho. You watch out for Tony. I can take care of myself."

Andy hoped he was right. He watched with admiration as McCawley walked out toward the corrals. The man's stern determination reminded him of Rusty Shannon and Sheriff Tom Blessing. He had seen both stand tall in the face of severe adversity.

Ranger Hewitt came out of Tony's room. Andy asked, "How's the patient?"

Hewitt shrugged. "I'd just as well find me a shade tree and sleep all day. He's not in shape to go anywhere."

"I'm not worryin' too much right now

about him leavin'. I'm worried about somebody comin' in after him."

Andy entered Tony's room. The young man lay on a cot, his face toward the wall. He did not acknowledge Andy's presence. He had lost a considerable amount of blood, and he still suffered from shock. Andy could imagine how much he must be hurting. A wound was usually more painful the second day than the first. Andy said, "Are you hurtin' too much to talk to Big Jim?"

Tony offered no answer.

Andy said, "He's worried about you. You're not bein' fair to him."

Tony did not look at him, but he murmured, "What the hell would you know about it?"

"All I know is that you're bein' an ungrateful young whelp and your family is too good for you."

"My real family is south of the river. I wish you'd taken me there instead of bringin' me to this place."

"If we'd tried, your mother and sister would be cryin' over you this mornin'. You'd be dead."

"You figure I owe you somethin'?"

"Not a thing except maybe to act like a human bein'. I'd give everything I own to have a family like yours."

Tony cursed. "Take them and be damned. Soon as I can I'm goin' back where I belong."

"If you can get past Jericho, and the Rangers, and me."

11

He appeared to be a ragged old Mexican beggar, riding up to the ranch house on a tired-looking burro the third day after the battle. The ancient saddle with its wide, flat horn appeared almost as large as the animal itself. The man presented no evident threat, but Andy looked him over for sign of a weapon. He saw none. The man spoke in Spanish. Andy did not understand him, so he beckoned to the McCawleys' middle-aged maid. She had stepped outside to shake crumbs from a tablecloth.

He told her, "I don't know what he wants."

She spoke to the old man in Spanish and listened to his reply. "He asks whose hacienda this is. I told him Señor Jaime McCawley is the *patrón*. He says he has heard that Señor McCawley is a generous man and kind to poor Mexicans."

"Tell him that right now Mr. McCawley is also a very suspicious man when it comes to strangers."

She and the gray-whiskered oldster conversed a bit more. She said, "He says he means no one harm, that he is simply a poor man on his way to see his son in San Antonio. He is hungry and wishes only for a little food. In return he is a *curandero,* a healer. He would work his magic on any here who may be sick."

"I doubt as his magic would help much on a gunshot wound. And I wouldn't suppose he's got some kind of charm that would improve Tony's sour outlook."

"Many of our people put much faith in *curanderos.* They have powers no one else can understand."

Like Comanche medicine men, Andy thought. Logic told him the shamans' magic was useless, but he had seen strange things happen as a result of it. Sometimes logic did not work well either.

The maid said, "I will go and tell *la señora.*"

"I wouldn't bother her." Andy found that he was talking to himself. The maid had hurried inside. Shortly, Juana and Teresa came out, the maid explaining to mother and daughter what the old man had said.

Big Jim's wife appeared intrigued. She asked something in Spanish. The man replied, *"Me llama Gonzales."*

Andy took that to be his name, though the rest of the conversation went past him.

Teresa said, "Mama, these *curanderos* are fakers. There's nothing he can do for Tony."

Her mother said, "There are many things we do not understand, child. What is to be harmed if he takes a look? Just a look, that is all."

"Papa may not be pleased."

"There are things your papa does not know either. We have never turned the hungry away from our door. I see no harm in feeding the old fellow."

Andy felt uneasy, but it was not his place to argue with Mrs. McCawley. He said, "It might be a good idea to search him and make sure he's not packin' any iron."

Teresa told the old man what Andy had said. The *curandero* made no protest. He lifted his arms to demonstrate that he carried no gun. He had a skinning knife at his waist. He removed it and its belt, hanging them over the horn of his old saddle.

Mrs. McCawley said, "He is a stranger. There is no reason he would want to hurt Antonio."

Andy replied, "Right now any stranger will bear watchin'."

The old man seemed a stranger to water.

Mrs. McCawley and the maid brought him a plate of beef and beans and a cup of coffee on the patio. He sat in the shade and devoured the food quickly without availing himself of a chance to wash his face and hands.

Teresa frowned. Quietly she told Andy, "These beggars all have some kind of story. If he is a true *curandero*, why does he not heal himself?" The old man had a swollen cut on his hand that he had said resulted from letting his knife slip while he butchered a fat goat.

Andy said, "Maybe he expects the dirt to heal it."

Teresa said, "I have a bad feeling about this man. Would you watch him?"

"I will." Andy suspected she would probably rather have asked Farley, but Farley and Hewitt were out at the corrals looking over some brood mares a couple of vaqueros had brought in to mate with McCawley's best stallion.

When he had eaten his fill, Gonzales asked to see the sick man. Mrs. McCawley led him to the room where Tony lay. He said his medicine would work better if everyone left. The two women withdrew, though Teresa's eyes begged Andy not to go. The old man frowned at him. Andy sat in a chair and said firmly, "I'm stayin'."

Tony seemed to brighten a little as Gonzales spoke quietly. Andy strained to hear, but it was a lost effort because he could not understand the language. Gonzales laid his hands on Tony and said words that Andy took to be some sort of incantation. He had witnessed similar performances by Comanche medicine men.

Tony had spoken little to anyone in the family, but he talked at length to the *curandero*. Afterward, though he said nothing to Andy, he appeared to have a stronger light in his eyes.

Maybe there's more to this magic stuff than most of us can see, Andy thought.

He stood at the front door, watching as the old man rode northward on the over-burdened burro. Teresa joined him, a question in her eyes.

Andy said, "I don't see as he hurt anything. Maybe he did Tony some good, even if it's only in his head."

She replied, "These are strange times. You never know for certain who are your friends and who are your enemies."

"I guess he's just a harmless old —" Andy caught himself. He had been about to say *harmless old Mexican*. She might have taken that as an affront to her mother's side of the family. It was the sort of thing he would expect from Sergeant Donahue, and perhaps Farley. He completed the sentence. "Harmless old beggar."

She said, "It will take him a long time to reach San Antonio on that poor burro."

"Time doesn't matter much to a burro."

The next time Andy looked in, Tony was sitting up, a pillow propped behind him. It was the first time Andy had seen him that way. Tony nodded, saying nothing though he appeared at least civil. His attitude changed when his stepfather came in hot and dusty from working cattle and stopped to ask how he was. Tony turned his face to the wall and made no comment. Big Jim looked dejected.

Andy followed him out into the parlor. He said, "If it's any comfort to you, a while ago he seemed like he was feelin' better."

"Seein' me spoiled it, I suppose." McCawley went into the kitchen. He poured a glass of raw tequila and drank half of it in one swallow. "His uncle convinced him that I married his mother just so I could steal this ranch. But it was the only way I could keep Jericho and some others of his kind from gettin' their hands on it. Once these border troubles are behind us, I plan to sign everything over to

Tony and his sister."

"Maybe you ought to tell him that."

"He'd want me to do it now. I'm afraid it's too early. The courthouse crowd would find a way to take it away from him, like they took so much away from old Don Cipriano and Lupe."

"They might do it anyway if anything happens to you."

"That's why I keep a crew of good men around me, so nothin' does."

Farley and Hewitt remained at the horse corrals until nearly time for supper. They proceeded to the patio to wash their hands and faces. Drying himself with a towel, Farley said, "We seen an old Mexican stop at the house this afternoon. What was he after?"

Andy explained that he claimed to be a *curandero*, and that he spent some time with Tony. That quickly caught McCawley's interest. He said, "Nobody told me."

Andy said, "Guess nobody felt like it was important. Mainly he just wanted to beg a meal, then be on his way to San Antonio."

Farley said, "San Antonio's north."

"That's the way he went."

Farley and Hewitt exchanged looks. Farley said, "For a little while. But after he traveled north for a ways, he took a turn to the west. Me and Hewitt seen him."

McCawley's jaw dropped. "West, toward Jericho's?"

Andy felt a stab of conscience. He realized he should not have allowed Gonzales into the house. "You reckon he was here to spy for Jericho?"

McCawley mulled over the question. "He might've been, but what could he find out that Jericho doesn't already know? That Tony is here? Jericho knows that. That we're keepin' a guard on him? Anybody with half a brain has to figure that we would."

Andy said, "He might've intended to do Tony harm, but I searched him for weapons before I let him come inside. I watched him all the time he was here."

"Did he say anything?"

"Not to where I could understand him. Most of it was sort of a chant."

"We could trail him," Farley offered.

McCawley shook his head. "We wouldn't likely catch up to him before dark. If he came here as a spy he probably won't stop till he gets to Jericho's place. Let's just be happy that there wasn't any harm done."

It nagged at Andy how the old man's visit had seemed to boost Tony's spirits.

Maybe Tony believed in *curanderos,* or perhaps the old man had told him something. He returned to the door of Tony's room and looked inside. He wanted to ask what the visitor had said, but if it had been anything significant he knew Tony would not tell him. It was frustrating that he could not figure the old man's motives, though by now he was convinced that Gonzales had been up to no good.

Burt Hatton hesitantly entered the office that Jericho Jackson considered his private sanctuary from the frequent disturbances which plagued his life. He stood a moment, unsure of Jericho's reaction to the interruption, then tapped his knuckles against the doorjamb. He said, "That pet Mexican of yours is outside."

Jericho set down an account book he had been working on and flipped a stub pencil deep into the rolltop desk. It annoyed him that Hatton had entered unannounced and uninvited. "A little wait won't hurt him."

"He says he's just come from over at Big Jim's. Got word for you about that boy."

Jericho shoved the account book into a drawer and locked it. There was no telling when some of the help might decide to snoop, including Hatton. His finances were nobody's business but his own. "All right, damn it, I'll see him. But outside. I don't want him comin' in this house. He's liable to be carryin' lice."

It had been dark for an hour. Jericho lighted a lantern beneath the roof's narrow overhang and beckoned to Gonzales. The burro stood droop-headed where the old man had stopped him.

Jericho asked impatiently, "What you got for me, Gonzales?"

His knowledge of Spanish was limited. He knew Gonzales understood English, though the old man acknowledged it to few people. The appearance of ignorance served his purposes. Gonzales said, "I have done as you asked. I have seen the boy Antonio. He is in the house of his stepfather."

"Hell, I already knew that."

"He is stronger than his family thinks. He tells me he will soon get away. He wants to go back to his *tío* Guadalupe Chavez."

"I've figured he'd try. Him and Big Jim don't get along. When does he intend to go?"

"He says he thinks after two more days he is strong enough to ride. The Mc-Cawley and the women are to go to San Antonio. Among the vaqueros the boy has

244

a friend who will bring his horse that night."

"Anybody watchin' him?"

Gonzales held up three twisted fingers. "*Rinches*. But they do not think he is strong enough to ride. He fools them. He has only to get out of the house while others sleep."

Jericho considered for a moment, then made a grim smile. "He won't go far. We'll get him as he leaves."

"It will be dark. He will be hard to see."

"Even if we lose him, he'll leave tracks. It's a long ways to the river. Come daylight we'll catch up to him."

"*Bueno.*" Gonzales extended his hand, palm up. Jericho dug several coins from his pocket. Gonzales counted them and looked pained. "What I have told you is worth much more."

"This is enough, you damned old bandit. You'll just get sloppy drunk on tequila. If I was you I'd buy me a young burro with it and feed that one to the hogs."

"But Señor Jericho . . ."

"Move along before I sic my dogs on you."

Looking as if he had bitten into a sour melon, Gonzales mounted the burro. His thin legs hung almost to the ground. He struck the burro across the hips with a rawhide quirt and cursed it as he rode southward.

Hatton said, "Kind of rough on the old reprobate, ain't you?"

"He'll take it. He likes my money too much not to. Anyway, I've got no respect for a man who betrays his own kind, even if his kind are Mexicans."

"How can you be sure he won't betray *you?*"

"He won't. He knows I'd skin him and nail his hide to the barn. I may do it anyway when I've finished with him. He leaves a stink wherever he goes."

The old burro was still wet from swimming the river when Gonzales quirted him up to the stone house. A man walked out and confronted him, holding a rifle.

"I am Fermín Gonzales. I have come with news for Don Guadalupe Chavez."

The rifleman studied him with distrust. "I know who you are. Get down. Let me see if you are carrying a weapon."

Gonzales said, "Only this poor knife. It is so dull it will not cut hog fat."

The guard looked him over carefully anyway. Gonzales said, "I am but a poor man doing a service for my good friend Lupe. Why would I wish to do him harm?"

"Perhaps someone has paid you to. We know you come from the Texas side. You have been watched since before you rode into the river."

"It is good to see everyone so careful. One can never be certain who are friends."

"Or enemies." The guard said, "Wait. I will tell Don Lupe." He walked into the stone house. Shortly he returned, followed by Guadalupe Chavez.

Chavez's eyes were as distrustful as the guard's. His voice was sharp and without friendliness. "What have you for me, Gonzales?"

Normally it would be custom to invite a guest into the house and offer him something to drink. Chavez did not. Gonzales was aware of the slight, but he hid his resentment. A wise man does not bite the hand that may soon offer him money.

"I have seen your nephew Antonio."

Chavez's attitude changed abruptly to one of eagerness. "Where is he? Is he well?"

"He is in the house of his mother. He is not well."

"But he is alive?"

"Yes. He was shot by the Jericho's men. Some *rinches* took him to the hacienda McCawley. But he gains in strength. It is his intention to slip away and come back here to you."

"When?"

"If all goes well, he will leave in two nights." He explained about his ruse to get into the McCawley house and speak to Tony. He told of Tony's intention to escape. He said nothing about Jericho, for that would risk revealing that he was working both sides.

Chavez frowned. "It will be a long ride to the river. Do you think he is strong enough to endure it?"

"He thinks he will be. I am not so sure. It would be well if you met him and made certain. The *rinches* are sure to follow him."

A disturbing thought came to Chavez. "Do you think Jericho knows where he is?"

"How could he know? Unless, of course, there is a traitor somewhere."

"I wish I could send word to Antonio that we are coming to meet him."

"I can go back. They accept me as a *curandero*. I can tell them I have come with medicine for the boy." That offer, and the risk inherent in it, should be worth a larger payment, he thought.

"Do that. Tell him to come to the old adobe camp. He knows where it is. We will meet him and see him safely to the river."

"It will be done." Gonzales hesitated, staring at the ground. "I have expenses, Don Lupe."

"Of course. Wait while I go into the house." Chavez came back in a few minutes with a small leather bag that clinked as he placed it in Gonzales's hand. "You have done me a service."

"*Gracias, patrón.* May you live well and die a very old man."

Gonzales hefted the bag. He knew without counting that it did not come up to his expectations. Disappointed, he started to complain but thought better of it and turned away. Chavez would probably chastise him for being greedy, as Jericho had done, and pay him no more. He reined the burro toward the river.

Chavez watched until Gonzales was a couple of hundred yards away, then crooked his finger and beckoned to one of the pistoleros who had fought the gringos with him.

He said, "I have no trust in Gonzales. It was he who told me Jericho was gathering a herd. It was a trap. He has promised to go to the hacienda of Jaime McCawley. Follow him. If he rides in any other direction he has lied to me. Kill him."

"*Sí, patrón*. It will be done." The pistolero went to catch his horse.

Gonzales crossed the river, but once out of sight he turned eastward. He had no intention of returning to the McCawley ranch and delivering Chavez's message. The risk was too great, the reward too small.

He saw some possibility that Chavez and Jericho might collide in their search for Tony. Perhaps if they had been more generous he would favor one or the other. As it was, beyond the loss of their meager bribes he would feel satisfaction rather than grief if either or both of them died. He was acutely aware that the two men held him in contempt, though they were not so contemptuous that they would not use him.

This was a game that more than two could play. It would serve them right if he were the instrument of their mutual destruction.

He would follow the river down to Matamoros, where a man with money in his pocket could debauch himself on the sweet fruit of the vine, dance with lissome señoritas, and be young again while the money lasted. He felt younger already. He could hear the music playing in his head.

He hummed along with it and for a while did not notice the horseman rapidly catching up from behind.

Awareness brought alarm, and he quirted the burro vigorously across both hips. It was of no use. The horseman pulled up beside him, a pistol in his hand. His eyes were those of a hawk swooping in for the kill.

Gonzales tried to cry for mercy, but his mouth and throat were dry. He heard the shot. He felt nothing when he hit the ground.

12

The sun broke over the eastern horizon as Big Jim McCawley helped his wife and daughter up into the buckboard. He turned back to Andy and said, "I hate to go, under the circumstances, but we've got to. I'm meetin' with a cattle buyer in San Antonio. Teresa needs books and things for teachin' when school takes up again. Tony seems to be comin' along all right. He just needs healin' time."

Andy said, "If anybody was fixin' to make a move against Tony, looks like they would've already done it. We'll keep a close watch over him."

Several of the ranch hands were going with the McCawleys to protect the family on the road. Travelers were beset from time to time by highwaymen who had no connection with either Jericho or Guadalupe Chavez. Andy, Farley, and Hewitt were staying.

Andy asked, "What do you want us to do if Sergeant Donahue sends for Tony?"

"How good are you at lyin'?"

"Never was much of a hand at it. The Comanches didn't have much use for a liar unless he was braggin' about a fight. They made allowances for that."

"Convince them that Tony is still too weak to be moved. We should be back in a few days. I know a good judge in San Antonio. I think I can get a court order to make Donahue leave him be."

That pleased Andy, though he wondered about the fairness of a legal system that would let a man of influence obtain favors unlikely to be available for the average poor citizen from the forks of the creek. He thought it probable that Donahue might know a judge or two himself.

The procession consisted of the buckboard, a wagon, and four horsemen. He watched it leave, then turned toward the house, where Farley and Hewitt stood beside the door.

In Andy's days at the ranch he had heard Tony say very little to anyone. He was surprised when Tony asked, "They gone?"

"They're just toppin' the hill. Why? Didn't they tell you good bye?" He let a little sarcasm creep into his voice.

"I'm glad Farley Brackett didn't go along. I don't like the way he keeps lookin' at my sister."

"Farley's got his faults, but he wouldn't harm a woman."

"My sister is half Mexican. He doesn't have much respect for Mexicans."

"She's also half gringo. Does that make you have any less respect for her?"

"That's different."

"Not much." Andy looked at a small bedside table where a cup of coffee was going cold. "Need anything?"

"I wish you'd open the shutters and let some air in here. It was awful warm all night."

"We've kept the shutters closed so nobody can slip up in the dark and shoot you through the window."

"But it's not night anymore. Nobody's goin' to try it in broad daylight."

"I guess not." Andy swung the shutters back and opened the window. "Me and Hewitt will be close by. Holler if you need anything."

"I just need lettin' alone."

That suited Andy. He had had about enough of Tony's sour attitude. He was tempted to saddle up and ride away, but he had given his word to Big Jim. He might go, however, when the McCawley family returned. They had plenty of help. They didn't really need him. And he had no obligations to the Rangers anymore. Sergeant Donahue had taken care of that.

Lately Andy had given considerable thought to Rusty Shannon and Alice. And Bethel Brackett. He did not feel at home in this hot and brushy borderland, so different in people, climate, and terrain from what he had known. He had been revisiting his old dream of settling down in a pleasant valley, perhaps in the hill country, somewhere along the San Saba or Llano rivers.

Idling had never suited him for long. He had a sense that time was a gift not to be wasted. Through the day he pitched in with a couple of Big Jim's Mexican hands in digging postholes for a new corral. He could keep an eye on the house while doing that. Physical exertion helped him sweat off some of his frustrations. The fatigue that came upon him toward the end of the day gave him a satisfying sense of accomplishment.

Despite his reassurances to McCawley, he felt a vague uneasiness as night came on.

Farley said, "I can't see what you're worried about. Ain't nobody made a try for the kid yet."

"Dark always worries me. You never

know who or what might be out there in it."

At dusk Andy and Farley made a wide circle around the house, walking to the edge of the brush and checking the out-buildings.

Farley said, "Like I told you, ain't no-body comin'. I'd bet my life on it."

"It's Tony's life we're bettin'."

Though he had seen nothing, Andy closed the shutters that covered Tony's window. Tony demanded, "Do you have to do that? I'll suffocate in here."

"Better than lettin' a Jericho man shoot you through the window. Maybe you'll think about this the next time you decide to pull a raid on somebody's cattle."

"I'll bet half of those cattle belonged to Tío Lupe in the first place."

"I'm not a judge. I'm just a Ranger. Or was. It's on account of you that I got fired."

Tony showed no remorse. "If you had any self-respect you wouldn't have been a Ranger anyway. The Rangers are a tool of the gringo land grabbers. They won't be satisfied till they've run all the Mexicans across the river." He scowled. "Who knows if they'll even stop there? I heard that to the day he died, Sam Houston was plottin' another invasion of Mexico."

"And I heard that the earth is flat, that if you go to the edge of it you'll fall off."

"Go ahead, make fun of what I'm tellin' you. You just haven't seen things from my side of the river. Someday some Mexican general will rise up and drive the gringos all the way north to San Antonio. Maybe farther."

Andy tried to think of an answer. "I guess you think that general might be your uncle Lupe?"

"Who knows? The strongest leaders we've ever had came up from the people. Like Father Hidalgo. He raised the cry for Mexican independence from Spain."

"As I heard it, they shot him."

"That was the Spanish. They were no better than the damned gringos. And we Mexicans beat them."

"And then the Texans beat you." Almost before Andy got it said, he wished he hadn't. He saw that he had touched a raw nerve.

Tony flushed. "You better watch out that when the stampede starts you don't get tromped in it." He turned his face toward the wall.

It was useless to argue with Tony. Andy felt foolish for trying. He went outside to be sure a proper guard had been set up. The face he saw at the front of the house was not the one he expected. He found a bronc rider whose name he remembered as Francisco.

Andy said, "I thought Toribio was standin' the first watch."

Francisco's grasp of English was tentative. He touched his hand to his stomach. "Toribio sick a little."

Andy remembered that Francisco had been in the house to visit Tony a couple or three times. Evidently their friendship went back a long way. "Well, you watch good. There may still be somebody lookin' to get at him."

"Good boy, Tony. I watch."

Andy had been sleeping on a cot in the hallway. An invader would have to go past him to get into Tony's room. Farley had spread his bedroll near the back door. Hewitt slept at the end of the hall nearest the front door. With guards inside and outside, Andy felt that Tony was well protected.

He did not remove his clothes, other than his boots. He would get up at least once in the night to check on the guards outside. The steady *tick-tock* of a tall grandfather clock in the nearby parlor slowly lulled him off to sleep.

He was jarred awake by gunshots from somewhere outside. Flinging off the light blanket that covered him, he dashed into Tony's room. Though it was dark he saw that the shutters were open. Tony was not in his bed. Andy rushed to the open window and tried to see out into the darkness. He heard a horse running. Somewhere out there a man shouted angrily. More shots echoed back from the brush.

He bumped into Hewitt as both tried to go out the front door at the same time. He saw the guard Francisco standing, looking off southward in the direction from which the shots had come.

Andy demanded, "What's happened?"

Francisco turned. To Andy's surprise he was smiling. "Antonio . . . he get away."

"But how?"

"I bring horse for him so he goes to his uncle. Men in the brush shoot, but I think they no hit Antonio. He is gone *por allá,* for the river."

Farley came running up. "Damn kid. I didn't think he was in shape to climb out the window, much less to ride a horse."

Andy said, "Looks like he fooled us."

Francisco chuckled. "Fool everybody."

Andy was tempted to hit him, but he saw

no gain in it beyond possibly venting a little of his frustration.

"Looks like Jericho's men were layin' for him." He heard more shots, farther away. "Sounds like they haven't caught him."

Francisco said, "Fast horse. Nobody catch."

Andy said, "Come on, we'd better see if we can help him."

Hewitt said, "We couldn't find an elephant out there in the dark."

"But we know he's headed south. He won't stop till he gets to the river unless Jericho's men overtake him." He had no doubt that Jericho or his men had done the shooting. He would give odds that the angry voice he had heard belonged to Jericho himself. "Maybe we can cut his trail and catch up to him."

Andy went back for his boots. He trotted toward the barn, Hewitt and Farley close behind him. Hewitt fretted, "Donahue will have my hide for this."

Andy didn't give a damn about Donahue, but he felt that he had let Big Jim down.

They saddled and set out in a lope in the direction from which the last shots had come. The firing had stopped. That could mean Tony had eluded his enemies in the darkness, or it could mean . . . Andy did not want to think about that.

Hewitt said, "What I can't see is why Jericho is so hell-bent on gettin' that kid. It's not like he's Lupe Chavez's right-hand man."

Andy replied, "It's somethin' about Jericho losin' a nephew. Even a man like him can have feelin's for his kin. He blames Chavez. Got a grudge against Big Jim too. Killin' Tony would give both men a kick in the teeth."

Patches of thick brush forced them to slow down to prevent thorns from injuring the horses. The men were not immune to them either. Andy heard Farley curse as an unseen mesquite branch slapped him across the face. "Damn near put my eyes out," Farley complained. "Every time I go somewhere with you, Badger Boy, somethin' happens to me."

The only saving grace was that Jericho's men were probably having the same trouble.

In the darkness and the brush it would be easy to lose the way and begin traveling in circles. Andy picked out a star he judged to be more or less due south. Whenever they had to skirt around an obstacle he kept reining back in the direction of the

261

star. He paused from time to time to listen, but he heard no more shots, no hoofbeats. He was fairly sure they had not gotten ahead of Jericho's men. He hoped they had not ridden past Tony.

"At least they ain't caught him," he said. "We'd hear shootin' if they did."

They continued riding through the night, though without any solid indication that they were on the right track. Andy began to be plagued by doubts, which he thought best not to confess to Farley or Hewitt.

Just at daybreak he heard desultory gunfire in the distance. He reined up to listen. "It's at least three or four different guns. Sounds to me like Tony is makin' a stand."

Farley said, "He won't hold out long if they've got him bottled up in the brush."

Hewitt pushed past Andy and Farley. "I've got to protect my prisoner."

The two quickly caught up with him. Andy said, "He's not anybody's prisoner, not till we pry him loose from the hole he's in."

They almost rode upon the Jericho men before they realized how close they had come. Andy heard the hiss of a bullet passing by his ear and clipping into a tangle of mesquite limbs behind him. He drew his pistol and fired a couple of shots. He had little expectation of hitting something he could not see, but it might give the pursuers something extra to worry about.

Farley said, "Let's surround them."

Another bullet sang as it passed by. Andy realized it did not come from the Jericho crew. "Look out. Tony can't tell us from them." He shouted, "It's Andy. We're comin'."

Jericho's men did not seem talented at hitting moving targets. They fired several ineffective shots as the three riders swung around them.

Andy saw that Tony's horse was down. Tony was lying behind it, pistol balanced across the saddle. Andy jumped to the ground. "Are you all right?"

Tony said crisply, "Hell no, I'm not all right. They shot my horse out from under me."

Andy saw blood on Tony's shirt and doubted it came from the horse. "Looks like they hit you."

Tony shook his head. "No, but the fall opened that wound up again. Been bleedin' some." His hand shook. "I can't hold my gun steady or I'd've gotten two or three of them by now."

"You ain't got a lick of sense or you wouldn't be out here in the first place. We're goin' to take you home."

"Like hell. You think you can get past them?" He nodded toward the Jericho men, less than a hundred yards away. "One of them rode off a while ago. I figure he went for reinforcements. The only direction we can go from here is south."

Andy realized he was right. They had caught Jericho's crew by surprise just now or they would not have gotten past them. They could not go back through or around them without heavy risk. He looked at Farley and Hewitt. "You-all ready for a swim?"

Hewitt said, "I'm still a Ranger. It's illegal for me to cross the river."

"Liable to be fatal if you don't."

"Since you put it that way . . ." Hewitt fired toward the men in the brush. "Just want them to know that we ain't gone to sleep."

Andy said, "Let's hoist Tony up into my saddle. I'll ride behind him."

Farley pointed out, "That means they'll have to shoot through you to get him. Are you sure he's worth it?"

"Probably not. But let's go."

Andy's horse fidgeted, made nervous by

the shooting and the smell of blood. Tony was as weak as a sick colt. Andy and Hewitt struggled to get him into the saddle while Farley watched for the Jericho men to move. Andy swung up behind Tony. He said, "Hold tight to the horn so you don't slide off. One more fall just might put you under."

"It'll take more than that."

They moved into an easy lope. Shortly Farley shouted, "They're tryin' to go around us. We'd better whip up."

Andy looked back. He saw six riders, somewhat scattered but spurring hard. "How far is it to the river, Tony?"

"It's just ahead of us."

"Then we'd better give them a horse race. If they get in front of us, we'll never be able to go through them."

The ground seemed a blur as Andy and Farley and Hewitt pushed their mounts for all the speed they could get. But Andy's was handicapped by carrying the weight of two riders. Once the horse stumbled and went to its knees trying to jump over a bush. Andy almost lost his hold on Tony. The horse regained its feet, but it had lost some ground.

They hit the river still barely ahead of Jericho's men. Andy held tightly to Tony as the horse began thrashing, plunging through the water. This was not an ideal place to cross. The river had narrowed, but narrowing made it deeper.

The pursuers' aim was spoiled by the motion of their swimming horses.

Andy and the others broke out on the south bank and resumed running. But Andy's hopes began to sink as he saw that they were going to lose the race. Jericho's riders were gaining rapidly. Gradually they maneuvered around to the front, fifty yards ahead. They stopped and faced about.

Andy brought his horse to a stop and slid off, reaching up to help Tony down.

The riders began firing at them. A bullet thumped against the cantle of Andy's saddle.

"Get behind the horse," he told Tony. That was difficult because the horse kept dancing about, trying to jerk the reins from Andy's hand and run away. "Then drop down low where they can't see you through the brush."

Farley said, "They don't have to see us to hit us."

"We don't have to make it easy for them." Andy raised up, trying to see a target. He saw a man moving around to the left. "Tryin' to flank us," he said.

Tony tried to aim. Andy took the pistol from his hand. "You can't hold steady enough to hit the side of a barn. Don't be wastin' shells. We'll need all we've got."

He fired at the flanker. He saw the man drop, then rise again and go hopping back toward the others.

Farley said, "Aim higher, Badger Boy. His leg is too far from his heart." He had his rifle. He leveled it, squeezed the trigger, and the man fell.

Hewitt said, "Good shootin'."

"I got a lot of practice back in the days of the state police. They learned to keep their distance."

For a while Jericho's men seemed confused and uncertain, unnerved by Farley's accurate shot. Every so often they would send a bullet whispering harmlessly in the general direction of the fugitives, who for the most part kept low.

Farley raised up a little, as if inviting a bullet. "Look yonder, up the river."

Andy had been concentrating his attention on their adversaries and had not paid attention to what was going on to the west. He saw at least a dozen horsemen loping alongside the river toward them. He asked Tony, "Some of your friends?"

Tony seemed to pick up strength. "That

old *curandero* must've told Tío Lupe that I'd be comin'."

Andy frowned. "But I'm thinkin' he told Jericho too. That's why they were waitin' for you soon as you left the house. Looks like he lit the candle from both ends."

Jericho's men exchanged a few shots with the oncoming riders, then broke and ran for the river.

Tony looked up at Hewitt. "You're still a Ranger. Tío Lupe had rather shoot a Ranger than eat. I don't know if I'll be able to stop him."

Hewitt seemed to be measuring the distance between him and the Mexicans. "I'd best go report to Sergeant Donahue that his prisoner got away. I'll be lucky if he doesn't fire me."

Andy said, "Tell him it was all my fault. He'll believe that."

Hewitt left in a lope, riding eastward to avoid contact with either Jericho's men or the Mexicans. Andy was relieved to see that no one from either group chased after him. He figured Hewitt would cross over at some shallow point. "He's a pretty good sort," he said.

Farley nodded. "At least he doesn't talk your ears off like Len Tanner. If I was to ever be a Ranger again, I wouldn't mind havin' him with me."

Farley must be mellowing, Andy thought. Usually he had rather have a boil on his butt than to pay anybody a compliment. First Teresa McCawley, now Ranger Hewitt. After this, Andy would not be surprised to see the sun rise in the west.

The first of the Mexican horsemen reined up. Andy was strongly aware of several pistols aimed at him. He raised his hands to shoulder level and tried not to betray any anxiety. Some people fed on others' fear.

He had never seen Guadalupe Chavez, but he thought he had heard enough to recognize him on sight. He would have picked almost any of the others before he would have chosen the one who turned out to be Chavez. To Andy's surprise, he was anything but imposing. He was a small, thin man, not much more than five feet tall and weighing perhaps a hundred thirty. His fierce eyes were so dark that they appeared black. A heavy mustache gave his face a fearsome look that belied his size.

He pointed to Jericho's fleeing men and shouted an order in a voice far stronger than his physical stature would indicate. Most of his men set out in pursuit, spurring into the river.

Only then did he kneel to look at his nephew's wound. Andy could not understand the conversation, but he sensed anxiety in the older man's voice. The only word he could pick out was *rinche*.

Tony explained, "He thought I was shot again. I told him I would've been if you hadn't come after me."

Andy saw no softening in Chavez's malevolent glare. Chavez shifted to English. "You would take my nephew to the Rangers?"

Andy said, "No, we intended to take him back to his mother and stepdaddy."

"But you are Rangers, no?"

Andy said, "We used to be. We lost our job."

"Not good enough even to be a Ranger? Tell me why I should not shoot you."

Tony spoke again in Spanish. Andy sensed that he was defending them. He thought it best to let Tony do the talking. Chavez seemed unlikely to listen with patience to a gringo, especially a used-to-be Ranger.

Chavez's grim countenance softened a little. "Antonio says you are friends of his. You are not friends of mine, but maybe I don't kill you for a while yet."

Andy hardly considered himself and

Tony to be friends, but he was not about to argue the point. He said hopefully, "Since Tony is safe now, me and Farley will go back and tell his folks what's happened."

Chavez narrowed his eyes. "Or maybe go and bring the *rinches?* I think you may be spies for them. I must think on whether I will shoot you or let you go."

Tony spoke again in Spanish. Andy looked at Farley, who was equally at a loss with the language. A pleading tone indicated that Tony was trying to dissuade his uncle. Chavez did not appear to be yielding much.

Gradually Chavez's riders began trailing back. Two rode over to look at the man Farley had shot. The others had left him behind. One shouted something to Chavez, who responded by making a slicing motion across his throat. The man leaned down from the saddle and fired once.

Chavez said, "He was not sure the gringo was dead. Now he is sure."

Andy flinched despite himself.

Farley said, "They do take their politics serious down here."

13

Chavez lighted a long black cheroot and stared up at Andy and Farley, his eyes unreadable. Though he was shorter than either man, he seemed taller to Andy. He held out his hand. "Your guns, please."

Farley hesitated. "I've got a sentimental attachment to my guns. I carried one of them all the way through the war. The other one I took off of a state policeman. He'd lost interest in it."

Andy cautioned, "You'd better give it to him, or he'll take it away from you the same way you got it." He forked over his own pistol to one of Chavez's lieutenants and nodded toward the rifle on his saddle. The man took it too. Farley then gave up. At Chavez's command a couple of his men helped Tony to his feet. Another led the unfortunate Jericho man's horse to Tony and carefully lifted him into the saddle. Chavez motioned for the Texans to get on their horses.

Tony slumped, weakened by the re-opening of his wound, though the bleeding had stopped. He said, "Sorry, boys. When Tío Lupe gets his head set on somethin', it's hard to talk him out of it. But I'll keep workin' on him."

When Chavez was out of earshot Andy said, "From all the stories I've heard I thought he'd be a lot bigger, at least as large as Jericho or Jim McCawley. He reminds me of a banty rooster."

Farley replied, "A fightin' rooster. Santy Anna was a little man too, and look at all the hell he managed to cause."

The Chavez riders kept Andy and Farley hemmed up in the middle as they rode westward. It would have been foolhardy to try to run. They had nowhere to go except the river, and they would be cut down before their horses got their bellies wet. Andy tried to rationalize that Tony would soften his uncle's attitude, but he did not convince himself.

Farley muttered, "You've gotten us into a fix this time, Badger Boy."

"Me? I didn't do anything more than you did."

"But you're a jinx. Always was. Everything you get into causes me trouble. It's a wonder I'm not dead."

"You could've lit out with Hewitt."

"I wish I had. If we was still Rangers

maybe Donahue would bring a rescue party and get us out of this. But as it is, I doubt he'll lift a finger. And it was you that got us fired."

Andy knew the futility of argument. For every answer he gave, Farley would come up with another complaint. He wondered how Teresa McCawley could see anything romantic about Farley. She would have a hard time gentling him if she managed to hook him, which she seemed to want to do. That was assuming he and Andy survived this scrape.

They came to a sprawling ranch headquarters, a mixture of stone and adobe buildings flanked by an expansive set of corrals built crudely but effectively of brush. It lay a mile or so south of the river. Smoke arose from several chimneys. The smell of burning wood reminded Andy that he had not eaten since last night's supper. He thought it best not to say anything that might be taken for complaint. He suspected that Chavez had a low tolerance for complaint, nor would he be hesitant in imposing a penalty. He had scarcely blinked when one of his riders had shot the fallen Jericho man.

Chavez barked a series of orders to his followers. Most dismounted and took up defensive positions while the others led their horses into a corral.

Chavez said, "One never knows what the Jericho may do. Come. We go to my house. I will tell the women it is time for *comida*."

Andy hoped that meant something to eat.

Chavez led them to a large stone house built along the same old Spanish lines as the home of Big Jim McCawley. He motioned for them to dismount and signaled one of his men to lead the horses away. He walked to the hand-hewn front door and beckoned the Texans and his nephew inside.

Farley muttered, "Like a fly into a spider's web."

Andy said, "You better do a lot of listenin' and damned little talkin'."

Two women came to meet them. Both were relatively young, and one was obviously pregnant. Chavez put his arm around her. The motions of his free hand told Andy he was talking to the women about the boy's wound.

Tony explained, "An old woman lives here, a *curandera*. She will make me well."

Andy said, "I hope she's cleaner than that old man who came to see you at McCawley's."

"That old man was no real *curandero*. He was a spy for my uncle. I told him when I would get away. Tío Lupe and his men waited for me at the river, but because of the Jerichos I could not cross where they expected me. That is why they were late."

Andy said, "They weren't the only ones who knew what you figured on doin'. Jericho's crew was layin' for you."

Chavez broke in. "The old man was two times a spy, sometimes for me and sometimes for the Jericho. He will not spy again."

Andy considered the implication and took no comfort in it. Death meant little to either Chavez or Jericho so long as it was not theirs.

Chavez went to a rustic old wooden cabinet and took out a bottle of some kind. He poured a drink for Tony and one for himself. He did not offer any to Andy or Farley. Instead he pointed to a pair of straight chairs. "You will sit. My men watch outside. If you try to go I will not have to concern myself with you anymore."

Chavez put his nephew's arm around his shoulder and took him down a long hall. The women followed. Farley continued to stand. Andy said, "He told us to sit."

Farley said, "I don't do somethin' just

because some Mexican tells me to."

"Might be a good idea this time."

Farley sat.

Andy looked about the room. Instinctively he sought any opening that might offer escape, though he knew he would be caught and probably shot the moment he stepped outside. The furnishings were generally of fine quality but showed age and wear. He guessed most went back to Spanish colonial times. The house itself certainly did. It bespoke a more prosperous period, when a don could afford to buy luxuries from Mexico City and even Spain.

Farley said, "Livin' pretty high for Mexicans."

"The old don was a big landowner on both sides of the Rio Grande before the Americans came. I guess he believed in spendin' his money."

"I would too, if I had any."

"Your family still has a right smart of land. The carpetbaggers didn't steal all of it."

"It belongs to my mother and my sister, not to me." Farley's eyes widened a little. "Now that I think on it, the carpetbaggers did to us Bracketts what the Americans did to the Chavez family. But there were people here before the Chavezes. The Spanish did to the Indians what the Americans did to the Spanish and the Mexicans later. And what your Comanches did to the Apaches and any other Indians that got in their way. The same things keep happenin' over and over again. It's just the people that change."

Andy wanted to argue but recognized the truth in Farley's comment. "The trouble you stirred up with the carpetbaggers and the state police was like what Lupe Chavez does to Jericho and the other gringos."

"But I never hurt no honest citizens. Chavez don't make much distinction as long as they're gringo."

"He still looks on it like a war. Wars always hurt innocent people."

Farley frowned. "That ain't no reason to sympathize with him."

"But I do, sort of. It'd be simpler if I didn't. Then I wouldn't be pulled one way and another over what's right and what's wrong."

An old woman entered the house. She carried a small cotton bag. One of the younger women met her and escorted her down the hall. Andy reasoned that she was the *curandera* Tony had mentioned. He could hear a buzz of conversation from the direction of Tony's room.

Lupe Chavez returned, a satisfied look on his face. "All is well now. When the old woman speaks, heaven listens."

Andy said, "Wouldn't it be better to have a real doctor look at him?"

"Doña María is a doctor. She has not the papers from the university, but she knows things that are not written in the university's books."

Andy shrugged. He had little doubt that Tony would survive anyhow. He had been well on the way to healing before his fall reopened the wound. With a *curandera*'s attentions it might just take a little longer.

Chavez said, "You doubt, but there is much you gringos do not know."

Andy said, "I spent several years with the Comanches. They had their own version of the *curanderos*."

That piqued Chavez's interest. "You are not Indian."

"They tried to make one out of me. Came awful close."

Chavez demanded to know more. Andy told him how Comanche raiders had killed his mother and father and taken him to raise as one of their own. He had been well on his way to becoming a warrior when he fell back into the white man's world.

Chavez became more animated. "There was a time we had to fight the Indians. In the days of my grandfather they drove many of our people off of their land. But not him. He built this house to be a fort. Never did they break in. Neither will the Jericho. Neither will the *rinches*."

"They tell me Jericho's house is a lot like this one."

"Because my grandfathers built it to stand against the Indians. But it could not stand against the lawyers and the Yankee land grabbers. They fight with paper, not with guns. So many lawyers, so many papers."

"Me and Farley, we're not lawyers. There ain't nothin' we can do to help you, and nothin' we can do to hurt you, either. I don't see any need in us stayin' here."

Chavez frowned. "I still do not know if you are spies for the *rinches*."

"We ain't. Even if we were, there's nothin' we could tell that would be of any use to them. They already know where this place is, and they'll pretty soon figure out that Tony is here. But they can't do anything about it. It's illegal for them to cross the border."

"It was illegal when the McNelly came with all his *rinches* across the river and in-

280

vaded the Rancho Las Cuevas. He killed many men who were not bandits. He killed them only because they were Mexicans. Some were of my blood. My very own family."

Andy had heard stories about McNelly's bold raid in pursuit of bandits. It was claimed afterward that he hit the wrong ranch and killed several innocent men before he found his intended target. By then he was surrounded by Mexican soldiers and vaqueros. Only intervention by the U.S. Army extricated him and averted the annihilation of his command. Even so, he provoked an international incident that raised smoke all the way to Washington and Mexico City.

On the positive side, the border raids stopped for a while. Under the circumstances Andy did not think it prudent to mention that. All he said was, "I wasn't here. Neither was Farley."

"But you are *americanos*. You share the blame."

Andy was familiar with the concept of collective guilt, though he did not agree with it. To the Comanches, a wrong by one white was a wrong by all whites. Vengeance could be exacted upon any who came in handy.

Chavez said, "Poor Mexico. So far from God and so near to Texas."

The two younger women came up the hall. Chavez spoke, and both answered him at the same time. He turned to Andy and Farley. "We will eat now. Not even a gringo *rinche* is to be hungry in this house."

Andy took this as a hopeful sign that Chavez did not intend to shoot them, at least not for a while.

Chavez led them into a dining room, where the women began placing food on a large handmade table that had legs thick as fence posts. Its varnish had darkened with age and was worn through along the edges and much of the top. "You will sit."

He bowed his head and spoke a prayer. Andy found that inconsistent with the shooting of the wounded Jericho man, but he had never understood the flexible interpretations given religion by people who considered themselves civilized. It seemed they could find biblical justification for almost anything they chose to do.

Finished eating, Chavez said, "It is true that you wanted only to take Antonio back to his mother?"

Andy nodded. "And his stepfather. Big Jim has been awful worried about him."

"That man's name is not spoken in this house."

"Why? He's your sister's husband, and he raised Tony like he was his own."

"But he is not of our blood. The Jericho took our land with lawyers and a gun. The McCawley took it with a wedding. In the end it was all the same."

"You're wrong. Him and your sister love each other."

"That I do not believe. What he loves is the land. Our land."

Andy quit arguing. To anger Chavez might put Farley and himself in deeper jeopardy. He pushed his chair back from the table and said, "What now?"

"I am still thinking. You will stay while I decide." He walked to the door and shouted to a vaquero who stood outside, watching the trail. "You will follow Porfirio. He will see that you go nowhere."

Porfirio was tall and lanky with dark eyes cold as January. He carried two pistols and a rifle, which he politely but firmly pointed toward a small stone outbuilding that had a front door but no windows. He motioned for them to enter, then closed the door behind them. Andy heard the clatter of a bar dropped into place.

He said, "Pretty dark in here."

Farley replied, "Kind of like our future."

"Don't give up. I believe Tony'll keep talkin' in our favor."

"He's not much more than a kid. You think Chavez will pay any attention to him?"

"Seems to me like these Mexicans put a lot of store in blood relations."

"Especially when you hurt one of them."

Andy's eyes accustomed themselves to the dark interior. He found a goatskin and spread it on the dirt floor, then stretched out on it. "After ridin' all night and finally gettin' my stomach full, I'm tired out."

"You may be fixin' to get a lot longer sleep than you figured on." Farley found a piece of canvas and made a bed of sorts. "Every time I try to do a good deed for somebody, I find myself in trouble all the way up to my chin."

Cracks in the stone wall and around the door admitted just enough light that Andy could guess at the sun's position. Just at dusk he heard a commotion outside: dogs barking, a babble of voices, several shouts of warning. He sat up, wondering if Rancho Chavez was being invaded by Rangers or perhaps Jericho's outfit. He heard no shots, however.

Andy went to the door and tried to peer

out through the narrow space at its edge. "Can't see a thing."

Farley said, "If it's good news we'll hear about it eventually. If it's bad we'll hear sooner."

After a while Andy heard the bar being removed. Porfirio swung the door open and beckoned, giving a curt command. Andy and Farley both blinked, for even at dusk the light seemed bright after their confinement in near darkness. Porfirio pointed toward the house. *"A la casa."*

A buggy stood in front. Several vaqueros were gathered around it or were watching the front door. They appeared to be having a heated discussion.

One of Chavez's young women opened the door and motioned for Andy and Farley to enter.

Teresa McCawley shouted, "Farley! Are you all right?"

Teresa and her mother stood in the parlor. Teresa rushed to Farley and threw her arms around him. Farley looked surprised and confused, keeping his arms at his sides for a moment, then raising them to embrace the girl. "Ain't nothin' wrong with me," he said. "What's all the fuss about?"

For the first time Andy saw Big Jim

McCawley over in a corner. He and Lupe Chavez were engaged in a silent staring match. It was not friendly.

McCawley asked, "You boys all right?"

Andy said, "We're fine. Been enjoyin' Mr. Chavez's hospitality. Kind of surprised to see you here."

"I'm surprised myself, but we had to come and see what happened to Tony. We had no idea we'd find you-all here too."

"Mr. Chavez insisted on us stayin'."

McCawley explained that one of the ranch hands had overtaken them on the San Antonio road with news of Tony's break. "Tony says he wouldn't have made it to the river if you-all hadn't come along at just the right time. I'm obliged to you. We all are."

Andy looked at Chavez, searching for any sign that he shared that gratitude. He said, "Me and Farley will escort you-all home when you're ready to go. You might run into some of the Jericho bunch." He looked to Chavez, half expecting to be contradicted.

In a cold manner Chavez told Mc-Cawley, "I offer you escort to the river. You will want to cross before dark. The women are welcome to stay as long as they wish."

Big Jim said stubbornly, "We'll all go together when my wife and daughter say so."

The two men stared hard at each other again until finally Chavez shrugged. "Naturally they will wish to stay with Antonio awhile. I do not like you, gringo, but you are safe under my roof."

"I've got a bedroll. I'll sleep outside and not contaminate your house."

Sternly Chavez said, "You stole our land by marrying my sister. So you will do the proper thing. You will sleep in a bed with the woman you married. She is your property now, just like our land."

Big Jim declared, "She's not property. Can't you get it through your wooden head that I married *her,* not your land?"

Juana McCawley's face flushed in anger. She lashed into her brother in rapid-fire Spanish that crackled like burning cedar. Andy did not understand the words, but their meaning was clear.

Chavez tried to stand up to her but finally slumped in surrender. He said, "I can defeat an army of *rinches* or the men of the Jericho. But I cannot stand against a determined woman."

Teresa held to Farley's arm. She launched a tirade of her own. Chavez shook his head sadly. "You also?"

"Yes, me too. Farley is my friend. You will not hold him any longer."

Chavez shrugged again. "You may all stay or you may all go. I wash my hands."

Andy spent two uneasy days until the two women were certain Tony would recover. They gave up hope that he would consent to leave his uncle and return home with them. Big Jim assured them, "He's probably safer here anyway, south of the river. Jericho might try for him again if Tony was at our place."

Juana and Teresa said their good-byes to Tony. Big Jim stood behind them, sadness in his eyes. Tony had spoken to him but little, and only in a formal, standoffish manner. He pointedly avoided addressing him either by name or by any version of the word *father*.

Farley muttered, "That boy needs a good whippin' with a wet rope."

Andy said, "He just ain't finished growin' up yet. Maybe he'll get better."

"If he don't get himself killed before that. I'll say this for him, though, he'd poke a bear in the eye with a willow switch and then try to skin him."

Teresa kissed her brother and told him, "We'll be back to see you real soon." She looked hopefully at Farley. "You're coming with us, aren't you?" She added as an afterthought, "You and Andy?"

Farley seemed a little flustered. "If you want us to."

"I do."

As he and Andy mounted their horses, Farley said, "You know how close we came to gettin' buried on this place?"

"The McCawleys saved our bacon. Them and Tony." He had to give Tony that much credit, at least.

Farley stole a glance at Teresa. "I swear that little girl gets to lookin' prettier all the time. If only she wasn't half Mexican."

"If it was me, I wouldn't let that make any difference."

"It oughtn't to, but it does."

Chavez sent an escort of vaqueros along to see the McCawley party safely to the river. None of the Chavez men would have dared molest them, but the region was infested by bandits over whom Chavez had no control. Several of McCawley's cowboys had camped on the north bank, waiting for their employer's return. They would pick up the escort duty. Andy and Farley were not really needed, but they had nowhere else in particular to go.

The procession crossed at a shallow ford.

Chavez had sent a messenger to alert the McCawley crew, so the cowboys were waiting as the buggy and the horsemen pulled up out of the water. Andy's horse shook himself like a dog, startling the buggy team. McCawley had to draw hard on the lines.

Andy saw that the reception committee was more than the McCawley cowboys. Sergeant Donahue was there with several of his Rangers, including Hewitt. He touched the brim of his hat in deference to the women and told Big Jim, "From what folks say about you and Lupe Chavez, I wasn't sure you'd come back alive."

McCawley acknowledged him with a nod. "Folks say a lot of things that aren't true, Sergeant. Lupe and I are kinfolks, sort of."

"Some of the worst fights I ever saw was between kinfolks." Donahue turned a stern face toward Andy and Farley. "Don't you two know that you had no legal right to go into Mexico?"

Andy said, "That was when we were Rangers, but we're just citizens now. You fired us."

"I sometimes say things in the heat of the moment that I do not mean."

"You hirin' us back?"

"I never took you from the rolls. The company is too far under strength."

Farley's eyes took on a calculating look. "Maybe you could see clear to give us a raise in pay."

"The pay scale is set by the state. I have nothin' to do with it."

"It was worth a try." Farley glanced at Andy. "What say, Badger Boy? Want to give the Rangers another chance?"

Andy was not sure what his reaction should be. He said, "I don't see where I've got anything better to do."

Jericho Jackson brushed away the marks of the saddle from his favorite gray horse as it cooled down from the afternoon's riding. Working with his hands helped him relieve some of his tension. He fretted, "I don't know what's become of that old man Gonzales. I'd sure like him to tell me what's goin' on down at Chavez's."

Burt Hatton stuffed a wad of chewing tobacco into his mouth. "He probably took hisself up to Laredo and got drunk. You know these Meskins. Put a little money in their pocket and you won't see them again till they drink it all up. It takes twenty of them chili pickers to make a dozen."

"I'd give a thousand dollars to know

what Chavez is up to."

Hatton said, "For a thousand dollars I'd go down there and ask him."

"Even if you got close enough to listen, you couldn't savvy what they said."

Jericho had not been among those who tried to ambush Tony as he left the McCawley house. Always leery of Big Jim McCawley, he had put Hatton in charge of that project. It had gone awry, as too often happened with Hatton. Jericho had come with the reinforcements who tried to stop Tony just short of the river, but he had been frustrated by the arrival of three Rangers.

For a time now Jericho had been on the lookout for a new lieutenant. When he found one he would send Hatton off on some mission likely to get him killed. The best thing to do with mistakes was to bury them.

Jericho said, "I can't help feelin' like that damned bandit is plottin' some kind of strike against me. He's bound to've figured out that we laid a trap for him with that herd of cattle. He'll be achin' to square up."

"Too bad we missed gettin' that nephew of his. At least we bloodied him up a little."

"All the more reason to wonder what Chavez may do next. I can't afford to leave here right now."

"Why would you want to?"

Jericho's eyes pinched. "That good woman of mine is still grievin' over her nephew. I been thinkin' about takin' her back to Missouri to spend some time amongst her kin. Maybe the change would ease her mind and set her to dwellin' on other things."

Jericho was about the strongest man Hatton had ever known, but he had one outstanding weakness in Hatton's view: he was excessively devoted to his wife. As unyielding as he might be to the men around him, he seemed almost subservient to her. Hatton believed women were emotionally unstable, so it was the man's responsibility to make the decisions. A woman's place was in the kitchen and the bedroom. She should keep her opinions to herself. That was little enough to ask if a man was expected to work and support her.

Hatton had been married once when he was young and foolish. He had left that nagging woman years ago and never looked back. He could not understand why Jericho bent backward to please his wife. Hatton would have told her to quit whining and get back to her knitting.

He knew that Jericho's fixation on avenging his nephew was prompted by his wife's grief even more than any of his own. Because of it, several Jericho men had died, and more might yet do so. Hatton would like to stop it, but he was boxed in. It might cost his life if he told Jericho who had really killed his nephew. He was not prepared to die for anybody, man or woman.

Jericho rubbed his red beard. "I've about made up my mind to hit Chavez before he can hit me again. I'll gather me a bunch of bold men, cross the river, and wipe out that Chavez outfit for good and all."

Hatton shook his head. "McNelly tried that once. Found himself up against a whole company of Meskin soldiers and come within an inch of gettin' slaughtered."

"Because he hit the wrong ranch and lost the element of surprise. By the time he got to where he meant to go in the first place, they were ready and waitin' for him. The way to handle Chavez would be to hit fast, hit hard, and leave nobody standin'."

Including some of us, Hatton thought. He did not relish being caught up in any such reckless venture. If need be, he could get along without Jericho. He had been skimming off some of the proceeds from cattle he had driven north for Jericho. He had a secret account salted away in a San Antonio bank. It would see him to a new life in some distant place beyond Jericho's reach.

He asked, "When you figure on doin' all this?"

"I don't see any reason to wait. Send out the word. We're hirin' fightin' men."

"Some of them will get theirselves killed."

"We won't have to pay the ones that don't come back."

14

Andy was trying to decide if he had made a mistake, remaining a Ranger. Sergeant Donahue's attitude toward him seemed no better than before. He realized he would not have been retained had Donahue not been too shorthanded to patrol the river properly. He sent Andy the farthest of all the Rangers, way upriver from the base camp. Given a pack mule to carry supplies, he had to set up his own rude camp west of Len Tanner's appointed area of responsibility. Every second day he rode east until he encountered Len, then turned back to the west.

He had cooked for himself before, but it made eating more a chore than a pleasure. He lost weight. Only his coffee had any appealing flavor. After a few days he became acquainted with several Mexicans who lived near the river. He communicated mostly with an improvised sign language. What he recalled of plains-Indian hand talk was of little use, for the Mexicans did not understand it any better than they understood his English. In spite of the language barrier he managed to arrange for a couple of the women to cook a meal for him each time he passed by, though it was costing him most of his meager Ranger salary.

His assignment was to watch for sign of any major movements across the river from either direction. So far he had seen none. After a time he was just going through the motions, riding his appointed circuit as ordered but expecting to find nothing. In his loneliness he found himself spending more and more time visiting with residents who farmed along the Rio Grande. He began picking up fragments of Spanish. He found that some of these people worked hard to scratch out a living from a land that was grudging in yielding up its gifts. Others did only as much as they had to. Some were cheerful; some were moody, distrustful, and made little effort to communicate, especially with a Ranger. In short, they were much the same as people he had known elsewhere, white, red, or brown.

The one characteristic almost all had in common was that they considered themselves to be Mexicans rather than citizens of American Texas. To them the border was a political concept that they usually ignored. He was conscious of small-scale smuggling in both directions, mainly of liquor and tobacco, horses and cattle. He saw no significant harm in it so long as it did not involve raiding and violence. Some small farmers worked land and raised livestock on both sides of the river just as they had done when Texas was part of Mexico and the boundary was only an imaginary line.

So what, he asked himself, if Austin or Mexico City lost a little tariff revenue? Politicians could waste more in a day than penny-ante smugglers might cost in six months. If Donahue wanted such small-scale traffic stopped, he would have to send somebody else.

One day as he paused at the river's edge to let his black horse drink he saw two men approaching from the east, one riding, one walking and leading a horse that limped. He took them for local Mexicans until they came close enough that he could see they were Americans, one tall, one short. The tall one, on horseback, raised a hand in greeting. His round, sunburned face looked genial. Andy responded in kind.

"Hell of a thing," the man said, "havin' a horse come up lame way out in this nowhere country. My partner's gettin' footsore."

The shorter man was limping about as badly as his horse. His weary face was lined in misery.

The tall one said, "We been lookin' for somebody who might make a trade with us. A good horse for a lame one."

Andy replied, "Might be hard to come by without you're willin' to pay some boot."

The walker came up even with the man on horseback. He rubbed a dusty sleeve across his face and blinked the sting of sweat from his eyes. He had a scraggly beard of uncertain color, longer in some places than in others, like a garden with a spotty crop. He asked, "Do you know Jericho Jackson?"

Andy was instantly wary. "I've met the gentleman."

"Maybe you can tell us where his place is at. We're thinkin' we've come too far upriver."

Andy gave both men a long study. He saw nothing in their appearance that would brand them as criminals. Their clothing was dusty and worn, holes unpatched at the knees. They looked like any number of working trail hands he had seen. Everything about them bespoke short rations and low pay. But he had to distrust anyone looking for Jericho. "You've come farther than you had to. From here you'd travel north and bear a bit to the east."

"How will we know when we're on his land?"

"You won't have to find him. He'll find you, or his men will."

The tall man in the saddle said, "Sounds like who we been lookin' for. Goin' to be hard to get there with a lame horse, though. I don't suppose you'd like to swap?"

"I don't suppose I would."

"You said we might need some boot. How's this?" So swiftly that Andy hardly saw the movement, the rider had a pistol in his hand. "Now, about that swap . . . we'd like it to be friendly."

His face no longer appeared genial.

Andy gauged his chances of successful resistance and knew they were next to none. Rusty had always told him there were times to fight and times to pull away. This was clearly no time to push his luck, not while he looked down the muzzle of a .44.

The man with the pistol said, "Before you get off, let's see you drop that six-shooter. Be real careful, or you could get a couple of holes in you that the good

Lord didn't put there."

Andy considered warning them that he was a Ranger but thought better of it. The two might decide to take no chances with him if they knew. It would be easy to murder him and drag his body into the brush, where it might not be found for months, if at all. He eased the pistol from its holster and let it fall. The rifle was still in its scabbard, but he knew he had no chance to draw it. He dismounted and stepped away from the horse but held on to the reins. "It's not a good trade unless both parties are willin'."

"Me and Devlin are willin'. I reckon two out of three ought to be enough."

The limping man named Devlin removed the saddles from both horses and put his on Andy's mount. He took Andy's rifle and scabbard. "I wouldn't want you to back out on the deal and shoot us with this Winchester. Me and Barstow will cut cards later and see who gets it."

Barstow grinned. The genial look returned but seemed tainted now. "No hard feelin's, I hope. At least we're leavin' you your saddle and a horse to put it on. I hope you won't abuse him. He's gettin' some age on him, but that ankle will heal if you give it time."

The two men were laughing as they rode off to the north. Angry words welled up in Andy's throat and stayed there. He saw no use in saying them aloud when nobody could hear. He turned to examine the brown horse. He saw nothing special in its conformation to mark it as anything except a working ranch horse. The lameness was in the right leg. He lifted it, hoping the cause might be nothing more than a stone caught in the shoe. There was no stone. There was no shoe. The ankle appeared swollen.

"Looks like I'm not goin' to ride you anywhere," he said. He led the horse to the edge of the river to see if it would drink. It took several swallows, then raised its head, water dripping from chin and steel bits.

He was a couple of miles from his campsite. He had left the pack mule there, staked on a long rope to allow it to graze. He considered the mule, but it was not broken to ride. It would probably balk and refuse to move if he tried to get on it. Or else it would throw him off and kick him hard enough to break his ribs.

Perhaps when Andy did not meet Len at their usual rendezvous site he would come looking. Then again, he might decide Andy was simply late and get tired of waiting.

Andy guessed that the sun was only a couple of hours short of setting. Chances were that the two horse thieves would stop and camp at dark, figuring they were safe. They might not appreciate how fast a determined man could walk.

They had not stripped his saddle of anything except the rifle, so he had his canteen and a chunk of bacon he had roasted but not finished at noon. He set off following the tracks. The thieves had taken the northeasterly direction he suggested. He was soon sweating. A southerly breeze found its way through his shirt and cooled him. At intervals he came across grazing cattle. Some shied away. Others, not used to seeing a man afoot, approached out of curiosity. A few even trotted alongside for short distances before they lost interest or he scared them off with a shout and a wave of his hat.

A coyote loped off a hundred yards, then turned to watch him. He had heard it said that coyotes could tell whether a man carried a firearm or not. He did not believe that, but he respected the Indian view of the coyote as trickster, a mischievous spirit always ready to foil the designs of men.

He stopped for short periods of rest, but impatience soon prodded him back to his feet. He wanted to go as far as possible before darkness. Though he intended to keep traveling after nightfall, following the tracks would be more difficult, perhaps impossible. Then he would have to depend upon his sense of direction. The two seemed to be traveling as straight a line as the uneven terrain allowed.

The stars indicated that it was somewhere around midnight when he spotted the faint glow of a dying campfire a little west of his line of travel. He indulged a moment in self-congratulation for managing to stay so close to the trail after darkness made him give up looking for it.

He hoped to catch the two asleep. He did not want to confront them in daylight with no weapon better than a mesquite club.

He moved carefully toward the glow, listening for any sound that might indicate someone was still awake. He heard nothing but distant night birds and the humming of nocturnal insects seeking to mate. He almost stumbled into the two horses. One snorted and pulled against the stake rope that held it. Andy sank to his knees and waited for a reaction from the sleeping men. He heard nothing.

He found the saddles. One of the thieves

had buckled Andy's scabbard to his own rig. He quietly slid the rifle free. He tried not to look into the remnant of the fire because it compromised his vision in the darkness. He located the two men, both wrapped in their blankets asleep. He saw a gun belt rolled up and lying by one man's head. Gingerly he drew the pistol from it and stuck it in his own holster, which the thieves had not bothered to take. He moved to the side of the other man. He too had a pistol in a belt, and a second lying beside his head. Andy assumed that was his own. He retrieved both and retreated to the smoldering fire.

To one side of it he found a can in which the men had boiled coffee. Some of it remained, but it was cold. He set the can on the coals to reheat it.

He could have awakened the men then but preferred not to take a chance with them in the dark. He sat on the ground, sipping the bitterly strong coffee and waiting for daylight.

They might have been trail hands, but if so they had given up the drover's habit of rising before dawn. The sun was breaking free before Barstow yawned and laid his blanket aside. He blinked and stretched his arms, then became aware of Andy sitting there watching him. He froze.

Andy said, "Sleepin' kind of late, aren't you? I heard a rooster crow somewhere an hour ago."

Devlin flung his blanket aside and grabbed for his six-shooter. He came up with an empty holster. Andy waved a pistol at him. "It's over here."

Both men stared at him in shock. Barstow slowly raised his hands. Devlin followed, his jaw sagging.

Barstow turned angrily on his partner. "Told you we ought to've taken turns standin' watch last night."

Devlin's tone was accusatory. "Mister, I didn't believe you'd be so mean as to follow us on a lame horse."

"I didn't. I walked."

"Walked?" The two looked as if such a foreign idea had never entered their heads.

Andy said, "I get the notion you two ain't been at this outlaw business long. You're not very good at it."

Barstow said, "We got awful tired of herdin' cattle for beans and bacon. We thought there must be an easier way to make a livin'. We heard Jericho Jackson was lookin' for men who can handle theirselves and that he pays good."

"Whoever told you that should've also

told you life can be short over at Jericho's. He's bad about gettin' men killed."

"Couldn't be any more dangerous than swimmin' cattle over a river when it's runnin' high."

"With Jericho you're liable to be crossin' stolen cattle over the Rio Grande with a bunch of mad Mexicans grabbin' at your shirttails. But I'm savin' you from that. I'm puttin' you under arrest."

"Arrest?" Barstow demanded.

"I forgot to tell you. I'm a Ranger."

Barstow turned on Devlin. "Damned if you ain't fooled around and got us in trouble again. It's easy, you said. Just swap horses, you said. If you hadn't been careless you never would've got yours lame in the first place."

"I couldn't help it. I didn't know he was so clumsy. He looked pretty good in the dark."

Andy surmised that Devlin had stolen that horse just as he had taken Andy's. He said, "I'm takin' mine back. You-all can switch around, one walkin' and one ridin'."

Devlin complained, "But I got blisters on my feet."

"The wages of sin. You-all get busy and fix us some breakfast. No use in startin' out on an empty stomach."

The meager meal consisted of coffee, bacon, and some dried-out bread the two had brought from somewhere. Done but hardly satisfied, Andy said, "Roll up your blankets and let's be movin'."

Devlin's stirrups were set a little short, but it would take time to unlace the leathers and retie them for Andy's longer legs. It was too far to go back for his own saddle. He hoped nobody would make off with it before he could get back to reclaim it.

Devlin complained constantly about his sore feet until Andy made Barstow change places with him. Then Devlin complained that Barstow's horse had a rough gait that shook his innards all the way up to his teeth. He reminded Andy a little of Farley Brackett.

Barstow trudged along, starting to sweat though the morning was only moderately warm. He argued, "Ranger, we ain't really done anybody harm. You got your horse back. We ain't robbed no bank or nothin'. Can't you see your way clear to just turn us loose? We'll take up our old jobs drivin' cattle and go to church every chance we get."

Andy said, "I know an old preacher man named Webb. He says that the church house is half empty as long as everything goes along smooth. But when there's trouble, people start comin' to meetin'. You two were all set to join Jericho's bunch of renegades. Now you're ready to sing in the choir."

"We'd been drinkin'. We're sober now, and things look different."

"Yeah. This time *I'm* holdin' the gun."

"I hear tell that the penitentiary is already overcrowded. I'd hate for us to make it worse."

Andy wondered how long the conversion would last when nobody was pointing a gun at the pair of would-be bad men. "It'll be up to a judge and jury to decide about that."

"Think how much a trial will cost the taxpayers."

Andy thought back on the prisoner he had seen shot in the Ranger camp. "Be glad it was me that caught you. Some Rangers wouldn't bother with a trial. Bullets come cheaper than lawyers."

Barstow shut up for a while, but Devlin kept whining.

Andy saw three horsemen approaching in a slow lope. He could not tell immediately whether they were Texan or Mexican, but instinct told him they were trouble. He drew his pistol and laid it across his lap.

Barstow said, "I hope them ain't some of your quick-trigger Rangers."

Devlin quit whining. His eyes were apprehensive. "We're your prisoners. You got to protect us."

Andy said, "They're not Rangers, at least none that I know. I'll bet they're Jericho hands."

The three reined up so close that Andy could have reached out and touched the one who by his manner appeared to be in charge. The leader demanded, "Who are you people? Don't you know you're on Jericho's road?"

It was not much of a road. It was more like a cow trail. Andy sized up the three and quickly decided they were not the kind he would lend money to. Like Andy, the leader held a pistol in his lap. The other two gripped rifles.

Andy said, "I'm Andy Pickard. I'm a Ranger. These men are my prisoners."

"I'm Orville Mapes, and your name don't mean a thing to me." He studied Barstow and Devlin. "These men ain't part of Jericho's outfit. What did they do?"

"They stole a horse. Mine."

Barstow spoke up with hope. "We was on our way to see Mr. Jericho Jackson about a job."

Mapes mused, "And you stole a Ranger's horse? Jericho ain't goin' to figure you're real smart."

"We didn't know he was a Ranger."

Devlin said, "If we had, we'd have shot him right off."

Mapes looked again at Andy. "Ranger or not, you've got no authority on Jericho's land without he gives you permission."

"Rangers don't have to ask for anybody's permission. They can go anywhere they decide to."

"Not on Jericho's property. I think you'd better hand me that six-shooter."

Andy knew he could not shoot his way out with three men at close range. He would be dead before the echo faded. He gave up the pistol and his rifle. They also confiscated the weapons he had taken from Barstow and Devlin.

Barstow asked, "What about us? You're goin' to turn us loose, ain't you?"

Mapes said, "I'm takin' you to Jericho. He'll decide what to do with you."

Barstow tried to speak with confidence. "He's just the man we wanted to see." A wavering in his voice betrayed doubt.

"Maybe. Then again, there's people who've seen him and wished they hadn't." Mapes jerked his head at Andy. "You-all seem to be short a horse. I don't suppose you'd object to this man ridin' double with you?"

His tone indicated that it was a command rather than a question. Andy saw no point in replying. He took his left foot out of the stirrup to allow Barstow to swing into position behind the saddle. The horse humped up a little, not liking the extra burden. Andy wished he would pitch Barstow off, but the horse settled down.

As they rode, Barstow continued pressing the case that he and Devlin could provide useful service on Jericho's crew. Mapes looked straight ahead and seemed to pay little attention.

Their conversion had been shorter than some of Preacher Webb's sermons, Andy thought.

At first he was surprised to see that Jericho's headquarters looked much like those of Lupe Chavez and Big Jim McCawley. On reflection he recalled that all had been built at about the same time and by the same people, the forebears of Don Cipriano Chavez. Designed for defense against hostile Indians, Jericho's place would still be a formidable fortress. Andy would not like to have to lead a charge against it.

Mapes pointed them toward an adobe barn backed by an extensive layout of corrals, much like Big Jim's. "We'll all wait out here till Jericho sees fit to come and look you over."

One of the men with him asked, "Why not take them up to the main house instead of troublin' Jericho to come to the barn?"

"Nobody goes up to the main house unless it's with Jericho's say-so," Mapes said. "He doesn't like his missus seein' the kind of men he associates with."

"You mean us?"

"If you was married to a pretty little woman from Kansas City, you wouldn't want her puttin' up with this grimy bunch."

Barstow asked anxiously, "What happens to us?"

"Who knows? He may decide to hire you, or he may decide to shoot you. With him you never know."

Devlin suggested, "Maybe we ought to've written him a letter before we came."

Andy wondered if he could write.

Mapes herded Andy and the two thieves into a corner of the barn. He said, "You-all had just as well sit. I'll go up and tell Jericho you're here. He'll get around to you in his own good time."

Andy sat on the dirt floor. Mapes left his two helpers to watch. One leaned against a saddle rack and spun the cylinder of his pistol. The other propped himself against the doorjamb and aimed his rifle casually at supposed targets outside. Andy compared their faces with those of Barstow and Devlin. They had a hard-bitten, determined look. They might at one time have been working cowhands, but now they fitted Andy's conception of hired pistoleros who would commit any crime if the pay was right.

He asked Barstow, "Think you-all have got it in you to qualify for a bunch like that?"

Barstow seemed too troubled to answer. Devlin stared apprehensively at the two Jericho men but tried to sound confident. "You're the one that needs to worry, Ranger. I doubt as they've got any patience for lawmen here. They're liable to cut off your ears and send them to Austin."

Barstow growled, "Shut up, Devlin. You may give them ideas about what to do with me and you."

Jericho seemed in no hurry to see his visitors. Andy waited in the barn for more than an hour before he saw a shadow fall across the threshold. Jericho's broad shoulders almost blocked the door. He walked halfway across the room and waited while his eyes adjusted to the poor light. Andy and the two thieves stood up. Jericho looked first at Barstow and Devlin, then at Andy. His eyes brightened with recognition.

"I've already made your acquaintance, Ranger. You had that boy Antonio. I wanted him, but you wouldn't let me have him."

He had seen Andy once before that, but Andy thought it prudent not to remind him of the day when one of his windmill towers had mysteriously burned down. Andy said, "It's against Ranger policy to turn a prisoner over for lynchin'."

"I wasn't goin' to lynch him. He'd have gotten a fair trial. We have our own court to try thieves and killers and trespassers."

"A kangaroo court."

"Nobody has ever appealed a rulin'."

"Maybe they haven't lived long enough."

Jericho's face darkened. "Don't be tryin' my patience. I don't have enough of it to waste."

As long as his blood was up, Andy decided to keep pushing. "They say you're runnin' a haven here for men in trouble with the law."

"Call it a sanctuary. The Mexicans hit somebody, then run to sanctuary on the other side of the river. You Rangers can't touch them there. I say if it works for them, it ought to work for me. I'm runnin' a sanctuary of my own here. I don't want the Rangers messin' with it."

"But you're in Texas. Lupe Chavez ain't."

"I'll say this for you, Ranger, you've got guts to come on my ranch and try to lecture me like that."

"I'm just sayin' what I think."

Jericho rubbed a big hand across his chin, squeezing his red-bearded face into a grotesque shape. "And most men in your place would've let me have that kid. Was you really prepared to die protectin' him?"

"I don't know. I never had to make that decision. Big Jim McCawley came along just in time."

The name brought a wistful look from Jericho. "Big Jim. You know, me and him used to be friends a long time ago, before he fell in with the Mexicans."

"But you still wanted to kill his son."

"Stepson. The boy ain't of his blood."

Jericho turned belligerently on Barstow and Devlin. "What about you two? What's your excuse for trespassin' where you wasn't asked?"

Devlin pleaded, "Me and Barstow came here hopin' we could work for you. We ain't got no truck with the Rangers."

"Work for me?" Jericho snorted. "What could you do?"

Devlin said eagerly, "We stole the Ranger's horse."

"And got caught. Damned little recommendation."

Barstow said, "We learn easy. Just tell us what to do and we'll do it."

Jericho beckoned to Mapes. "Take these two to Burt Hatton. If he can find a use for them, they can stay. If he can't . . ." He did not finish. Andy knew by the apprehension in the two men's faces that they were finishing the sentence for him in their minds.

Jericho turned his attention to Andy. "I've never been friends with the Rangers, but maybe it's time I tried to be. I can see where they might be of use to me."

"It's our job to enforce the law. We're not supposed to play favorites."

"I'd just ask you to lean a little in my direction in case a dispute was to come up. Most of my trouble has been with Mexican border jumpers, so that oughtn't to be hard for you to do. They're illegal anyway, the minute they set foot on the Texas side of the river."

"I'm just a private. Even the camp cook doesn't ask my opinion about anything."

Jericho asked Andy's name, and Andy told him. Jericho said, "I don't suppose you're a married man, Pickard?"

"I haven't had time for such as that."

"Any prospects?"

"Maybe, if I was to ask her. But it wouldn't be much of a life for her, bein' married to a Ranger who's always movin' around from one camp to another."

"You'll get tired of that sooner or later. Every man ought to get married. Havin' a wife gives you somethin' to come home for instead of spendin' all your time with the likes of the men you've seen around here."

Andy was surprised to hear that kind of talk from a man everyone branded as an unredeemed outlaw. It did not fit the image he had built in his mind. Lupe Chavez had not fit his preconceived notion, either. Both men aroused doubts about the validity of public opinion.

Jericho said, "Havin' a good woman can be the salvation of a man. I'd have you come down and meet mine, but she's not in a mood for company right now. She never could have any children herself, so she took her nephew under her wing after her sister died. Some of the Chavez gang killed him a while back."

"Sorry."

"I've had to watch that good woman grieve herself half to death. That's why I've wanted to get my hands on Chavez's nephew. I want Lupe to know how it feels."

"Would it make your wife feel better to know Tony's mother was grievin' the same way she does?"

"*I'd* feel better. Blood for blood. An eye for an eye."

Andy asked, "Is that why you're so dead set against Mexicans?"

"My feelin' about Mexicans goes back a lot further than that. It goes all the way back to when Texas fought for independence from Mexico."

"You're not old enough to've been in that fight."

"I'm old enough to remember it, though. I remember seein' my daddy take his rifle down from over the mantel and ride off to join the rebellion. Mexican soldiers caught him and stood him against a wall. Shot him down like a dog.

"My mother put me on a mule. We started runnin' for the Louisiana border to get away from Santy Anna's army. It was rainy and cold, and we bogged in mud plumb to our knees. She taken pneumonia and died. Left me all by myself, just a shirttail young'un. Damn near starved to death before I learned to take whatever I needed, however I had to. Lie, steal, whatever it took. I've been at war against Mexicans ever since."

Andy could think of a few arguments, but he knew they would not make a dent against so deep a hatred.

Jericho said, "I suppose you've got an old mother somewhere, puttin' a lamp in the window every night, waitin' for you to come home."

"Indians killed my mother. I was so little I can't hardly remember her."

He thought he saw a flicker of sympathy in Jericho's eyes, though it was gone as soon as the man blinked.

Jericho said, "Too bad. I still remember mine, twenty times a day. My wife looks a lot like her." He quickly changed the subject. "I suppose you're anxious to get back to your company."

"I was figurin' to turn in those two horse thieves, but I guess you're goin' to keep them and put them to work."

"I'll leave that up to my foreman, Burt Hatton. He'll escort you off of my ranch."

"I can find my own way."

"He'll see to it that nobody gives you any trouble. He'll have your horse waitin' for you at the corner corral." Jericho pointed. "And you tell your fellow Rangers that if I ever want any of you on my place again, I'll send for you."

Irony edged into Andy's voice. "Sergeant Donahue will appreciate hearin' that."

Jericho went out the door. Andy followed. After being in the dark barn so long, the bright sun hurt his eyes. When his vision cleared, he saw three men and four horses at the corner corral. Two of the men were Barstow and Devlin. Andy did not recognize the third until he reached the gate. Jericho had disappeared.

Andy said, "I know you."

Burt Hatton said, "And I know you."

This was the man who had led the nighttime attack on Andy, Len, and Farley as they rode south from San Antonio to join the Ranger company on the river.

Andy said, "The night you-all tried to hit us, we suspected you belonged to Jericho's outfit."

The man did not reply.

Andy said, "We heard somebody holler like he was shot. Was he?"

Hatton growled, "Get on your horse.

We're takin' you away from here."

"I can go by myself."

"Jericho wants to be sure you're gone. You can go peaceful or we can tie you in the saddle." He poked the muzzle of a pistol in Andy's direction for emphasis.

Andy said, "I believe that six-shooter's mine."

"You'll get it when I'm ready. Or you'll get what's in it."

Devlin was holding a paint horse with a huge Mexican brand across most of its left hip. It had undoubtedly come from across the river, probably on some dark night. Though Indians fancied paints for their unusual coloring, Rusty had taught Andy to regard them with suspicion until they proved themselves. Andy said to Devlin, "Looks like they gave you a new saddle, and a horse to put under it."

Devlin said, "He ain't as good as your black. I'm thinkin' about another swap."

"You'd have to shoot me first."

"I've been thinkin' about that too."

Hatton snapped, "Come on, I got other things to do."

Andy followed him out the gate, the other men riding behind. They took a southeasterly course, in the general direction of the Ranger company's camp. Andy

322

doubted that Hatton intended to go all the way there. He simply wanted to be sure Andy got off to a good start.

They rode for about an hour. Hatton pointed to a thicket of mesquite and catclaw. "Over there."

Andy saw no sense in riding into a thicket, but he looked into the muzzle of Hatton's pistol and decided against asking questions.

Hatton reined up just at the edge of the thicket. A javelina sow and four pigs snorted and went clattering into the brush. Their backs bristled and their short legs moved in a blur. Hatton beckoned for Barstow and Devlin to come closer. "Jericho left it up to me to decide if you boys have got a job. You want it bad enough to earn it?"

Both men nodded. Barstow said, "Just tell us what to do."

"I want you to prove yourselves. I want you to shoot this Ranger."

Barstow's mouth dropped open. Devlin looked as if he had just swallowed a scorpion. Barstow said, "You mean kill him?"

"Here and now."

Andy felt helpless and cold. Hatton's eyes were grim, leaving no doubt that he meant what he said. Barstow and Devlin appeared to be near panic. Barstow's voice was strained. "I ain't never shot a man. I can't do it in cold blood."

Hatton scowled. "I figured you two for counterfeit as soon as I saw you. You'll shoot him or I'll shoot all three of you. You'll make a good meal for those javelinas."

Hands trembling, Devlin drew his pistol.

Hatton said, "Steady down. You're as liable to hit your horse as to hit that Ranger."

Devlin held the pistol in both hands. It continued to waver.

Hatton cursed. "I told Jericho that neither one of you is worth the rope it'd take to hang you with."

Barstow bent down and came up with a rifle. "I reckon we rate a little higher than that." He swung the muzzle toward Andy.

Andy's mouth felt as if it were full of cotton.

Barstow moved the rifle a little farther. It pointed at Hatton.

Hatton demanded, "What're you doin'?"

Barstow was sweating as if it were the Fourth of July. "Never kill a Ranger. If you do, the rest of them will come after you. They never forget, and they won't give up till you're hangin' off of a tree limb or shot full of holes."

Hatton declared, "I'll have your heads on a pike."

Devlin trembled. "For God's sake, Barstow."

Andy took advantage of the moment to push his horse forward and grab Hatton's pistol with both hands. They wrestled. Hatton squeezed off one shot toward the thicket. A javelina squealed. Andy managed to twist the weapon free.

Hatton wheeled his horse around and spurred away, bent low over the horn of the saddle to present a poor target. Barstow took one shot but was too nervous to hit him.

Devlin complained, "You spilt it now, Barstow. We'll never get a job with Jericho."

"It's a damned poor job that says you got to kill somebody in cold blood, and him lookin' at you the whole time. There ain't enough money between here and San Antonio . . ."

Andy slowly regained his composure. "Thanks, Barstow. For a minute I felt like an angel landed on my shoulder."

Barstow was still sweating. He lowered the rifle. "If there's any angels around here, they're lost." He looked puzzled. "I was afraid Jericho wouldn't hire us, but I didn't expect he'd send his foreman out here to kill us."

Andy said, "I believe Hatton did that on his own." Killing Andy would have eliminated one witness to the attack on him, Len, and Farley. "And even if you had shot me, he'd have killed both of you and left us all lyin' here for the hogs. Dead men don't testify."

Barstow removed his hat and rubbed his sleeve over a face dripping with sweat. "Workin' cattle gets to lookin' better all the time. Maybe we can get our old jobs back."

Devlin said nothing. He was too busy losing his breakfast.

Barstow asked Andy, "You goin' to turn us in for stealin' your horse?"

"I would've, but you saved my life. I owe you a chance to get yours straightened out."

Barstow said, "Me and Devlin was just lookin' for a little more excitement than we been havin'. I think we've had enough of it to last us a long time."

"If I was you-all, I'd take a wide swing around Jericho's country, then head north . . . way north."

"That's what we'll do. And if I ever get arrested again it'll be for singin' too loud in church."

Andy watched them ride off in an easterly direction, then he turned southward. He wanted to recover his own saddle. This one, which had belonged to Devlin, could be traded to one of the poor Mexican farmers who had been selling him food down by the river. Devlin's horse, if it got over its lameness and didn't turn up on a list of stolen property, would give him an extra mount so he could alternate and always have one resting.

All in all, he had come out a little ahead on what had seemed to be a stroke of bad luck. He hoped that someday he might see Burt Hatton again under circumstances more in his own favor.

He had also seen another side of Jericho Jackson, a side that left him conflicted. Things had appeared much simpler when he'd seen Jericho simply as a cold and calculating land-grabbing outlaw. He did not know how to handle this unexpected complexity.

Burt Hatton entered the outside door to the room Jericho used as an office. He was seldom asked into the main part of the house. Jericho was strict about insulating his wife from the ranch help. Hatton's shirt was torn. A long red scratch marred his cheek.

Jericho looked up from his ledger book. "What happened to you?"

Hatton delayed his answer. "Mind if I get me a drink?" Jericho nodded, and Hatton went to a cabinet where he knew the whiskey was kept. He poured a small glass half full and swallowed it with a sense of urgency. "Horse cold-jawed on me. Ran through the brush."

Jericho often had a feeling that Hatton said only what he thought his boss wanted to hear, but the story was plausible enough. No man worth his salt worked in the brush country without taking scars and getting thorns imbedded in his hide. "Did you set the Ranger safely on his way?"

"Last I seen of him he was headed south."

"Good. I'd like to have a friend or two in the Ranger camp when the bullets fly again."

"I don't think you'd better count on him for a friend. We oughtn't to have let him get off of this place alive. We'll have trouble with him yet."

"Dead Rangers are bad for business. What about them two cowhands? Did you put them to work?"

Hatton frowned. "I sent them on their way. They didn't have enough sand in their

328

craw for our kind of business."

"Too bad. We'll need all the help we can get when we make our big push on Lupe Chavez."

Hatton poured another drink. "And when is that to be?"

"I don't know yet, but it'll come. It'll be like the battle of the Alamo all over again, only this time it'll end different."

Hatton had a worried look. "Maybe we ought to leave Chavez alone. You've got more land already than you can rightly see after. What do you want with land in Mexico?"

"This is about more than land. It's an old fight that never got settled. And there's the business about my wife's nephew. Lupe has got to pay for that."

"Maybe I was wrong about them Meskin outlaws that killed him. Maybe they wasn't Lupe's men after all."

Jericho's brow furrowed. "You scared, Burt?"

"Not scared. Just thinkin' about the men that might get killed."

"They're bein' well paid for it."

"There's some things money ain't enough for."

"Money can buy anything. You just have to be willin' to pay the price."

15

Len Tanner was at Andy's makeshift camp-site when Andy rode in. "Where you been?" the lanky Ranger demanded. "I found your saddle where you left it. Been worried that some Mexican bandits might've drug you off and cut out your gizzard."

"I've been up to Jericho's."

"What in the hell for?"

"Gettin' another saddle." He waited for Len's puzzled expression to come to full flower, then explained about the horse thieves and Jericho's men taking the three of them to headquarters.

Len said, "It's a wonder Jericho didn't shoot you."

"The funny thing is that I got along right decent with him. He wasn't what I expected. I never once saw him breathe fire."

"You never saw no halo around his head, neither. He's a bad hombre."

"So everybody says. It's odd, but he reminded me of Lupe Chavez. Neither one of them has any idea how much they think alike. They just look at things from oppo-

330

site sides of the river."

"They'd both cut your throat in a minute. But right now you'd better report to Sergeant Donahue before *he* cuts your throat. He suspicions that you swum the river to join up with Lupe Chavez."

"What would make him think that?"

"You took up for that boy Tony. You helped him get back to his uncle."

"I'd have done that for a lost pup. And I did it for the McCawleys, not for Lupe Chavez."

"Donahue ain't goin' to see the difference. As far as he's concerned they're all Mexicans, even Big Jim."

Andy said, "I'll go downriver and report to him. First, though, I'm hungry. Want to help me scare up some wood for a fire?"

While they ate, Len told Andy that the river had been quiet. "Ain't been sign of any raiders crossin' that we could see. Just the usual traffic. A few farmers, kinfolks passin' back and forth. I picked up a lame horse wanderin' around here. Don't know who he belongs to."

Andy said, "One of those horse thieves had him. I guess he's mine if we don't find out who he was stolen from."

They rode down the river past Len's camp. Halfway to the next Rangers' post they came upon Sergeant Donahue riding the line. Len said, "Here's your stray, Sergeant."

Donahue gave Andy a look that for a culprit would mean five years in prison. "Absent without leave. What's your excuse, Private Pickard?" He bore down on the word *private*.

"It wasn't by my choice," Andy said. He repeated what he had told Len about the horse thieves and being escorted to meet Jericho.

Curiosity erased Donahue's scowl. "I've never seen Jericho's headquarters. Not many Rangers have ever been there."

Andy gave him a rough description. "It looks a lot like the McCawley ranch, and Lupe Chavez's."

"I've never seen Chavez's either, but I'd sure like an excuse to go there and give them Meskins a good whippin', the way McNelly did." His eyes brightened at the thought. "By the way, what about them two horse thieves?"

Andy shrugged. "The last I saw of them they were headed in the direction of Canada." He thought it best not to divulge that he had made no effort to stop their going. He had probably broken some unbreakable Ranger rule.

Donahue said, "You should have pulled the trigger on them. Nothin' cures a thief better than a forty-five slug."

"I figured on bringin' them in as prisoners."

"Chances are fifty-fifty that some judge would turn them loose, and they'd go right back to what they were doin'. Death is pretty damned permanent."

"I'll try to remember that."

Donahue nodded, satisfied. "Since your goin' was not voluntary, I'll reconsider filin' charges. But consider yourself on probation."

Andy had considered himself on probation ever since Donahue took temporary command of the company. He asked hopefully, "Any word on when Lieutenant Buckalew will be back?"

"None. I think they may have found somethin' else for him to do. I'm lookin' to be advanced to lieutenant any time now. Maybe even captain."

"That'd be nice." Saying so put a sour taste in Andy's mouth.

Donahue said, "Go back to patrollin' your section of the river. I expect you're about out of supplies?"

"Pretty near."

"I'll send a pack mule out tomorrow

with coffee and sugar and salt. As for meat, I see lots of cattle and hogs runnin' loose."

"They all belong to somebody."

"Meskins. If they holler, tell them this is a tax they owe for us keepin' them safe."

Safe. Andy considered the irony. These people along the river were subject not only to banditry from both sides but to harassment by those Rangers who considered every Mexican suspect. The few American settlers were not much better off, for they were particular targets of Mexican outlaws still trying to avenge Santa Anna's defeat.

At times Andy thought seriously about giving this part of Texas back to the horned toads, the scorpions, and the sharp-toothed javelinas. They had a prior claim.

Donahue turned downriver, and Andy proceeded upriver. He found the lame horse contentedly grazing in the river's grassy floodplain. The limp was less pronounced. Andy tossed a loop around the animal's neck and led him to his makeshift camp. He found his saddle hanging from a tree limb so wild animals would not gnaw on it. Len's work, he guessed. Now Andy had two horses and two saddles. He was coming up in the world.

An old man crossed at a shallow point, urging a burro along with a willow switch. He saw Andy and veered away. Andy had seen the old man and the burro before, and the old man knew Andy to be a Ranger. Everybody up and down this stretch of the Rio Grande did. It would be a long time before these river people trusted the Rangers, Andy thought. And some Rangers would never come to trust the people who lived along the river. The gulf between the two cultures was too wide to bridge, at least for now.

A trail led northward from this shallow crossing. Andy saw a procession coming from the north. He counted four men on horseback. A buggy trailed behind, carrying two women. As it came closer he saw that they were Juana and Teresa Mc-Cawley. One of the horsemen was Big Jim. The others were some of his cowboys.

Andy rode out to meet them. The riders drew guns, then put them away as they recognized him. He suspected he knew their mission before they told him. "Headin' down to see Tony?" he asked McCawley.

"We haven't heard a thing about him since we were down here the last time. The womenfolks are worried."

"I always figure if it's bad news you'll

hear about it soon enough. Since I haven't heard anything, I'll bet Tony is all right." He tipped his hat to the two women.

Mrs. McCawley said, "You look thin, Andy."

"Eatin' my own fixin's, ma'am. Nobody would ever hire me as a cook."

"If you'll come up and spend a few days with us, we'll put some weight back on you."

"It'd pleasure me, ma'am, but I don't see as I can."

Teresa asked, "Have you seen Farley?"

"Now and again. He's closer to the main camp, so he slips down there and gets himself a decent meal when he knows the sergeant's not around."

Mrs. McCawley said, "It isn't far from here to my brother Lupe's ranch. He knows you now, so you could go over there when you get hungry."

"He might not like havin' a Ranger show up. Anyway, it's illegal for me to cross the river."

She frowned. "It's too bad people have to draw boundaries. There was a time when the river made no difference."

McCawley drew up beside Andy. "The trail has been unusually quiet. I've heard that Jericho has been hirin' a lot of men,

336

but we didn't run into any. Not them or hardly anybody else. Makes me wonder."

"I had a visit with him. Maybe he's reformed."

"I wish I could believe that, but I know him too well. He has a hunger that can't be satisfied. Most people get drunk on whiskey. He gets drunk on acquisition."

Andy watched Big Jim and the buggy go into the river. The cowboys remained behind.

Andy asked one, "You-all aren't goin' to stay with them all the way?"

A cowboy replied, "Big Jim said we wouldn't be welcome down there. He feels like they'll be safe enough since the womenfolk are kin to Chavez."

Andy feared McCawley might be stretching his luck in view of Chavez's dislike for him. Perhaps Chavez would not raise a hand against his sister's husband, but some of his followers might not be so reluctant. The McCawleys were almost out of sight when several riders came up from the south and met them. They halted briefly, then went on, escorted by what Andy assumed must be Chavez men. He saw no sign of hostility. Soon the procession moved beyond his view, hidden by the brush.

Andy asked the cowboy, "You-all goin' to stay and watch till they come back?"

"No, they figure to be there for several days. We'll come back to meet them when it's time."

Andy considered. "Maybe things'll stay quiet for a while. Chavez wouldn't seem likely to set up any raids while his kin are there. He wouldn't want his sister to see him as a bandit. She thinks of him as a hero."

The cowboy said, "I've got a cousin who steals horses, but I keep tellin' myself he's not a thief. He just knows how to get them cheap."

Len was waiting at the rendezvous point where he usually met Andy. He said, "Got orders from Sergeant Donahue. He says for everybody to gather their stuff and go back to the main camp."

"Does he think the raids are over with?"

"He ain't one to explain why he does things. He's generally got a reason whether it's a good one or not."

The change suited Andy. His stomach had complained for days about his short-comings as a cook. Maybe now he could get a few solid meals. "I'll be along as soon as I can. Meet you at your camp."

"I'll see if I can catch a couple of fish while I'm waitin'." Len had grown up on a river. Fishing was second nature to him.

Andy said, "If a fat little shoat was to wander by with no earmarks on him, that'd suit me better than fish."

"I ain't even seen a javelina lately."

It was almost dark when they rode into the main camp. Len suggested they report to the camp cook first. The sergeant could wait. Pablo bade them welcome and gave Andy a pitying look. He said, "Pretty soon you get so thin the wind carries you away. You better take two plates."

When they carried their food to a wooden table, Farley came over. He said nothing in greeting but came right to the point. "Seen anything of the McCawleys?"

Andy knew which McCawley Farley was really interested in. "Several days ago. They went over to Lupe Chavez's to see about Tony."

"To Chavez's?" Farley looked as if Andy had struck him. "And they ain't come back?"

"Not unless it was today, after I left."

"From what I hear, there's fixin' to be bad trouble down there. They're liable to get caught in the middle of it."

Disturbed, Andy put down his fork.

"What kind of trouble?"

"The sergeant ain't talkin' but some of the boys say he's pulled all of us back so we won't get in Jericho's way. His spies have told him Jericho's fixin' to hit Chavez like Sam Houston hit Santy Anna."

Andy found the idea hard to accept. "And Donahue figures to just let it happen? The Rangers are supposed to try and stop that kind of thing."

"Donahue's been chompin' at the bit, wantin' to go down there and do it hisself. But the law don't allow it, so he's standin' back and lettin' Jericho do it for him."

"Jericho's pulled raids over there before."

"Not like this. He's been hirin' men anywhere he can get them. They don't have to be cowboys. They've just got to be ready and willin' to use a gun."

Len listened gravely. "Maybe it's just as well to let the thing get settled for once and for all. It's been brewin' a long time."

Farley said, "But once the shootin' starts, a bullet won't care who's in the line of fire. Women, kids . . . that girl of McCawley's."

Andy tried to rationalize. "Chavez is nobody's fool. Maybe he's already got wind of what's comin'."

"He's not God. He can't know every-thing. His people will be outnumbered. They won't stand a snowball's chance in hell."

Andy wrestled with his conscience. The simplest course would be to remain neutral and let things play out on their own. The conflict was inevitable. The only question was when and where. It was not his busi-ness. He had no kin in the fight. Nobody could fault him if he could do nothing about it.

Well, there was one thing he could do. He could carry a warning to Chavez. At the least he could try to get the Mc-Cawleys out of harm's way before the at-tack. He felt he owed them that. But to do so would violate his orders and the prohi-bition against Rangers crossing the river.

He did not ponder long. He rose from the table, leaving his supper half eaten. "Tell the sergeant I've just resigned."

That would take care of the legalities.

Len spilled half a cup of coffee. "What're you fixin' to do?"

"If I don't tell you, you won't have to lie to him."

Farley smacked the palm of his hand upon the table. "You're thinkin' the same thing I am. I'm goin' with you."

"Every time we ride together, you get yourself hurt and then blame me for it. You'd risk it for Lupe Chavez?"

"To hell with Chavez. I'm thinkin' about the McCawleys."

"One McCawley, anyway. Are you forgettin' she's a Mexican?"

Farley said, "She's just half." He told Len, "Tell the sergeant I resigned too." He hurried to saddle his horse. Andy had to hustle to catch up with him.

Both horses had been ridden during the day, so Andy had to caution Farley to slow down. "We can't help anybody if we kill these horses."

Farley reluctantly pulled down to a brisk trot. "First shallow crossin' we come to, we better take it. The sergeant can't stop us if we're on the other side."

"Good idea," Andy said. Farley still had the wily instincts cultivated during his long hide-and-seek relationship with the state police after the war. They put the horses into the river half a mile farther on.

Stopping on the south bank to let the animals rest, Andy saw several riders moving at an easy lope on the other side. He sensed that they were Rangers. "Donahue didn't waste much time comin' after us."

"We've rained on his barbecue. He's figured on Jericho wipin' out Lupe Chavez and his whole outfit. The border would quieten down after that, and Donahue could claim the credit."

"And get a promotion."

Farley said, "I've got no use for Chavez, and Jericho ain't any better. The border would be better off without them. But I'd hate for somethin' to happen to the McCawleys."

"Especially Teresa."

Farley did not respond.

They skirted along the Rio Grande. The terrain and thorny vegetation were similar to that on the Texas side. The sandy soil was the same, the air the same, but Andy had an uneasy sense of being an unwelcome intruder, treading on forbidden ground. A couple of hundred yards made a tremendous difference.

Farley had the same reaction. He said, "I feel like a carpetbagger at a Confederate reunion. We're a couple of gringos on the wrong side of the river. Targets for any Mexicans that come along."

Andy still saw Rangers riding along the northern bank. "Better here than over there. Donahue could probably chew up an iron bar and spit it at us."

He pondered the incongruity of his being on this mission with Farley. He had ridden with the dour Ranger before but always because he had been obliged to do so. Neither he nor Farley had ever pretended to like each other. At best their relationship had been one of forced tolerance.

He knew Farley was correct about the risk. The hostile feeling here against Americans in general and Texans in particular ran strong. A man could be killed for nothing more than being light-skinned and blue-eyed, just as on the other side some had been murdered for no better reason than that their faces were dark. Unreasoning hatred was not confined to one race.

Darkness overtook them. Farley said, "This part of the country ain't overrun with landmarks, even in the daylight. In the dark, how're we goin' to know when we reach the road to Chavez's place?"

"I think I'll recognize it."

"Think? Thinkin' ain't knowin'."

"If you've got a better idea, tell me about it."

They rode most of the night, stopping once to rest the horses. Andy tried to sleep but could not. His skin prickled with anxiety. For all he knew, this might be the day

Jericho planned to attack. However, daylight brought no sign of invasion, no distant gunfire. He said, "Looks like we'll make it in time."

Five armed horsemen suddenly appeared like apparitions out of the brush and confronted them face to face. A strong voice demanded, *"Quién es?"*

Andy raised his hands. "Friends. *Amigos.*" He chilled at the sight of five guns pointed toward him and Farley. He hoped somebody spoke English, for under his current stress he could not muster a dozen words in Spanish. "We've got a message for Lupe Chavez."

One of the men demanded, "What message?"

Andy tried to think of the Spanish word for *danger.* "*Pel . . . pel . . .*" The rest would not come to him. "We've come to bring warnin'. Jericho's fixin' to invade him."

He feared the meaning was not getting across. The men talked quietly among themselves. Andy had a troubling sense that some advocated shooting him and Farley here and now. Their undisguised hostility told him it would take but little to tip the scales in that direction.

A tall, thin man began to dominate the conversation. Andy recognized him as

Porfirio, who had held him and Farley at the Chavez place. So far as he remembered, Porfirio had not spoken English, but he seemed to be swaying the other four away from the notion of killing.

After several minutes of talk Porfirio motioned with the muzzle of his pistol. *"Vámanos."*

Andy said, "I suppose that means we're goin'."

Farley replied, "But where? To Chavez's, or to hell?"

They angled southwestward. In a while Andy saw the buildings he knew were the headquarters of the Chavez ranch. "I hope they'll believe us."

Farley said, "Even if they don't, Jericho's got to ride over me to get to the McCawleys. I ain't lettin' that girl and her mother be hurt because Lupe Chavez is too thickheaded to listen."

Andy thought Farley should know a lot about thickheadedness. He had about the hardest head of anyone Andy knew.

They rode up to the wide front door of the sprawling stone house. Porfirio dismounted and raised his hand. *"Esperen."*

He banged a heavy door knocker twice before a heavyset maid appeared, cautiously peering out through a narrow opening. He spoke quietly, and she admitted him inside. Andy looked at the other men who had brought him and Farley here. Their grim faces told him not to move.

Shortly Porfirio returned. Lupe Chavez stood in the open doorway, picking his teeth. They gleamed a brilliant white against the heavy black mustache and the dark brown of his face. Andy hoped for a sign of welcome but saw none. Chavez said, "You know *rinches* are not welcome. What brings you to my door?"

Andy said, "We've come to warn you about Jericho."

Farley put in, "He's fixin' to hit you like a hailstorm. If he can, he'll kill everybody here."

Chavez shrugged his thin shoulders. "He has come before. He has not found us easy to kill."

Andy argued, "From what we hear, he's raised enough fightin' men to do the job this time."

"He drove us out of Texas. Does he think now he can also drive us out of Mexico?" Chavez dismissed the notion with an oath that did not need translation. "He will leave here with his guts dragging on the ground, if he leaves here at all."

The mental image was graphic but not reassuring.

Farley asked, "Are the McCawleys still here?"

"They are."

"Do what you want to about Jericho, but I'm takin' those womenfolks away." Farley looked at Andy and corrected himself. "*We're* takin' them out, me and Andy."

Anger flared in Chavez's eyes. "You will not come to my house and tell me what I must do. It is for me to decide."

Farley flared back. "Then you'd better decide right."

Big Jim McCawley came out and stood a few feet away from Chavez. He reacted with surprise upon seeing Andy and Farley. "What's all this row? Aren't you-all too far south for Rangers?"

Andy said, "We're not Rangers now, we're just citizens. We're tryin' to tell Lupe Chavez that Jericho is comin' to settle old scores, and bringin' plenty of men with him. Things are fixin' to get woolly around here."

Farley interjected, "We come to tell you to gather up your womenfolks and take them away."

McCawley said, "I've never run from Jericho."

Andy said, "This is one time you'd better."

Chavez dismissed the idea with a wave of his hand. "We are not rabbits, to run from a pack of hounds."

"Even hounds run when somethin' bigger is after them."

Chavez asked McCawley, "Should I listen to these *rinches?* I do not want to look foolish."

Andy said, "Better to look foolish and alive than be layin' here dead."

No friendship existed between McCawley and Chavez, but they quickly came to a mutual agreement in the face of a common threat. Chavez said, "It is not that I have fear of Jericho, but I am a cautious man. I will send the women and children away." He gave an order to Porfirio. Porfirio relayed it to his companions, who quickly scattered.

Chavez turned back to Andy and Farley. His eyes narrowed in threat. "If you are playing me false and the Jericho does not come . . ."

Soon several wagons and a couple of buggies began picking up excited women and children at the clutter of stone and adobe houses that made up the Chavez headquarters. A vaquero drew McCawley's buggy up to the door of the Chavez home. The maid and two younger women came out, followed by McCawley's wife and daughter. Tony appeared, pale and thin, still hunched over from the effects of his wound.

Juana McCawley told her husband, "Tony says he will not go."

Tony said, "I want you to take my mother and sister away."

McCawley said, "We'll all go. You too."

"No, I will stay and stand beside my uncle. You and these Rangers do not belong. This is not a gringo fight."

Juana told her husband, "I will stay with my son, but I want you to take Teresa away from here."

McCawley held firm. "Go off and leave you? You know me better than that. I'll send Teresa with the other women, but I'm stayin' with you and Tony."

Teresa placed her hands on her hips. "My place is with family. If you stay, I stay." She looked at Farley. "You will be here, won't you? If you are here I will not be afraid."

Farley said, "I think you're all playin' the fool. I was figurin' on takin' you out of here."

"You would have to drag me."

Some of the wagons were already leaving, carrying refugees to a safer place. Andy made one more attempt to persuade the McCawley women. "We rode all this way to see that you get out of danger."

Juana said, "You brought warning. That is enough. Jericho will not take this place by surprise. Now you should go, the three of you." She touched her husband's hand. "As Tony said, this is not a gringo fight."

McCawley's face colored. "I've always hated that word *gringo*. I've never answered to it, and I don't now."

She retreated. "I say it only to make you go."

"Not without you two. And Tony." He bent forward and tapped a forefinger against Tony's chest. "Your uncle didn't raise you. I did. Like me or hate me, I'm the only father you've got."

Tony did not budge. "I'm stayin'."

McCawley shrugged. "Then I guess we all will."

Farley looked at Teresa. "I still think you ought to go. But if you don't, I don't either." He glanced back at Andy.

Andy said, "I'm not leavin' by myself."

After most of the women and children were gone, Chavez sent Porfirio to the river to watch for sign of Jericho. He sent other riders to rouse the neighbors. As the day wore on, men from nearby ranches drifted in to augment Chavez's limited force. Whatever endangered Chavez endangered them all.

Chavez was too busy to pay attention to Andy and Farley until far into the afternoon. He seemed then to notice them for the first time. "You are still here? I thought you *rinches* were long ago gone. I do not need you."

Andy said, "We're not here for you. We stayed because of the McCawleys."

"Then stay close to them. Let no harm come to my sister and her daughter and I will try to forget that you are gringos like the Jericho."

Late in the afternoon Big Jim McCawley came to sit beside Andy and Farley in front of the big house. He carried a rifle and wore a pistol on his hip. "I guess this outfit is as ready as it'll ever be. Lupe has set up a heavy ring for defense. He would've made a good general in the big war."

Andy said, "The trouble with defense is that you have to stand and take whatever comes at you. You don't carry the fight to the enemy."

"You see somethin' you'd change?"

"I might try a little Comanche strategy.

They used to set up decoys to draw the enemy in. Then they'd swoop down from both sides."

"A flankin' maneuver?"

"I guess that's what you'd call it. Instead of lettin' the enemy surprise you, you surprise him."

McCawley thought it over. "I'll talk to Lupe. He might not like it if he knew you thought of it, so I won't tell him that."

McCawley returned after a time. Andy knew by the satisfied look on his face that he had been successful. McCawley said, "I just led him along a little at a time till he came up with the rest of it himself. Now he thinks it was his own idea."

Andy asked, "Did you ever think about goin' into politics?"

16

Jericho heard a laugh from somewhere behind him in the blackness. He looked back angrily. "Burt, go tell them to keep quiet. This won't work worth a damn if we don't catch Chavez by surprise."

Hatton rode only as far as the first half dozen men behind him. He told them to pass the word back for silence. They were within half a mile of the river. Though predawn darkness and the brush still shielded them from view, sounds could carry to the other side.

Jericho had counted thirty-seven men when they left headquarters. So far as he knew none had had a change of heart and turned back. He had taken the precaution of telling the newly hired hands that they would be paid after the mission was completed, not before. He was by necessity dealing with a class of men in whom he felt little faith. Honor was a stranger to most of them. Some would accept his money, then disappear. He did not even trust Burt Hatton, his next in command. He had purposely delayed paying Hatton all the money due him. He had a strong feeling the man's loyalty was so shallow it had to be bought anew over and over in the form of wages.

Hatton returned, grumbling. "I got a bad feelin' about this."

Jericho was in no mood to listen to Hatton's recitation of misgivings. "You've had bad feelin's as long as I've known you. This'll be over so quick that we won't even break a sweat."

"You never know where the Meskin soldiers are at from one day to the next. Somebody's liable to fetch them, like they done that time to McNelly."

"We have to see to it that nobody gets away. Then they won't tell the soldiers anything."

Jericho could see that he had not calmed Hatton's fears, but it didn't matter much: Hatton had little choice but to go along. "Once this is over, Burt, we won't have to put up with Chavez anymore. Him and his bunch won't keep nippin' at us like a bunch of heel flies."

"You ever see a firin' squad, Jericho? I did once, down at Matamoros." He shivered. "Them soldiers stood two poor fellers up against a gate and shot them.

The blood spilled like water."

"We'll finish up and be back across the river before they can even blow a bugle."

The sun dropped low, then set without sign of intruders. Porfirio sent back word from the river that he had seen no activity on the other side. Andy began to sense restlessness in the men stationed around the house. They had been primed for a fight, and no fight had come.

Farley expressed a thought that Andy had considered but rejected. "Reckon Sergeant Donahue's reports were exaggerated?"

"Nobody said exactly when Jericho was comin'. They just said that he would."

"If he don't pretty soon, you'll see things start comin' unraveled. A lot of the neighbors will start wantin' to go home and do their milkin'."

"Ain't likely he'd come in the night. Neither side could see their targets in the dark."

"When we fought the Yankees it seemed to me like the best time to attack was at first light. It generally caught them half asleep."

After dark Andy heard several men ride off to the west. Several more rode east.

Farley said, "They're desertin' already."

Andy said, "I don't think so. I believe Chavez has sent them off to wait out of sight. When Jericho strikes, they'll come in on the flanks."

"Sounds like Confederate military tactics."

"Or Comanche."

"Makes sense. Most of these Mexicans are more Indian than Spanish. If Lupe Chavez would shave off that mustache I'd take him for a Comanche."

The night was long and restless. Despite his fatigue from yesterday's ride, Andy found it difficult to sleep. He would doze, then awaken abruptly in a sweat, thinking the attack had begun. He realized he had been dreaming. He and Farley had taken a position behind a three-foot adobe wall that ran parallel to the front of the house.

Farley grumbled, "I don't see how you can sleep."

"I can't, much."

"I keep thinkin' about that little girl in there. If anything was to happen to her . . ."

"Those walls are thick. Ain't likely any bullets will go through."

"But what if Jericho managed to break into the house? The walls wouldn't help much."

"We have to stop him before he gets that far."

The stars began fading in the east, and several roosters crowed. Andy's nerves began to tingle. Farley had finally gone to sleep. Andy started to wake him, then changed his mind. Farley would wake up quickly enough if Jericho came.

Lupe Chavez emerged from the house and walked around his defense perimeter, cautioning the men to stay low and avoid being seen as the morning light improved. He came at length to Andy and Farley. "You are still here? I thought you might slip away in the night."

Andy said, "We told you we were stayin'." He repeated what he had told Chavez the day before: "We're not here for you. We're here for the McCawleys."

Chavez turned a disapproving gaze upon Farley. "Especially my niece, I think."

Farley said nothing.

Chavez sniffed. "Young women can be foolish. She should look to someone better than a gringo *rinche*."

Farley declared, "Show me somebody better."

Porfirio galloped in from the north and shouted for Chavez. Andy could not understand the words, but he understood the excited look and the way Porfirio pointed as he reported to his *jefe*.

Farley had dozed again. Andy shook him. The Ranger was suddenly awake and alert, his rifle ready.

Andy pulled the skin at the corners of his eyes, trying to sharpen the image. He thought he saw movement to the north, toward the river, but he could not be sure.

Farley thumbed back the hammer of his gun. To Andy the click sounded as loud as a gunshot.

McCawley came out of the house and took up a position beside them. Andy asked, "What about your womenfolks?"

"Tony's inside with them. He's standin' at a window."

Andy saw a rifle balanced upon a windowsill.

The sun had not yet broken over the horizon, but the predawn light was enough that now he could clearly see movement to the north. Jericho's horsemen had fanned out in a line over a space of more than a hundred yards.

Chavez gave an order in Spanish. McCawley said, "He's tellin' everybody to keep down. Let Jericho think he's caught us asleep. And he would have if you-all hadn't brought warnin'."

Andy rough-counted the riders. He saw around forty. "There's more of them than there is of us."

The Jericho men were within fifty yards of the Chavez defense line when a defender raised up. A Jericho rider fired at him. Andy heard Jericho shout, "Pour it on them."

The invaders spurred into a run, coming on like a whirlwind.

The defenders began rising, taking aim at the mass of horsemen coming at them. Gunfire crackled all around Andy. Riders pitched from their saddles. Horses fell, some struggling to regain their feet, some lying on the ground and kicking. To Andy's left a defender screamed and went down.

McCawley staggered backward, a bullet in his leg. Andy ran to help him, easing him to the ground.

He heard a curse. Farley held a hand to his side. Blood oozed out between his fingers. The impact had knocked the breath out of him. He gasped, trying to get air back into his lungs. Andy started toward him, but Farley waved him away and pointed in the direction of Jericho's men.

Powder smoke rose like a patchy fog, hiding many of the adversaries from one another. Andy was sparing with his ammunition. He fired only when he could see something to aim at. Bullets smacked into the adobe wall or whispered past his ears to sing off the stone wall of the house behind him. The incessant firing made his ears throb with pain.

The attackers came near breaching the defense line, then wavered. He heard a shout in a voice he thought was Jericho's. The invaders began pulling back, shocked and badly bruised by the determined defense.

About now, Andy thought, Jericho must be wondering what could have gone so wrong with his plan. Ordinarily so large a force should have overrun this ranch in a matter of minutes. They should have swept through the buildings with relative ease, cutting down the inhabitants before they had time to mount any creditable defense. Jericho was probably cursing, asking himself if he had a spy in his ranks.

The invaders took cover wherever they could find it, behind corrals, behind outbuildings, in the fringes of brush. They began a desultory firing. The defenders fired back. None of the shooting now was doing much damage to either side so far as Andy could see. He knelt over McCawley, pressing a handkerchief against the wound to slow the blood. He then went to Farley, but Farley refused help. He had regained enough breath to say, "It ain't that much."

Andy heard a drumming of hooves from the east, then from the west. The flankers were coming in, attacking Jericho's men from both sides. Many invaders hit the saddle and beat a fast retreat toward the river. Andy could hear Jericho's angry voice calling for them to come back and fight. Shortly he was left with only a handful of men unable or unwilling to quit the scene. They were well concealed but not in a position to carry the fight forward.

The shooting died away. Neither side offered many visible targets. An uneasy quiet fell over the contested ground.

Lupe Chavez raised up a little, looking over the wall. He cupped his hands around his mouth and shouted, "You, Jericho, you give up now? You bring with you too many cowards. They run like rabbits."

Jericho answered, "You don't see *me* runnin'. I come to settle things with you, Lupe. I ain't leavin' till I do."

"You are welcome to stay. I give you six feet of ground. It will be all your own."

"You damned chili picker, you ain't seen the day you can put me under."

The two men went quiet for a bit. Andy returned to McCawley. "I'll help you into the house."

McCawley put up no argument. Andy got the rancher's arm around his shoulder and boosted him up onto his feet. He half carried, half dragged him to the door. Juana opened it and cried out in alarm. The two women helped Andy bring McCawley into the house. They laid him upon the floor, well below the windows through which a bullet might reach him.

Tony looked down on his stepfather, his face softening. "He ain't goin' to die, is he?"

Juana said, "You have struck him in the heart, but the bullet did not. Do you just stand there, or do you help?"

Tony went to his knees. "I'll help." He ripped his stepfather's bloody pants leg open with a knife blade.

Andy went back outside, where only an occasional wild shot was being fired. Crouching, he returned to Farley, on his knees behind the wall, his shirt off and wadded up, pressed against his side. He did not give Andy time to ask questions. He said, "I told you, Badger Boy. This happens every time I'm with you."

"I'm not the one that shot you."

"No, but I'll bet they was aimin' at you instead of me. You're the damndest jinx I ever saw."

"I'll help you into the house."

"It ain't so much. Clipped my ribs is all. Might've cracked one, the way it feels."

Andy's patience was strained. "Don't be so stubborn. Teresa will patch you up, her and her mother."

Mention of Teresa had a positive effect on Farley. "All right, but soon as I can I'm goin' as far from you as I can get. A hundred, two hundred miles. Maybe more."

Teresa gasped as Andy brought Farley in. She appeared even more concerned over Farley than over her father. Andy tried to explain that the wound was not all that serious, but he saw that Farley was enjoying her attention. He went back outside.

For a while all was quiet. The shooting had stopped. Andy was sure the remnant of invaders remained, though they were well hidden.

He heard Jericho call again: "Chavez, you still there?"

"I am here, *diablo Tejano*. What you want now?"

"I got a proposition for you. We can make a deal."

"You came here to kill me, and now you

want to deal? You got no cards."

"I have one. I'm bettin' I've got more guts than you do."

Indignant, Chavez stood up to his full height, just a little over five feet. He shook his fist. "I got plenty guts, gringo."

"Then let it come down to just me and you. We step out into the open, both of us. Best man wins. Either way, everybody else goes free."

"It would not be an even fight. You are a bigger target than me."

"Maybe I'm a better shot. It'll be easy to find out."

Chavez hesitated. "Why should I do this? You are in a trap. When you try to get away my men will kill you."

"I thought you wanted that pleasure for yourself. When it's over everybody will say you were too much of a coward to face me."

Chavez bristled. "I am not a coward."

"Then show me."

Chavez shouted in Spanish. Andy assumed it was an order for everyone to stay put, to take no part. Jericho shouted for his men to keep hands off. "This is between me and Chavez. Whichever way it goes, everybody else rides out of here peaceful. You hear me, Burt?" He paused, looking around. "Burt?"

Burt Hatton was not there. Andy wondered if he had been shot or if he had fled.

Jericho stepped out from behind a small shed, carrying a rifle. He walked toward the wall. Porfirio handed Chavez a rifle, then stood back as Chavez went out through an opening and stood waiting. Jericho walked to within twenty feet of him, then stopped.

Chavez said, "A long time we have been enemies, Jericho. But never did you come against me like this. For why now?"

"Some of your bandits murdered my wife's nephew. It was like she'd lost a son. I couldn't stand still for that."

"I know nothing of it."

"I had it in mind to kill your nephew in return, but it's better this way. I'd rather kill you."

"If you can, gringo. If you can."

For what seemed several minutes the two men stood glaring, taking each other's measure, each waiting for the other to move. When it happened it was so fast that Andy could not tell which man moved first. Two shots sounded as one. Chavez staggered, eyes stricken as he dropped his rifle and clasped both dark hands against his stomach. He tried to speak, but no sound came except a groan. His knees buckled. He went down on one shoulder.

Jericho's left arm hung at his side, shattered. Blood soaked a torn sleeve and dripped from his fingers. He swayed like a tree about to fall.

Porfirio moved toward him, fury in his eyes, but Chavez called to him in a weak voice. Porfirio dropped on his knees beside his fallen leader. The language was Spanish, but Andy surmised that Chavez was telling him to let Jericho go.

Tony hurried out and knelt beside his uncle. Quiet words passed between them. Tony looked at Jericho with hatred and seemed about to move against him. Chavez grasped Tony's sleeve and stopped him. A deal was a deal.

Chavez coughed and went limp. Tony folded his uncle's hands across his chest and pulled his fallen sombrero over the still face. He pushed to his feet, his eyes profoundly sad. "You'd better go, Jericho. I can't hold Uncle Lupe's people back very long. I may not be able to hold myself."

Jericho looked toward Andy. "What about you, Ranger? You got somethin' to say?"

"I ain't a Ranger anymore, but I expect there'll be Rangers waitin' for you at the river." He did not know what the Rangers could do about Jericho, however. His invasion of Mexico had not been a violation of Texas law.

One of Jericho's men took his boss's good arm and led him away.

Several of the Chavez men stood over their fallen *jefe* and removed their hats. One made the sign of the cross. Porfirio said something in a low voice. Three men carefully lifted Chavez and carried him toward the house.

Andy walked up to Tony. "I guess you're the boss here now. What comes next?"

The thought seemed to take Tony by surprise. "I don't know. I'll need time to think it through. I wish Uncle Lupe hadn't made that deal with Jericho. If we don't kill him now, we'll have to reckon with him sometime later on."

"He took a whippin' he won't get over any time soon. And that arm is bleedin' bad. He might not make it home."

"If he does, bein' crippled may just make him meaner."

Andy watched Jericho ride away with a few of his followers. The rancher was hunched over, in obvious pain.

Andy said, "This didn't have to be. It happened because of two hardheaded men.

Either one of them could have stopped it years ago."

Tony said, "No, they couldn't. It wasn't just them. It was the Alamo and San Jacinto and the Mexican War. I was able to pick sides, but most people never got a choice. Their side was picked for them the day they were born — American or Mexican."

"You're some of both. Maybe you can help bring all this to some kind of settlement."

Tony shook his head. "It'll take a lot of time and a lot of funerals before that happens. I picked the Mexican side. I can't turn my back on it. I can't help my belly firin' up every time I see a gringo push some Mexican around. I want to kill him and all the blue-eyed gringos around him."

"What about Big Jim? He put up a good fight on your uncle's side, and he got himself bloodied for it."

"He's still a gringo. I'd like to forget that, but I can't. Every time I look at him, I'll remember what the gringos did to us."

"But a lot of Americans took abuse from Mexicans too. Remember Santa Anna? Remember the Alamo and Goliad?"

Tony looked at ground darkened by the blood of Guadalupe Chavez. "We re-

369

member what we want to remember, and we forget whatever makes us ashamed. There won't be peace on the river until no one is left who remembers these times."

Jericho Jackson's arm was afire. The pain brought blinding tears to his eyes. He turned his head, trying not to let Jesse Wilkes see them.

Wilkes said, "We better stop and do somethin'. You're bleedin' plumb to death."

Jericho felt drained of strength, but he did not want to stop before they crossed the river. He realized he stood a good chance of not reaching it at all. "Tie it off so it won't bleed so much," he said. "It's way too far to a doctor, but I know where there's a *curandero*. He'll fix me up till I can get to somebody better."

Wilkes tore a sleeve from his own shirt and wrapped it tightly above the wound. "Maybe that'll slow it down a little. In the war I seen doctors saw off arms that didn't look as bad as yours."

Jericho grunted. Wilkes was almost as pessimistic as Burt Hatton had always been. "Got any idea what happened to Burt?"

Jericho could see that Wilkes wanted to

speak but was hesitant. He demanded, "Tell me somethin'."

Grudgingly Wilkes said, "I hate to say this, but I seen Burt turn his horse around and run for the river right after the first shots was fired. He wasn't in favor of this raid in the first place."

"Damned coward." Jericho tried to spit, but his mouth was too dry. "I've always suspicioned that he didn't put up much fight the time Lupe Chavez's bandits killed my wife's nephew. I wouldn't be surprised if he turned and ran then just like he did today."

Wilkes seemed to be summoning courage. Reluctantly he said, "Burt lied to you about that fight. He said he'd kill any of us who ever told you the straight of it."

"He ain't here now. Tell me."

Stumbling over the words, Wilkes managed to say, "It wasn't none of Chavez's men. What happened was, we came onto three travelers, and Burt wanted their horses. Thought they might be carryin' money too. Said we could rob them on the quiet and lay the blame on Mexican bandits. And we wouldn't have to divvy up any of it with you. He figured on jumpin' them after dark and takin' them by surprise. They surprised us instead. We didn't know it then, but it turned out they was Rangers."

A building anger almost made Jericho forget the pain. "He told it a lot different."

"He didn't know but what you might shoot him — and maybe us too — if you found out he got the boy killed on a fool stunt like that. It was a lot easier to drop the blame on Lupe Chavez."

Jericho slammed the palm of his good hand against his leg. "The lyin' son of a bitch! The main reason for this raid was to get even with Lupe for killin' that boy. And now you tell me it wasn't even his bunch that done it."

Wilkes hung his head. "I ought to've told you a long time ago."

"Yes, you should. But get me back to the ranch. If Burt is there, it'll pleasure me to shoot him between the eyes."

Approaching the river, he saw strangers waiting on the north bank. They were Rangers, he guessed, and they appeared to have taken several of his men into custody.

Jericho said, "I can't see clear enough to tell if Burt Hatton is amongst them."

"I don't think he is."

"Maybe he went upriver and crossed where there ain't no Rangers. We'll do the same."

Wilkes argued, "Them Rangers might be able to do somethin' about your bad arm."

"To hell with the arm. We're goin' after Burt. If I start to fall off, you grab me. I ain't stoppin' till I catch him."

Burt Hatton reined up and studied the Jericho headquarters. The place looked deserted. All able-bodied men who could handle a gun had gone on the raid. He had known as soon as the opening volleys were fired that the expedition was a failure. The surprise Jericho had counted on had gone sour somehow. Chavez had been ready with a lethal defense.

The early fire cut down several men on either side of him. Hatton quickly decided he did not intend to join them and die for someone else's folly. Jericho had allowed his hatred for Chavez to trump his judgment. Hatton had turned his horse around and quirted it most of the way through the brush and the sand to the river. Just in time he spotted a party of men waiting on the other side and guessed that they were Rangers. He rode farther west and crossed at another shallow point.

Now he surveyed the Jericho headquarters. He did not know if Jericho had survived, but chances were that he had. The boss had always enjoyed better luck than any two men were entitled to. Hatton sometimes suspected he had made a pact with the devil.

Well, Jericho would not put Burt Hatton in harm's way ever again. Hatton intended to gather up what belonged to him, plus some that didn't but should, and hunt for greener grass. The farther from Jericho, the better.

If he was lucky, he thought, no one would be in the house except Jericho's citified wife. Hatton had always resented her because Jericho thought she was too good to associate with the common hands. That old black maid of hers would probably be there too, but she was harmless. She was likely to do nothing except holler. The two might give him a little sass, but he did not expect them to offer any physical resistance. Chances were they would cower in a corner and cry.

He tied his horse outside. He started to push through the outside door into Jericho's office, but he changed his mind. That was the way he had always entered because Jericho did not want him venturing into the rest of the house where that pampered woman might have to look at him. This time Jericho was not here to make him go in like a servant. By God, he would go in the front like white folks should.

He shoved the door open and waited a moment, letting his eyes adjust from sunlight to the darkened interior. Hearing a gasp, he turned. Jericho's wife stared at him, her mouth open in surprise. Hatton had never studied her closely before. He found her skinny and frail-looking. He wondered what Jericho had ever seen in her. He could buy the favors of better-looking women in any town for the change in his pocket.

She demanded, "What are you doing here? Where is my husband?"

"Maybe in heaven, maybe in hell."

Her hands were clasped at her flat breasts. "He's dead?"

"A bunch of them are. I don't know about him. Things was a lot worse than we expected, so I lit a shuck."

Her face tightened in anger. "You are a coward, sir."

"If I wasn't, I'd be gettin' dirt shoveled in my face. Them Meskins are damned good shots." He made his way from the parlor to Jericho's office at the end of a corridor. He knelt in front of the safe and exercised his fingers.

He had never opened the safe before. Jericho allowed no one to touch it. But he had watched Jericho many times, and he had made a mental note of the combination in case a situation like this might arise.

Mrs. Jackson followed him, the black maid just behind her. She demanded, "What are you doing at that safe?"

"I'm fixin' to open it."

"Why?"

"It's got money in it. I ain't leavin' here with my pockets empty. I've spent too much of my life that way."

He turned the knob one way and the other, trying to remember the sequence of numbers. He missed once, but on his second try he swung the door open. Inside was a metal box in which he had watched Jericho place large sums of money from time to time. He did not bother to count. He could do that later, when he was well away from here. He rifled through the papers and ledgers to be sure he was not overlooking any currency. Satisfied, he tucked the box under his arm and rose to his feet.

Mrs. Jackson gripped a pistol with both hands. It was a big Navy Colt, heavy enough that she had trouble holding it steady. "You are not going to rob my husband," she said. "Put that back."

Instead, he threw the box at her and jumped aside as she pulled the trigger. The explosion shook the room. Smoke blossomed around her. Before she could thumb the hammer back he grabbed the warm barrel and twisted the weapon from her small hands. He raised it and swung it down hard, striking the top of her head and slanting down the side of her face. She dropped like a sack of corn.

The black woman screamed and came at him with a poker from the fireplace. He deflected the blow with his left arm and pointed the pistol into her face. "Back away, Mammy, or you'll be a dead nigger."

The maid dropped to her knees beside the unconscious woman. "Miz Jackson. Wake up, Miz Jackson."

Hatton retrieved the metal box and backed toward the door, still carrying the Navy Colt. He said, "When she wakes up, tell her I didn't come here to do that. But I don't stand for anybody pointin' a gun at me — man, woman, or child."

He tied the box to his saddle, patted it as he might a dog, then mounted and rode north in an easy trot. He whistled an old tune he had heard in a San Antonio dance hall.

A day that had gotten off to a miserable start had completely changed complexion. It looked now like a sunny day in spring. All it needed was a rainbow.

Jericho's arm hung stiffly at his side. Every heartbeat sent pain drumming through his body as he rode up to his stone house. Jesse Wilkes had been obliged several times to hold him and keep him from falling. His head ached, and he felt fever rising. Before long he was going to be sick as a calf with the yellow scours.

"Help me into the house, Jesse. I don't want to fall down in front of her."

He had always tried to let his wife see nothing but strength and purpose from him. He hated the thought of her seeing him in this deplorable condition. He had sent one of his riders to fetch a *curandero*, but it would be a couple of hours at best before the healer could get here. Tomorrow he would have Wilkes start with him to San Antonio, where an honest-to-God medical doctor could tend to that arm.

Wilkes opened the door, then supported Jericho as he crossed the threshold. They stopped abruptly just inside. Jericho's wife lay on a divan. A cloth covered most of her face, but not so completely that he did not see a deep bruise across her jaw.

"What the hell? Did she fall?"

The maid burst into tears. "It was a man done it, that man you call Hatton. He was takin' money out of your safe, and she tried to stop him."

Staggering, Jericho made his way to his wife's side. She appeared to be only half conscious, but she recognized his voice. Her fingers closed weakly over his hand. She murmured, "Jericho? Is that you, Jericho?"

"It's me. I'm home." Jericho lifted her hand and kissed it, then turned back to the maid. "How long since Burt left here?"

"Not long. I ain't kept track of the time."

"Which direction did he go?"

"I was too busy to watch him leave, but it sounded like he went north."

Jericho said, "Wilkes, help me back to my horse. We'll catch him if we have to trail him plumb to San Antonio."

"Jericho, you ain't in no condition. If you don't take care of that arm, it's liable to kill you."

"Damn it, I didn't ask you, I *told* you. If the Lord decides to take me, that's all right. We all got to go sometime. But I want to see Burt Hatton go ahead of me.

Hand me that shotgun from over the mantel."

"Like as not he's got a rifle. He may not let you get close enough to use a shotgun."

"I'll get close. I don't think I can hold a rifle steady, but that scattergun will get him."

"You may not live that long."

"Ain't nobody ever killed me yet. It'll take a better man than Burt Hatton to do it."

Hatton had put several miles behind him. The day's excitement had drained him. He knew he had to keep going, because if Jericho had survived the shooting at the Chavez ranch he might have reached home by now. Hatton wondered which would anger Jericho more, his wife's injury or the safe with its money box gone. It was a cinch that if Jericho was alive and on his feet he would sooner or later follow Hatton's trail.

But Hatton was in dire need of a drink. He could have taken a bottle from Jericho's house if he had thought of it, but his mind had been too involved with grabbing the money and getting away. His path would carry him by a crossroads general store that dealt in groceries, cheap whiskey, and sometimes destitute young Mexican women desperate to make a living any way they could. He saw the place ahead, a flat and ugly structure built of pickets and plastered to keep the wind and rain out.

It was his intention simply to buy a bottle and drink while he rode. But once he was inside, the metal box pressed firmly under his left arm, he decided to linger long enough to savor one drink at leisure. Then he could ride on. The first drink led to a second. By that time a slender young woman had sidled up to him at the rough plank bar and put an arm around his waist. He did not understand much she said, but imagination filled in the gaps. He poured a drink for her and another for himself. His fear of Jericho began to fade as the whiskey and the woman's big brown eyes warmed his blood. The bottle was more than half empty when he grabbed it by the neck and followed her through the rear of the store. She led him into a small picket shack in the back.

He lost sense of time. He swung his legs down from the bed and knocked over the empty bottle. His head felt light, and the room did slow circles around him. He tried to pull his britches on but had trouble keeping both feet from going into the same pants leg. The woman had to help him. He knew she had dipped into the metal box. He did not know how much she took out of it, and at the moment that did not matter. It came back to him that the box was Jericho's, and that Jericho was sure to come looking for it. He buttoned his shirt wrong but left it that way. He strapped his gun belt around his waist, part of the shirttail hanging over it.

The woman was rubbing against him and making what he surmised was love talk in Spanish, but he was feeling an urgency to move on. His fear of Jericho began to penetrate the fog raised by whiskey and lust.

He said, "*Adiós*, sweet thing," and staggered out the door into the daylight. His heart took a leap as his bleary eyes discovered two men standing there. They were Jericho and Jesse Wilkes. The metal box fell from his hands and burst open on the ground. Paper currency began blowing away.

Jericho carried a shotgun under his right arm. His left arm hung stiffly at his side. The sleeve was the rusty red of dried blood, and in the center it glistened with blood still fresh. The voice was not what he was accustomed to from Jericho. It was a little man's voice, strained and weak, but the words crackled with hate. "Burt Hatton, you are a woman beater, a thief, and a liar."

Hatton saw the muzzle of the shotgun coming up. He drew his pistol and squeezed off one shot before the blast slammed him back against the picket wall. As he slumped to the ground he heard a woman's scream from inside the shack. A green bill drifted in front of him. By reflex he reached out, but his fingers were too weak to grasp it. The wind carried it away.

17

Andy stood beside his horse and looked back toward the Chavez house. He had tried to help Farley saddle up, but Farley had stubbornly waved him away though his face was twisted in pain. He managed to saddle his horse by himself.

Teresa stood just outside the front door, watching.

Andy said, "She doesn't want you to go."

Farley did not reply. He went about tightening the cinch, mumbling under his breath.

Andy said, "That wound is liable to get infected. Why don't you stay here and let them take care of it for you till you're sure it's goin' to heal all right?"

"Why don't you mind your own business, Badger Boy?"

"Personally, I don't care one way or the other. But that girl has got feelin's for you, and it's hurtin' her to see you go. I think you've got the same feelin's for her."

"What if I do? What kind of life would people let us have together, me white, her

Mexican? Half, anyway."

"I'll bet Big Jim and his wife had some doubts too, at first. But it looks to me like they've done pretty good together."

"I ain't Big Jim."

"No, you sure ain't." Andy felt a flicker of resentment, seeing the sad-eyed girl watching from the house. "If you was, you wouldn't worry about what other people say. You'd only think about what *you* want, you and her."

Farley groaned as he pulled himself into the saddle. His hand went to his side, pressing against the wrapping that bound his ribs. "If we hurry up, maybe we can catch Jericho before he crosses the river."

"What for? We're not Rangers anymore. What Jericho does is none of our business."

Farley grimaced. "It just rubs me raw thinkin' about what he done here today. There's been people killed and a good many more shot up on his account. He ought to be called to answer for it."

"He took a bullet. Wouldn't surprise me if he loses that arm."

"It ain't that I got any sympathy for Lupe Chavez. I don't. But he's dead, and Jericho's still alive. Everybody would be better off if they was both dead. Maybe the border would finally settle down."

The border would not settle that easily, Andy thought. Two people, even those as powerful as Jericho and Chavez, would not make that much difference.

Andy had seen Jericho ride away with one of his men. Jericho had appeared to be in a bad way. He said, "Like as not the Rangers will pick him up as soon as he crosses the river."

"What can they do to him? Any law he broke was on this side of the river, not in Texas."

Andy admitted with regret, "You're probably right."

Before the house faded from sight, Farley shifted in the saddle and looked back. Andy suggested, "It's not very far. You could still turn around."

"I've made up my mind."

They rode in silence most of the way to the river. As they approached it Andy could see horsemen on the far side. He guessed there might be thirty or more. "Some of them are Rangers. Looks like they've been pickin' up Jericho's men as they cross over."

Farley drew rein. "I expect Sergeant Donahue is with them. Looks like we're in trouble, me and you."

"Might be. We left word that we'd resigned before we went over, but he didn't accept that the last time I did it."

Farley appeared to wrestle with his conscience. Finally he said, "Go on by yourself if you want to. I'm turnin' back."

"Thought you'd made up your mind."

"It's *my* mind. I can change it if I want to."

Andy smiled. "Just be sure you don't ever say or do anything to hurt her, even if she is a Mexican."

"Just half," Farley said. He turned and started back toward the Chavez headquarters.

Andy watched until Farley was out of sight, then put his horse into the river. Len Tanner rode to the water's edge to meet him as he came out. "Awful glad to see you, Andy. I was afraid you might've got yourself shot in the big doin's over there."

"They tried, but they missed."

"Was it Farley that I seen turn back? I hope he didn't get his grouchy self wounded." His tone of voice indicated that he wished otherwise.

"Once in the side and once in the heart. The one in the heart is a wound he's apt to carry the rest of his life."

Len understood and shook his head in

disbelief. "Well, I'll swun. After all the things he said."

Andy saw Sergeant Donahue riding toward them. "What has Donahue been sayin'?"

"About you, nothin' that falls easy on the ears. But about today, he's grinnin' like a possum. He's sure this is fixin' to earn him a promotion."

"I don't see Jericho in that bunch."

"Ain't much he can do about Jericho anyway, seein' as everything he done was in Mexico. But he's got most of Jericho's men, the ones that made it back across the river. He's holdin' them till we can check all of them against the fugitive list. The ones Jericho didn't lose on the other side of the river, he's apt to lose over here."

Donahue stopped his horse and gave Andy a hostile study. "You're under arrest, Private Pickard. In goin' across the river you violated a direct order."

"I resigned before I went."

"That resignation was not delivered directly to me. I do not recognize it." He looked past Andy. "Where is Private Brackett?"

"He's stayin' over there for a while. He got himself wounded."

Donahue said, "Serves him right. What about Jericho? He has not crossed."

"He left before we did. Had a few men with him. They probably saw the Rangers waitin' and decided to find a quiet place farther up the river."

Donahue frowned. "Then he's probably on his way back to his stronghold."

"He looked like one arm was shot to pieces. I'm guessin' he headed for home to get it taken care of."

"You've been to his headquarters before. I want you to guide me there."

"But I'm under arrest. And I'm not a Ranger anymore."

Donahue snorted impatiently. "I told you I do not accept your resignation. But take me to Jericho's and I will consider you no longer a Ranger."

"What about that arrest business?"

"I'll drop the charges."

"If we find Jericho I don't see much you can do about him. Not legally."

"I just want him to know that he's not the cock of the walk around here anymore. I'm goin' to tell him the Rangers can go anywhere they want to. From now on Jericho's road is open to the public."

Donahue did not wait to see if Andy would accept. He called, "Tanner, I want you and Bill Hewitt. You are goin' with me and Pickard."

It struck Andy again how similar Jericho's stone house was to those of Lupe Chavez and Big Jim McCawley. He saw a man sitting on a bench at the edge of a colorful flower bed, just to the right of the front door. The man watched the Rangers' approach but made no move to get away. He sat until they were within stone-throwing distance, then stood up to wait for them.

Donahue demanded, "Who are you?"

"Name's Jesse Wilkes."

"We've come to see Jericho Jackson."

Wilkes jerked his thumb toward the door. "Inside."

Donahue dismounted and said, "Hewitt, disarm him, then stay out here and watch him. We do not want any interference."

Wilkes said with glum resignation, "Ain't nobody fixin' to interfere with you. Just go ahead in."

Pistol in hand, Donahue motioned for Andy to open the door. "I'll be right behind you."

Andy felt a momentary queasiness about going in first. If Jericho was waiting with a drawn weapon, Andy would take the first bullet. Donahue was using him for a shield.

He blinked, for coming in from the sunshine made the room appear dark the first moment. He saw two women standing in the parlor, facing him. One was black. The other was white, a tall, thin woman Andy knew must be Jericho's wife. He saw a deep bruise on her swollen face.

Donahue stepped out from behind him. "We've come to talk to Jericho Jackson. Where's he at?"

Mrs. Jackson remained silent but pointed down a dark hall. She led the way. Donahue said, "Pickard, Tanner, you-all stick close to me. No tellin' what Jericho's reaction may be."

Mrs. Jackson stopped at an open door and motioned for the Rangers to go inside. Andy saw Jericho Jackson lying on a bed. A candle burned on a stand beside him. Beside the candle lay a Bible.

Andy did not have to move closer to see that Jericho was dead. He turned toward the woman. The grief in her eyes told him to ask her no questions.

Donahue's eagerness was gone. Soberly he said, "You men can bear witness that the fugitive is deceased." He puzzled, "But how could a wounded arm have killed him?"

Mrs. Jackson summoned enough voice to say, "Ask Wilkes."

Outside, Wilkes explained that he and Jericho had followed a man named Burt Hatton. Andy recognized the name. Though Jericho had blasted Hatton with a shotgun, Hatton had managed to put a bullet through Jericho's lung.

Wilkes said, "Wasn't nothin' anybody could do for him except bring him home to his woman. I done that. Now, if you-all have got no further business with me, I'll see to his buryin'."

Donahue said, "Somebody else will have to do that. You'll be goin' with us. We'll want to check you against our fugitive list."

Mrs. Jackson had come out to stand beside the door. Andy asked her, "You goin' to be all right, ma'am?"

She shook her head. "No, but I'll get by. I still have a home back in Missouri."

Donahue asked, "What do you figure to do with this ranch and everything that belonged to your husband?"

"I've not had time to give it thought. I'll probably sell what was legally his. As for that which was not, I'll try to find who rightfully owns it."

Donahue frowned. "Be careful who you

let have it. This is a white man's country now."

She stiffened. "The kind of outlaw white trash my husband surrounded himself with? He tried to shield me, but I am not blind. I was always aware of his shortcomings. Where I can, I'll make amends."

Donahue warned, "You could be askin' for trouble."

"If trouble comes, I'll call on the Rangers." She went into the house and closed the door.

Donahue cursed under his breath. "She'd better not call on *me*. Be damned if I'll answer."

Andy said, "If you don't, you may have to hunt for honest work."

They returned to the main camp, where the Jericho men had been escorted for screening to determine which of them might be wanted somewhere. Len had searched his fugitive list and found Jesse Wilkes was sought on a murder charge. Several others held in the camp had already been identified as well.

Sergeant Donahue was jubilant. "This will look great in the newspapers. I can see the headline: BIG CLEANUP ON THE BORDER."

Then he saw something else, and he froze to attention. Major Jones of Austin walked out of the headquarters tent and beckoned. "Sergeant, I want to see you."

Flustered, Donahue made a halfhearted salute. "You've come just in time, Major. We've done a good piece of work here."

"So I see."

"We've broken up two of the worst bandit gangs on the border, one on each side of the river. The people of Texas can be proud of my Rangers."

"Well and good, but I think the adjutant general will want to know why you didn't do it sooner."

Donahue blinked. "What do you mean?"

"I am given to understand you had advance word that Jericho was gathering a hard crew for that invasion. You stood by without making any effort to interfere. If these men are wanted today, they were wanted then. Why didn't you round them up before they went into Mexico?"

"Nobody's ever invaded Jericho's little kingdom."

"You had good reason to do so. All you lacked was the will."

Donahue slumped. "At least Chavez and Jericho are both dead. The country is well rid of them."

Jones nodded. "True. But many others are dead too, white men and Mexicans both. You will have a chance to explain all that in Austin. Perhaps the adjutant general will see fit to keep you in the rank of sergeant. Or he may suggest that you seek employment elsewhere."

The major turned and walked away, leaving Donahue standing with his head down.

Andy waited until the major went back into the tent, then followed him. He said, "Sir, I've already tried twice to turn in my resignation. What do I have to do to get it accepted?"

The major stared in surprise. "You can't mean you want to leave the force."

"I think I've been a Ranger about long enough. The time has come for me to try my hand at somethin' else."

Jones's voice was regretful. "I can handle the resignation for you. But are you sure?"

"I've thought on it a lot. I'm sure."

Outside, Len Tanner put his hand on Andy's shoulder. "I'm goin' to miss you."

"And I'll miss you. Don't you ever consider quittin' too?"

"Nope. Never had so much fun in my life." He gripped Andy's hand so hard that it hurt. "Tell Rusty and them I said howdy."

Andy's heartbeat picked up as he saw Rusty Shannon's double cabin ahead. He had grown to manhood here. He felt that he was home, though he knew he would not stay for long. He looked over the fields, expecting to see Rusty working there, but in this he was disappointed. He rode up to the cabin, dismounted, and shouted, "Anybody home?"

Alice Shannon stepped out onto the dog run that separated the two sections of the cabin. She shaded her eyes and called, "Andy? Can that be you?"

"Sure is. You got anything to eat?"

"If I don't, I'll fix somethin'." She hurried out to meet him. As her apron flared in the wind he noticed that her stomach was extended. He hugged her but took care not to squeeze too hard.

He said, "Looks like pretty soon there's goin' to be another mouth to feed around here."

"Two of them if you're stayin'."

"I just came for a little visit. Wanted to be sure the two of you are all right. I can see that *you* are. How's Rusty?"

"Fine. He's tickled over the prospect of bein' a daddy. He went over to Shanty's. Ought to be home pretty soon. Come in

396

and have some coffee. We'll eat supper when Rusty gets back."

Andy heard a rattle of trace chains and looked toward the road. He saw Rusty's wagon. "I'll wait out here for Rusty." He frowned, trying to think of a delicate way to ask her. Finding none, he blurted, "Last time I was here you were still wonderin' if the reason Rusty married you was because you reminded him of Josie."

"Josie will always be with him. I don't try to take her place. But I've made my own place with him now." She touched her stomach and smiled. "The baby and me." She went back into the cabin.

Rusty hauled the mule team to a stop and jumped down from the wagon, wrapping the reins around the brake. He rushed up to pump Andy's hand. "Thought you were way down on the border. Are you on leave?"

"No, I'm not a Ranger anymore. I decided it's time to find out just where I belong."

"You've got a place right here as long as you want it."

"No, this is yours and Alice's. And however many little Shannons may come along. I've thought a lot about that country out west, along the Llano and the San

Saba. I took a likin' to it while I was stationed there."

"It's a pretty country. But it's a long ways from here."

"Everything around here is settled up. That's a new country. Lots of room to grow in."

"Not by yourself. You'll need somebody to help you, somebody to come home to of a night. It took me a while to realize that myself, but I know it now." He looked toward the house, where smoke rose from the kitchen chimney. "I didn't realize how lonesome this place used to be till I brought Alice to share it with me."

Andy looked at the ground. "Seen Bethel Brackett lately?"

"Saw her in town a few days ago. She's prettier than ever."

"Anybody courtin' her?"

"If they're tryin', they're not gettin' anywhere. First thing she did was ask me all about you. She hadn't heard from you in a long time."

"I ain't much hand at writin' letters." He glanced at the house. "Reckon Alice would take it badly of me if I was to skip supper and go on over to see Bethel?"

Rusty grinned. "She'd think it's the smartest thing you've ever done."

Andy moved quickly into the saddle. "I may not be back tonight." He spurred the horse into a long trot. He looked behind him once. Rusty and Alice stood in the yard, arms around each other. Alice waved.

Andy put the horse into a gallop.

The sun was going down as he reined up in front of the Brackett house. He yelled, "Bethel! Are you in there?"

He heard a cry from inside. She stepped out onto the porch, then hurried down the steps. She skipped toward him with out-stretched arms as he swung from the saddle. When they broke apart he asked, "Ever been out west to the hill country?"

"Never have."

"How would you like to go?"

She hugged him again, hard. "Just tell me when we're leavin'."

About the Author

Elmer Kelton is a native Texan and an author of forty novels. He has earned countless honors, including a record seven Spur Awards from Western Writers of America. The organization has voted Kelton the greatest Western writer of all time. He lives in San Angelo, Texas.